Praise for the Daughters of the Crescent Moon Series

Read2Review on Destiny's Past: "The flow of the story was very well planned; I didn't want to stop reading! I loved the characters; each one had heart and their own voice. However, what really stuck out for me was that while I was reading I could actually picture the places the story was set in and I could clearly picture the characters. Patricia's use of description, for me, helped bring this brilliant story to life."

From the Paranormal Romance Guild: **Reviewer's Choice 2016 2nd place winner** "This is an amazing series and I can't recommend it enough...it has everything you could want if you love paranormal and fantasy." *Linda Tonis*

Destiny's Past

Book 1
Daughters of the Crescent Moon

Patricia C. Lee

Phoenix Literary Publishing
phoenixlitpub@gmail.com

Cover design: Taria Reed Cover Artist (www.tariareed.com)
Cover model: Alyssa Edelman

ISBN: 9781777156329   print
ISBN: 9780994851208   epub

DEDICATION

To the "Ari" in my life, who, with his lovable but demanding ways, led me to Leisos. Thank you, my prince. I miss you.

And to my husband, K. - my akitra. Your endless support, love and confidence in me cannot be put into words. My heart is yours - always and forever.

Glossary of pronunciations

Akitra (Ah-kee-tra)
Ariki (Ah-ree-kee)
Daylen (Day-len)
Feldar (Fel-dar)
Jarek (Jer-ek)
Laisa (Lay-sah)
Laleen (Lah-leen)
Larennia (Lah-ren-y-a)
Leisos (Lay-sos)
Malik (Mal-ick)
Midwisfel (Mid-wis-fel)
Narena (Nah-ree-nah)
Nafstahd (Nahf-schtad)
Ravell (Rah-vell)
Rayja (Ray-ya)
Rehema (Ree-mah)
Saltera (Saul-ter-ah)
Selaya (Sel-ay-ah)
Surduata (Sir-due-ah-ta)
Tabibu (Tah-bee-boo)
Tavarian (Tah-ver-ee-an)

Chapter One

Kelly Richards was at her best when surrounded by death. Calm, centered, and confident, she was exactly where she was meant to be.

She plucked a pair of surgical gloves from a box on the counter, snapped them on, walked over to the open file on the desk and glanced at the information. Caucasian male, mid to late thirties, died of an apparent drug overdose.

Although she couldn't understand or agree with people trying to find answers in chemical substances, she felt a momentary pang of sadness at the needless loss of life.

She'd dreamed of becoming an MD because she wanted to help others. Taught to maintain emotional distance from her patients, their pain and grief brought her own inner struggle to the surface—the one buried deep to avoid living it day after day. Unwilling to turn her back on aiding people, she switched careers and became a Medical Examiner to assist families of the dead achieve closure.

Working the evening shift alone at the county morgue was preferable to being with people who made idle conversation, mainly about stuff she had no interest in. It also provided a way to prevent coworker's well-meant intentions to set her up. Her job offered escape from them, allowing her to hide from her past. And herself.

Five metal drawers occupied the far wall of the room, each containing bodies to be autopsied. Kelly pulled open the door to number three, rolled out the drawer, revealing the man she would work on.

Her eyes widened. Most of the time, the prep crew stripped cadavers of their clothing before putting them in the cooler, but if the autopsy couldn't be performed right away, they didn't bother. His clothing wasn't the issue. It was the type of garments that caught her attention. He wore a short sleeve shirt, almost like a tunic, made of a fine, silky material. His loose fitting pants were woven from an odd cloth, not the usual denim or twill. Dust covered dull tan sandals strapped to his feet.

He was foreign, exotic looking. Dark brown hair, longer than the norm, barely brushed broad shoulders. His skin was light bronze, yet the file classified him as Caucasian. A frown pursed her lips. Odd. The people in admitting didn't usually make mistakes. This male appeared of mixed Mexican or Spanish descent, maybe Cuban. She leaned closer. Hmmm. His skin didn't have the ashen grey pallor of death either. She reached out to touch his arm.

The phone on the desk screamed two jangling blasts.

Kelly started, heart pounding against her ribs. Muttering a soft curse, she answered the phone and gave the caller information on a body she'd autopsied earlier.

She braced the desk with a trembling hand. She hadn't been here long and working evenings still made her jumpy.

Her attention reverted to the file on the body she was supposed to autopsy. What the hell? The measurements were all wrong. No way was the body on the slab five-five. More like about six-three. Did she pull the wrong drawer out? The information at the top of the page confirmed no mistake. There must have been some kind of screw-up. Surely someone didn't switch bodies? Checking the others would be the only way to find out.

Kelly marched back to the bank of drawers. As her hand closed around the handle of the second one, a wheezing breath not her own interrupted the silence of the room. She turned in slow motion to the cadaver lying on the slab beside her. Her throat closed. Similar to a scene out of a horror movie, the dead man's chest rose and fell. Not the final gasp of air escaping lungs at death, he inhaled and exhaled in a slow, shallow rhythm.

Grabbing the edge of the slab for stability, she shut her eyes.

Easy girl. Calm down, it's just your imagination. When you open your eyes, there will be a dead person on the slab, and he will not be breathing.

"Oh, for heaven's sake. This is ridiculous. He's dead."

"Not yet," the body whispered.

With a scream that could have broken glass, Kelly's eyes flew open. She stumbled backward, scrambled toward the autopsy table, desperate to find a weapon. Her hand clasped the hilt of a scalpel and she whirled to face her adversary. But no one attacked. The cadaver was where she'd left him, only very much alive.

"Who the hell are you, mister?" Her galloping heart zinged adrenaline into her bloodstream.

He turned his head, staring with beseeching eyes. "Please, help me."

Kelly almost hyperventilated. What the bloody hell was going on? He was alive for God's sake. Was this some kind of a joke? An initiation gag for the newcomer? She relaxed her stance a bit but kept the scalpel clutched tight in her hand.

"I'm going to ask you one more time before I call the cops. Who are you?"

"My name is Jarek."

"What are you doing here?"

"I do not know," he panted out through clenched teeth as tremors shook his body.

Kelly wavered. Despite that the tremors were symptoms of

5

something it could all be an act. A ruse to lower her guard and come closer before he sprang.

"That's it, I'm calling the police." She walked backwards to the desk, eyes vigilant for any change.

"Please. I need your help."

The phone was within her reach.

"I am dying."

She hesitated, torn between the inherent desire to help and the need for safety. Self-preservation took precedent.

Her fingers started punching numbers. A grunt made her head snap up. Jarek struggled to a sitting position and toppled to the floor.

His cry of agony cut through her defenses as the 911 operator's voice came on the line. She slammed down the receiver, rounded the edge of her desk. She was a doctor, had taken an oath to aid.

"Damn, damn, damn." She needed to have her head examined she thought, inching closer to the body writhing on the floor. Why was she always a sucker for someone in pain?

Ignoring the ringing phone, she took another cautious step closer to Jarek.

"Hey buddy, you'd better not be yanking my chain." Her false bravado wouldn't fool anyone. Even in his weakened state, this man could still hurt her. A lot. The scalpel in her hand gave her courage.

"I will not harm you." Jarek's futile attempt to raise a hand in supplication failed before his body buckled again.

Kelly pushed caution aside. She knelt down, rolled Jarek onto his back, and examined him. Cool, damp skin trembled beneath her fingers.

"Do you know what's wrong?" She lifted his eyelids, noted dilated pupils.

He curled his arms around his abdomen. "I think it is poison."

6

"What kind? Who did this to you?"

Jarek shook his head, winced, clutching his stomach.

"How long ago?"

"Have been unwell for some time." He wheezed for a few breaths. "It has gotten worse."

"Shit." Kelly tossed the scalpel onto the table. She raced to the bookshelf, grabbed a diagnostic volume listing symptoms and treatments, and returned to Jarek's side. Pages of the book flipped through her fingers.

"Did you get bitten or inhale anything?"

He shook his head.

"Eat something out of the ordinary?"

Again no.

"Do you have any nausea?"

Jarek frowned, shrugged. "What is..."

"Sick. Have you been sick to your stomach? Have you thrown up?" she barked in frustration.

He nodded. Her hand barely encircled his wrist as she counted the weakening heartbeats. Not much time. Jarek's eyes fluttered closed.

"Hey, no you don't. Jarek, that's your name, right? Listen to me, Jarek. Do you have a headache?"

A feeble nod.

No bite, no inhalant, no known ingestion. The toxin must have been administered through food or liquid. "Okay." She checked the book once more. "Have you had diarrhea?" She wanted to scream at his frown. Didn't he know anything? "Have you had to go to the bathroom a lot—to relieve yourself?" Good grief, it was like talking to someone from Mars.

"Yes," he whispered.

"Okay. I think I know what it is."

"You think?" he said incredulously, his eyebrow shooting upward.

"Would you rather I wait and see what happens?" she snapped.

He glowered before giving her a curt nod.

Kelly's mind raced along as she ran from the room and down the back hallway to the Head Coroner's office. A couple of things could be poisoning Jarek, but she had to combat the seizures and tremors first by flushing his system with medications. She grabbed a ring of keys from the desk drawer, sped out of the Head Coroner's room and up the two flights of stairs to the doctor's clinic above.

She fumbled with the key, unlocked the door of the office, sprinted into the examination room and flicked on the wall switch. The fluorescent neon glare revealed a medicine cabinet hung on the wall for a multitude of drugs. She jabbed a small key into the lock, opened the door, and scanned the bottles. Phenobarbital. Perfect. She snatched a bottle and a few other medications listed in the book as treatments for poisoning. A unit to her right held hypodermic needles and IV bags. She took some of those and fled the room.

As her quickening steps took her back to the morgue, the logical part of her brain kicked in. How much trouble was she about to get into? Staff, for a variety of reasons, could use the keys to the upper clinic. Hopefully her boss would have an open mind about the situation. How was she going to explain a body in the morgue was still alive? And instead of following procedure—was there even a procedure for this type of thing?—she'd acted on instinct. Yes, she should have completed the 911, but by the time the paramedics arrived it would have been too late. He already had the tremors. Seizures came next. Then death.

As she knelt beside Jarek, she breathed a quick sigh of relief. He hadn't started convulsing yet. It was a good sign. Since she didn't know how much poison he was given or when, waiting for results of a tox

8

screen was not an option. Sweat beaded on her brow, either from exertion or adrenaline. With quick precision, she assembled the IV with the Phenobarbital. Jarek's breathing became shallower.

"Don't die on me now." Kelly injected the needle into a vein on his right hand. Since he hadn't moved, the extracted metal cooler drawer above provided the best place to put the IV bag so gravity could do its work.

"Do not leave," Jarek rasped as she rose.

"I'm not going anywhere. I need to secure the IV so it won't come out of your hand." Instead of hunting for surgical tape, she snapped a piece of transparent tape from the dispenser on the desk and used it to stabilize the needle.

"The Phenobarbital will counteract the tremors. You should be okay, but I'll stay for a few minutes to make sure. It will afford you some time before we get you to a hospital where they can take better care of you."

"Is that a healing place?"

What, this guy didn't go to school? He had a slight accent, but maybe they didn't have a hospital where he was from. "I guess you could look at it that way. You've never heard of a hospital before?"

He avoided her eyes, looked around the room. "I owe you my life."

The flat statement miffed her. Talk about a left-handed thank you.

"Well, I've gotta say, having a live corpse in the cooler is a change of pace," she commented with a touch of mirth.

Jarek's tremors began to subside and his muscles started to relax. "What is this place?"

She followed his gaze to the autopsy table, the multiple instruments required for dissection, and the suspended metal spray hose.

"It's the morgue."

"What is a morgue?"

"You're joking, right? You don't know what a morgue is?"

"Should I?"

A placating smile rose on her lips. "That's okay. Don't worry about anything. We'll get you to a hospital in no time." Not wanting to agitate this strange man, she changed topics. "So, where are you from?"

"I am not from here."

"I kind of gathered that from your clothing. Although, you could have been at a costume party or something. The armband is a nice touch."

Jarek's fingers touched the bronzed piece of jewelry around his well-developed bicep. "Where am I?"

"I told you, you're in the morgue."

"Where is this morgue?"

What a strange way to phrase a question. "Lackton, in Wesslyn County. The building used to be a jail and a lawyer's office. It was converted at the turn of the century. The lawyer's room is now a doctor's clinic and the former jail below became the morgue."

"And where is Wesslyn County? I am unfamiliar with that place."

Okay. "It's in North Carolina. You don't know where you are? How did you get here?"

"I am not sure, but I believe I was brought here."

"By whom? Is there someone I can call? There has obviously been a mistake if you ended up alive in the morgue and you're not sure how you even got here." Scenarios jumped through her mind. He was too old for a college keg party. A stag maybe. Under the pretense of taking a pulse on his neck, she leaned forward, sniffing for telltale signs of alcohol. Nope.

Instead of answering her question, Jarek asked another. "What is the date?"

"The date? As in the day of the week?" The pulse beneath her fingers beat stronger.

"What is the year?"

Okey-dokey then. The man either had a case of amnesia but remembered his name or was a crackpot from the loony bin. This just kept getting better and better. She drew away.

"Listen, I'm going to make a quick call, and I'll be—"

Loud knocking on the morgue's front door interrupted her.

"I'm going to need to get that."

"Please. I can sense you are frightened. I wish you no harm. I need your help."

"I have helped you. I just saved your life, in case you've forgotten." Gee, that was the thanks she got for playing the Good Samaritan.

"I am grateful. But I must get back to Leisos to find out who poisoned me and why."

"What? Back to where?" Where the hell was Leisos?

The knocking turned to thumping.

"This is the police. There was a 911 call placed from here. Please open the door."

God, could this get any worse?

Jarek snagged her wrist. "I see you do not understand. But I will explain it to you."

Her eyes darted between his face and the hand holding her. Had she just put herself in danger by saving his life? "Look buddy, the cops are here." Kelly's head swiveled to the murky black shapes outlined through opaque glass.

Jarek's hand tightened. "The birthmark on your neck. It is a crescent moon with a star. I know where it originated."

Chapter Two

"I can explain everything. I truly wish you no harm. You must believe me," Jarek pleaded.

The woman snatched her hand out of his grasp. "Be right there, guys," she yelled, yanking down the white sheet from the autopsy table and covering him with it. "Not one bloody word, and don't move a muscle, do you understand?"

At his nod, she grabbed the fluid-filled bag, slapped it on his chest, put the rest of the items beside him, and covered his face.

"I'm going to regret this," she muttered.

Jarek lay motionless. He had to find a way out of this room. Out of this world. His mind was willing, but his strength was gone. It galled him to be this weak, and worst of all, to depend upon this stranger to help him. Where he was from he'd never had to rely on others.

The cloth covering his face stuck to his lips with every breath. He tried to relax, but the cold from the floor seeped through his thin clothing, chilling his skin.

The woman spoke to the men who had arrived. Cops, she had called them. He didn't know what cops were, but they must have commanded some type of authority or else his savior wouldn't have rushed to the door. Maybe she let them in for another reason. Could she have lied to him? Would she tell these men about him and have them take him away? But, if that was the case, why cover him up and tell him to keep quiet?

"Look, I'm really sorry about this, but, it's, ah, it's just a mistake." A thin, pinched strain of laughter accompanied her words.

"So you had no intention of phoning for help? The 911 operator called back but received no reply."

"Oops, sorry. Everything is fine."

"Well then, you won't mind if we take a look around."

"Uh, is that really necessary?"

"Why, do you have something to hide?" another male said.

"No."

Was that panic he heard in her voice?

"Then you have nothing to worry about." Footsteps echoed closer.

Apprehension tripped up Jarek's spine. He slowed his breathing even more. Did these men want to harm him? He had a feeling the woman did not. He was powerless to help her and he wasn't strong enough to get away. Not yet, anyway. But she did say everything was fine. His best bet was to remain as quiet as possible.

In other words, look dead.

"You mind explaining this." The sole of the man's shoes squeaked beside Jarek's ear.

"Well, umm, I kind of had a bit of an accident."

"I gathered that. Isn't the body supposed to be on the slab, not on the floor?"

"Okay, you have to promise not to say anything. Since this was my first autopsy alone, I kind of got excited and yanked on the drawer too hard. It hit the end of the track, and the body bounced. Well, that just totally freaked me out, and then I stumbled into the drawer, knocked the body over and onto the floor."

"So where does the 911 call come into play?" Amusement filtered through the question.

"I panicked."

The words were so soft, the men asked her to repeat them.

"I panicked. I can't very well do an autopsy on the floor, so I was going to call a friend to help me lift the body back onto the slab. When I dialed nine to get an outside line, my fingers shook. I must have dialed 911. When the operator came on the line, I realized what I had done and hung up. I didn't think they would send you out."

"What took you so long to answer the door?" The other man was farther away.

Jarek willed himself not to fidget. Hearing men's voices and not seeing them was like spirits whispering in the wind.

"Once I calmed down, I remembered we have lifts for cadavers. I was on my way to get one when you guys came. I was embarrassed, so I threw the sheet over the body and hoped you wouldn't come in." Her voice softened. "You're not going to tell anyone are you? I mean, it's my first time alone, and I need this job. If my boss found out about this, he would probably think I was fooling around and might fire me."

The brusque-voiced man chuckled. "I think we can keep this one under wraps. Do you need help with the body now?"

"No. No, I'm good. We get training for this type of thing, and there's the lift down the hall."

Jarek smiled. This woman was quick. Determined. Maybe she could help him after all.

"It wouldn't be any—"

A crackle cut off the next words.

"Car Twelve, what's your status?"

Jarek's ears perked at the different female voice. Had someone else come into the room?

"Twelve here. False alarm on that last 911 call."

"Car Twelve, if you're available, see the man at Darlington and Fifth for a possible B and E."

"Twelve, roger. Hank, let's go. Gotta run, lady. Next time, be a little more careful, okay?" Heavy footsteps echoed away.

"Yes, officer." Her voice drifted across the room. "Thanks again. And remember, you said you wouldn't tell anyone."

There was a soft click, like something slipping into place, followed by muttering he strained to hear.

"It'll be all over the station by the end of their shift."

The sharp clack of footsteps signaled her approach, yet the woman stood by his side and did nothing.

"Are you going to uncover me?"

"I haven't decided yet. Do you have any idea how much trouble you caused me? I could get fired for this."

She paced the floor near him. "And I came across as sounding idiotic and inept."

"You are the only one who can aid me."

The sheet lifted from his face. She had blonde hair cut in a strange fashion. Her azure-blue eyes narrowed, and her lips pressed into a hard line. They reminded him of the passion berry from his homeland.

"Are you done staring?"

Her question shook him out of his daydream. "What is your name?"

"Why?"

"How else am I to address you?"

"You sure have a strange way of speaking. I can't place your accent, either. My name is Kelly. Do you have enough strength to get off the floor and back onto the slab?"

"A chair would be preferable. The 'slab,' as you call it, is quite cold, as is the floor."

Raising an eyebrow, Kelly retrieved a chair on wheels from behind a table-like structure, helped him sit down, and draped the sheet across his lap. She took the bag of clear fluid from his grasp, as well as the other items, and placed them on the drawer above his head.

"Okay, spill it. I've put my job in jeopardy for you, and I lied to the police. I want answers, and I want them now. Who are you?"

"I have already told you, my name is Jarek."

"Yeah, I got that. I mean who are you, as in what? Are you a cop? An actor? A drug dealer? Or are you just someone who happened to end up in my morgue?"

"I do not think you will believe me."

"Try me," she said testily.

Jarek sighed. He'd need to tell her everything. "I am a prince."

"A prince?"

Her disbelief irritated him. He was unaccustomed to having his word questioned. "Yes, I am the Prince of Leisos."

"Never heard of it. Where is this Leisos?"

"Far away from here."

"Oh, really."

Her skepticism made him grit his teeth. "Yes. Now I will ask you a question."

"It's not your turn yet. How did you get here?"

His eyes narrowed into a glare. Impertinent woman. "I do not know."

"Don't play with me, I'm not in the mood."

"I am telling you the truth. I do not know."

"Fine. We'll get back to that one later. Why did you come here?"

"I was dying." Jarek bit back a snarl. He wasn't sure what irritated him more, her constant questions or having to repeat himself. However, the snap of anger in her blue eyes and determined set of her chin showed she had strength, both inside and out. Intriguing.

"You can wipe the wolf grin off your face. If you were dying, why didn't you go to a hospital?" Kelly countered.

"What is a hospital?"

She stepped away, crossed her arms, the clothing stretching snugly over her breasts. Very intriguing.

"I said don't play with me."

The acid in her tone brought him back from dreamland. "Since we do not seem to be frolicking, I assume the word 'play' in this instance means 'lie.' I am not playing with you."

"You don't know what a hospital is?"

"Despite what you may think, no, I do not." Who was she to question his integrity?

"I don't believe you."

This was getting nowhere. "What is the year?"

"I'm not finished asking the questions."

"Yes, you are. I have answered some of yours. Please do me the courtesy of answering one of mine. What is the year?" he pressed.

She told him.

He felt the blood drain from his face as his world tilted. Impossible.

"Hey, you okay?" She knelt beside Jarek's chair. "I didn't mean to be so pushy, but what's going on?"

He took a deep breath. The span of time was irrelevant. He was brought here to escape death and had succeeded. Now he needed to get back. "I have come farther than expected."

"How far is that?"

"Over two thousand years into the future."

Kelly sprang up. "See, I really hate that. I asked you not to lie and then you tell me that you're from the past. What do you think I am, stupid?"

Jarek's temper flared. He had to make her understand how important it was for him to return to his time. Whoever tried to kill him didn't succeed. They might go after his brother next. He couldn't let that happen.

Narena had mentioned things would be very different, but in his weakened state, he couldn't remember much. It was obvious when he awoke he was no longer in Leisos, even before Kelly said this was North Carolina, wherever that was. For instance, an acrid odor he could taste in the back of his throat replaced the sweet smell of forsythia in the breezes of his homeland. He lay on sleek, icy metal instead of hard, packed earth. Not to mention the strange devices around the room. On the wall, a white round unit with numbers encircled a thin black stick ticking in a circle. A long, curved silver stalk hung from the ceiling. That wasn't like any of the hallowed reeds by the riverbank at home.

His fingers brushed an armlet on his left bicep. The sorceress must have put it on him before he left Leisos. She'd said sending someone through time was a tremendous strain on her. It had been a great sacrifice, and she was successful, but at what cost? Was she all right? Did she even survive?

Just before Narena had sent him forward in time, she warned him magic and sorcery didn't exist in the future. He had to be careful with how and what he revealed.

"I do not think you are stupid. I am truly from the past, from the land called Leisos. I do not know if it still exists in your time. Someone poisoned me, but I do not know whom. I was sent here to be cured. Now that I have escaped death, I will return to Leisos and have my vengeance."

"How'd you get to this time?"

"The sorceress Narena."

"A sorceress. Is she married to Merlin?" she snorted.

His patience snapped. This was futile. Kelly wasn't going to help him no matter what he said. She asked for the truth, and he told her.

18

Now she looked at him with derision.

"Narena is a very good friend. I advise you to tread with caution," he warned. If she chose not to believe him, fine. He'd find someone else to help him. Be damned if this wisp of a woman would stand in his way.

He stood. The room spun.

Kelly caught him as his knees buckled and eased him back into the chair. "You need to sit, rest for a while. Then if you want to leave, go ahead. But you won't get far in your condition."

Jarek put his head in his hands. Where would he go? He knew nothing beyond this room. In Leisos, he wouldn't hesitate to strike out alone. He stared at Kelly and said the one thing that might give her pause.

"The birthmark on your neck—the one of the crescent moon and a star—it runs in your family, probably the women. Am I correct?"

Her mouth dropped open.

"If you follow your lineage back through time, you would find the name Narena. Whether you believe me or not, you are a direct descendant of a sorceress."

Chapter Three

Kelly's world teetered. Her clinical, analytical domain was safe, for the most part. Everything of comfort could be explained by physical evidence. Science was her strength, her salvation. There was proof for everything. But the man before her defied the very core of her belief system. She refused to believe time travel existed.

"If you're from two thousand years ago, how come you can speak and understand English so well? English didn't really start until the fifth century." See if he can explain himself out of that one.

"Just before Narena sent me forward in time, she gave me a potion to drink and told me it would help me communicate in the future." Jarek replied.

Kelly reined in her temper. She didn't appreciate being patronized. And he was giving it to her in spades.

The ringing phone quelled the retort she felt like saying to his convenient answer. Between her irritation and keeping an eye on her guest, she had to get the caller to repeat the information before she got it right.

"You just got a lucky break," she said hanging up the phone. "I have to pick up a body, so we'll finish this discussion later." As angry as she was at Jarek, medical ethics wouldn't allow her to leave without administering an antidote to the poison in his system. Phenobarbital had done its work by combating the tremors and stopping him from slipping into convulsions or a coma.

She reviewed the list of possible candidates. "Did you eat anything that tasted strange?"

"No."

"Hmm, that means the poison had to be administered over time. Considering where and when you claim to come from narrows the possibilities considerably." Not that she believed his time travel tale, but he believed it. Best not to antagonize someone she considered wasn't all there.

"Can you remember what you ate?"

"By the time Narena came to me, I could not eat much. Mainly broth and vegetables," he replied.

That dismissed most of the other poisons on the list, leaving a couple that were plant-based.

"Did your broth taste sweet, like almonds?"

"No, it was strong. I do not like sweet soups."

"I'll keep that in mind," she noted dryly. According to her studies on alternative medicines, the most logical plant was hemlock. Considering the plant had been around for thousands of years, it was, in all likelihood, the culprit. Since there was no true antidote to hemlock poisoning, her course of action was to treat the nausea and dehydration.

Hesitation and indecision invaded her thoughts as she administered a dose of Metoclopramide into the saline solution in the IV bag. Jarek should be taken to a hospital where he could rest and be monitored, but his insistence at being acquainted with her ancestry plagued her rational mind. Did he really have this knowledge, or was he playing her for a fool?

"I will come with you."

His words stalled her mental argument. "I don't think so. I can't keep an eye on you and do my job at the same time. And I'm not letting you sit here. The morning shift will come in soon, and the last thing I need right now is to explain what you're doing here. Unless you want to run the cock-and-bull story by one of my co-workers and see if they will help you." Kelly snatched a set of keys from the desk and ripped off the address of the body pickup from the notepad.

"What do fowl and beef have to do with what I am telling you?"

She wanted to smack the guy but his innocent yet confused expression brought her temper under control.

"The only thing stopping me from tossing you out of here or calling the cops again is your claim you know about my birthmark and family history. Taking you with me may bring unwanted attention." She considered her options, gnawing on her lower lip. "You'll have to climb back onto the slab, and I'll lock you in."

Jarek's eyes widened.

"I'm sorry, but it's the only way. I'll get you another sheet to keep you warm."

Clutching the linen she retrieved from the closet, he eased onto the rolling slab, pulled the sheets up to his chin, and lay down, giving her a look of wary apprehension.

She almost felt sorry for him. "Relax. Compared with traveling through time, this should be a piece of cake. I'll get back as soon as I can. I'm going to lock you in and take the keys so no one will mistakenly pull you out." She tried to sound encouraging, but her mind spun with a thousand questions. Was this guy for real? If so, how would the scientific world take the discovery of time travel? Would anyone believe her if she told them? Other than his word, she had no hard data.

"Try and keep as quiet as possible." Kelly removed all but a couple of the vials and hypodermics he would need for later, rolled the drawer back into the wall and started to close the door.

22

He stopped her before she could latch it. "You will return." There was a hint of desperation in his demand. Maybe he wasn't so tough after all.

"I won't be gone long. You should have more than enough air to breathe. Get some sleep. I'm sure this has been quite an ordeal for you and you're tired from your long journey." She snapped the door shut, locked it, and deposited the keys in her pocket.

Kelly returned the remaining medical supplies to the doctor's office, replaced the clinic keys, and walked to the loading bay where the van — the meat wagon, as they called it — was parked. She sat in the front seat but didn't start the vehicle, staring ahead, past glaring streetlights, into darkness beyond.

Could someone actually travel through time? And if so, how? Through witchcraft, sorcery, or whatever the hell you called it? And what about science? If Jarek was right, then everything she had come to understand, know, and rely on was a lie.

A passing vehicle on the street broke her line of vision, snapped her attention back to what she needed to do. With a turn of the key the van came to life and she eased out of the loading bay onto the street. Lack of traffic during pre-dawn hours made navigating thoroughfares of the city easy. Her mind wandered back to the morgue and the man lying on the slab, very much alive. The time traveler. The hunky, sexy time traveler.

No. She wasn't going there. Not again. She'd been sucked in before over good looks and a killer body, and look at what happened with David. She was still paying the price.

Yet Jarek sounded so sincere, a part of her wanted to believe him. Even if she did, she didn't need him relying on her to get him back home.

Her younger sister had relied on her once.

But at the time when her sibling needed her most, Kelly had failed.

Pushing errant thoughts of painful memories and sexy men aside, Kelly pulled over to the curb in front of an apartment building. She jumped out of the van and went around to the back to collect her bag.

This was her job. This was real — not time travel. This was science – and it kept her sane.

Sensory deprivation inside the morgue drawer threatened Jarek's sanity. In Leisos, he was always around people. The palace was massive, employing a great number of staff that went about their duties at all hours, so he was never alone. Even in the dead of night when he returned home from enjoying a lovely maiden's touch, gentle murmurs of kitchen staff or echoing footsteps of guards on patrol broke the silence.

Leisos. Home. The need to return was as important to him as breathing. Had someone in the palace poisoned him? Someone close? Possibly a family member?

Quick shallow breaths hissed in the oppressive darkness surrounding him. He couldn't see his hand touching cold metal. Despite the cool temperature, trickles of sweat beaded down his nose, pooled at the base of his throat. His hands began to shake. Panic whipped up his spine, exploded into his heart.

Kelly had just left him there. What if she didn't come back? He'd be trapped. He couldn't tell how long she'd been gone. He hadn't come so far to die anyway. He slapped his palms along the walls, desperate to find a way out of his tomb. He reached above his head, thumping his fists against metal.

"For goodness' sake, take it easy." Kelly flung open the door.

Blessed white light fell onto Jarek's face. "You're gonna wake the dead with all that noise." She gave the drawer a hefty tug.

Before the unit came to a stop, Jarek bolted upright, tossed the sheets to the floor and gulped in a lungful of air. "You will not put me in there again."

"Sorry you had to go through that, but I had no choice." Kelly dragged a chair over. "Here, sit on this. We need to figure out what to do with you."

Jarek sat with the bag of clear liquid close to his chest and willed the unsteady beating of his heart under control.

Kelly gathered up the small bottles, shut the chamber, scooped the linen from the floor and tossed it into a blue container in the corner. "So, what now?"

He stared at her blankly.

Kelly continued. "What are we going to do?"

"You have cured me. Now I must return to Leisos and find out why I was poisoned and ensure the same fate does not befall my brother. How that can be done, I do not know. This is your world."

"Would you please stop making it sound like you're from another planet?" She pushed a hand through her short hair.

Jarek grew silent, thinking. After the experience in the cold tomb, he wouldn't survive long here without help.

"Okay. We need to leave. Now. The morning shift will be here any minute, and I have no clue how I would explain you. I guess you're coming with me." She retrieved her bag from the desk and tossed in the bottles of medication.

"Where are we going?" He followed Kelly out and down a dimly lit corridor, trying not to gape. The overhead lights were harsh, not like the warm glow of torches he grew up with in the palace. And the smell. How did she work here with that awful stench?

"My place. I just worked a double shift and I need some sleep. Maybe then I can figure out if I'm hallucinating or if you are for real."

"I am not imaginary, I assure you." He gestured to the bag in his hand. "What of this?"

"Keep it close and above your hand so it will flow. You were pretty dehydrated. It will replenish your body fluids." She pushed open a door and walked outside.

Jarek crossed the threshold, took two steps, when his blood turned to ice. A roar unlike anything he'd ever heard reverberated through the night air. Something was about to attack. His gaze locked onto Kelly. She was the only one who could help him. He had to protect her.

He lunged, clamped his hand on her arm, and dragged her behind him.

Chapter Four

"What the hell?" Kelly struggled away from the vise around her arm.

She'd been right, Jarek was nuts. And now he had her outside of the morgue, he'd probably drag her to a waiting car.

"There is danger." He whipped around, checking behind them, to the left and right.

"What are you talking about? What are you looking for?"

He wasn't herding her into an alley as she expected from his actions. By his determined expression and battle-ready stance he must be thinking they were in danger. She mimicked his movements, but nothing was out of the ordinary. They were in the parking lot at work, and everything seemed to be okay. It was just before dawn. Only a few cars plus an extra work van were in the area. She gazed into the murkiness where the streetlights didn't reach.

"A beast approaches. Did you not hear the roar?"

Beast? She glanced around again before stopping her cautionary inspection. Her lips pressed tightly to conceal a smile. The low drone of an aircraft faded into distance. That must have been what he heard. To him, the sound probably resembled a horrific animal.

"It's okay, Jarek. It's only a plane."

"One of them?" He pointed across the lot.

"No, those are cars. A plane is...uh...never mind. I'll explain later. But we're fine. No beasts." She continued toward her vehicle.

"What is a car?" He trotted beside her.

Kelly stifled a groan and stopped. "You're just going to have to trust me." She took out her remote, unlocked the unit. Jarek's step stuttered at the short chirp and quick blink of lights, but she kept going.

"This is how we get from place to place." She lifted the handle, swung open the door. "Think of it as an enclosed chariot. Oh, and once we get underway, you should close your eyes. I don't want you going into sensory overload and passing out on me."

When she strapped her passenger in, the seatbelt's click reminded Kelly of cocking a revolver. Taking Jarek with her was like having a loaded gun to her head. Where was her head? She didn't know this person from Adam, and she was giving him a lift. To her place, no less. She must be the one who was insane. No way was his time travel story believable, but she was a pretty good judge of character. Jarek didn't seem like the axe murderer type. Though it wasn't like sickos wore signs.

With a rueful smile, she stole a glance at her passenger while driving. No, not an axe murderer, but he could be a heartbreaker. Straight nose, strong jaw line, kissable mouth. *Stop. Just stop. You are not going there.* Kelly snapped her eyes back to the road and concentrated on driving. Soon she arrived at the parking lot of her brick three-story apartment building, switched the vehicle off and turned to her passenger. He stared straight ahead, lips compressed into a thin line.

She smothered a smile, placed a light hand on his shoulder. "What did you think?"

Facing her, he paused before answering with a gleam in his eye. "This mode of transportation will take some getting used to. Can it go faster?"

She quirked a brow. "Let me guess, you're the Mario Andretti of the late Iron Age, right?"

28

Without giving him a chance to respond, she angled out of the car, walked around to his side, and opened the door. Anyone watching would think chivalry had taken a full one-eighty. After Jarek got out, Kelly locked the doors and started toward her building. The smell of the dumpster coming from the back of the structure reminded her she missed garbage day again. Damn.

Jarek gaped at the vehicles parked in the lot. "Do all these, cars as you call them, function the same way?"

"For the most part, but don't expect me to explain it. I'm not a mechanic. I work on dead human bodies, not car bodies. But there are days when I wish I could. Especially when I get the bill. Are you coming?"

She held the door open, waiting for him to reach her side. The stairs might be less shocking, but in his weakened state, Jarek would have to take the elevator. Not that she believed his story. Not by a long shot. She stepped to the metal door, pushed the "up" button on the panel. A tone heralded its arrival. The door opened and she walked into the waiting car. He stood rooted to the floor.

"What's wrong?"

His look of skepticism was identical to the one he'd given her when she locked him in the morgue drawer earlier.

"What do you call this contraption?" He scanned the metal box's perimeter.

Breathe. Just breathe. She chanted the mantra silently while her finger depressed the 'open door' button.

"An elevator. It takes people to other floors of this building. Get in."

"Is there not another means of getting to your apartment, as you call it?"

"It's three flights up. I wouldn't advise it in your condition, but if you want to walk, go right ahead."

He glanced down the hallway.

"Don't you trust me? Did I not save your life?" She paused, unable to resist baiting him. "You're not scared, are you?"

In typical male fashion, he glowered as if offended she would even think such a thing and stepped inside the elevator. His head swiveled to inspect the interior before facing forward, staring ahead into the front lobby.

Kelly released her finger, punched the third floor button. The metal door slid shut, the car gave a slight lurch, and the box traveled upward.

Instead of the gasp she expected, Jarek only grunted. His eyes were shut, jaw tightly clenched. Just like when she locked him in the morgue drawer, she almost felt pity for him. Almost.

Maybe he was claustrophobic. Lots of people, especially mentally ill ones, had fears. She should call local hospitals and institutions later to see if anyone was missing a patient.

They arrived at the third floor. The door slid open, and Kelly led Jarek across blue-grey industrial carpeting in the hallway. A muffled whir indicated the elevator door shut behind them. Dark brown eyes stared coldly down at her.

"That was almost as bad as the tomb you made me lie in. Is everything here so unpleasant?"

Her paper-thin patience ripped in half. She wanted to crawl into bed and get some sleep. With more iciness than intended she said, "I didn't invite you to 'my world,' pal. If you don't like it, go back to where you came from."

He slid a wounded glare at her. "I would like nothing more."

Damn. "I'm sorry. I'm hungry, tired, and irritable. Instead of arguing in the hallway, let's go inside. Try not to make too much noise. My neighbor is a little coo-coo for Cocoa Puffs, and who knows what she might think is going on here." At least the older woman next door didn't think she was from a different time.

Kelly led the way down the hall, unlocked her door and walked in, leaving it open for him to follow. Purse and keys landed on the hall table. With a groan of relief, low pumps were toed off. The feel of thick carpet was heaven against her sore feet as she padded to the linen closet. One night on the couch, she told herself, carrying the pillow, blanket, and sheet into the living room.

After placing the items on the couch, she turned, brought a hand to her mouth to cover the giggle threatening to erupt. Jarek was intently staring at her lava lamp, his finger following the blob of wax as it distorted and lifted to the top. He studied the back and front, hesitantly touching the glass.

"Cool, huh?" she said.

"The red reminds me of what flows from the mountains in Leisos."

"A volcano?"

He shrugged, continued to watch pop art in the form of technology. "What is its purpose?"

"Good question. Some people like them for mood. It's a knick-knack from the seventies."

"What is a knick-knack?"

Lord, this could go on for hours. "You can sleep on the couch. I'm heading to bed. Be careful of the IV in your hand. It needs to stay there. Later today I'll add another dose of medication." She walked past him, paused, remembering an earlier conversation. "If you need to relieve yourself, the washroom is through that door," she said, pointing down the hall. "I'm sure you can figure it out."

His confusion plucked at her guilt. She couldn't imagine how tough this would be if he couldn't communicate. "Get some rest, Jarek." She patted his arm, went into her bedroom, and closed the door.

Wonderful, Jarek thought. Not only was he in a strange world, but he wasn't allowed to sleep in a proper bed. Instead, he had to stretch his long frame onto a cloth-covered piece of furniture. His feet would surely hang over the edge. He pressed down on the cushion. At least it felt soft. With pillow and blanket, he made up his bed and lay down. Sleep was far from coming.

Now that he was out of immediate danger, he tried to comprehend all he'd experienced. The sights, like tall building, modes of transport to move people place to place, the invasion of light everywhere made his mind swim. And there were the smells; the unpleasant odors at Kelly's workplace and general smothering pall in the air. However, he noticed the stink of rotting garbage when they crossed to the building earlier was similar to that at home. Perhaps a bit more odorful. But what bothered him the most was the noise, a varying level of harmonics that wouldn't stop. Even now his ears could pick up a low level hum that rose and fell. It was irritating and made him pine for the peace of his homeland.

He jockeyed for a better position and surveyed the room. A large black box stood against the opposite wall with a thin silver rectangle on a shelf below it. Another set of shiny silver squares were stacked on top of one another in the corner. Pictures with unfamiliar scenes hung on walls. This place—Kelly called it an apartment—was definitely not like the palace in Leisos. But he was warm, dry and in a considerably better situation than before.

Visions of his last days at home danced behind his eyes. His muscles had clenched as he rode wave after wave of pain. It had taken every effort not to cry out.

During the darkest time he'd lain in bed, damp sheets tangled around his legs, thinking it a shame his final days would be spent alone without the scent or touch of a woman beside him. How many fathers in his land would be grateful he couldn't pursue their daughters any longer? Did one of them try to kill him? No, they didn't have access to the palace unless invited, and Jarek wouldn't have asked one of his lover's parents to come for a visit.

Another theory rattled around in his brain. If he died, his twin brother, Rayja, was next in line to the throne. Would his brother kill to rule? He dug deep, searched his heart. Rayja couldn't be his assailant. Born within hours of each other, they were closer than mere brothers. Jarek would know, deep within his soul, if his twin wished him dead.

The question remained. Who would have the most to gain from his death?

The armlet's circling drew his attention. He inspected the wide metal band, fingers tracing the unfamiliar, intricate design. What was its significance? His hand slid across his chest to a hard object. When he was in the cold tomb, he noticed it but wasn't able to see. He tugged the thin strip of leather from under his tunic. Although he couldn't see the pendant very clearly in the pre-dawn light, it had the shape and texture of stone. Had Narena given him another item while he was so ill and couldn't remember? Why would she give him these things and not tell him their functions?

When death had seemed imminent, he'd called to her in a dream, and she'd come in the middle of the night, risking her very life. No one was allowed in the palace unless summoned by royal family member.

She was the only chance he had. Jarek brought the hazy memory forward.

"Prince Jarek, wake up." Narena's *urgent whisper pulled him out of a painful*

sleep.

"Ugh." He turned his head back and forth in restless slumber.

"Jarek, it is Narena. I am here. Please, you must awaken."

Jarek turned over slowly, pain-filled eyes fluttering open to gaze upon her face. "I always knew you wanted to get into my bedchamber."

"Do not count me as one of your other maidens."

He smiled, struggled to sit up. "You came."

"I received your message. How could I not come? What is wrong? I knew you were ill, but assumed since under the royal healer's care that you were getting better. Is it not the case?"

Another spasm of pain twisted through his body, like a hundred knives shredding him from the inside out. "I am being poisoned."

She gasped. "You are sure? Do you know who?"

"No. Although it could be one of the maidens scorned."

"Now is not the time to be making such foolish statements. Could it be Rayja?"

Even through the pain, he heard dread in her words.

He was next in line to the throne, but the king was in good health. The possibility of it being his brother seemed remote.

"No, I am certain my twin did not plot to kill me. Unfortunately, I will not live long enough to find out who did."

"Have you spoken to the king about this?"

Jarek shook his head. He didn't want to believe his father could have a hand in the slow death of his own son, yet he hadn't seen him in days.

"What is it you wish me to do?" Tears pooled in her eyes. "I cannot heal you unless I know what poison was used."

"There is not enough time to heal me and you are in great danger if caught within the palace walls. You must help me escape."

"Escape? For what purpose?"

Jarek reached out, pulled at Narena's wrist for her to sit down and leaned closer so he wouldn't be overheard.

"You must send me away."

"What do you hope to accomplish by leaving? It would be best for you to stay here. I can try and find out what poison they used. Only in that way can I help you."

"As a sorceress, you must know of a place where I can be cured. Send me to someone who knows how to combat the poison. I know you can do this, Narena. I have great faith in your powers."

Her eyes widened. When they were young, Narena had boasted her powers were growing and she might be able to send herself through time. After all her years of serving as the king's personal advisor, Jarek had no doubt she'd mastered her magic. If anyone could send him through time, it was she.

"Jarek, I cannot. I do not have the ability to do such a thing."

"Then you lied to me."

"I have never lied to you, nor do I wish to do so now."

"Then it can be done."

She hesitated, averted her gaze.

Her reluctance made him smile in satisfaction. "Ah, you do have the power."

"Yes, I have done it. Once. But it was only me, and only to the previous day."

"Does a time exist when healing is strong?"

"I have seen a brief vision of the future, but I do not know if I can send you forward so far in time or whether there is a cure."

"So, I am to die without knowing who or why."

"Please do not ask this of me, Jarek." A single tear trickled down her face.

The pain in her voice nearly broke his heart. What choice did he have? To do nothing would mean his death. If she could send him away from here, maybe she might be able to find out who was poisoning him. But, what then? How would she know when to bring him back, if he even survived?

Jarek brushed away the telltale sign of her sadness. "I have great faith in you, Narena. I always have."

"I do have great faith in you, Narena." Jarek sighed, fingering the armlet. "Sending me to the future gave me a chance to live. Now I need you to bring me back home."

Chapter Five

Kelly's heart raced, and tears flowed down her face when she woke from her dream. Or rather, her nightmare. It was always the same. That was the problem when you lived a nightmare; you never got a chance to change the ending.

She lay in bed, brushed tears away with the back of her hand. A shuddering breath escaped trembling lips as her hand found its way over her heart. Would it ever stop hurting? Did she want it to? She feared the moment the pain left, Stephanie's memory would fade, and she wouldn't allow that.

She snatched a tissue from the box on her bedside table. Late afternoon sun filled the room with warmth. Too bad it didn't have the same effect on her soul.

It was time to move on, let the memories of her younger sister's death fade, and replace them with memories of her life. But the bloodstains were forever embedded in Kelly's skin.

Getting out of bed, she strained to decipher the sound from behind the closed door—a light whirring, followed by a soft thump. It repeated a few times before her sleep-fogged brain came to life. Holy crap, someone was in her apartment.

Soft male laughter stopped her from lunging to the phone and dialing 911. Oh yeah, she'd let company sleep on her couch. Jarek. It sounded like her guest was awake and rummaging around in her kitchen.

So much for a quiet cup of coffee.

"Guess I'd better see what's giving him the giggles." As she reached for the doorknob, her hand brushed the silky peach-colored teddy she wore. Oops. She unhooked her robe from the back of the door, slipped it on. No need to give the guy a thrill.

A quick finger comb through her short crop of hair and she was out of the room.

The source of male chuckles was in the kitchen, enamored with her utensil drawer, pulling it out, pushing it slowly back.

"Not everything is so unpleasant, is it?" she said, echoing his comment from earlier that day. The boyish grin he flashed caught her breath. In that moment, the morning stubble on his jaw, that sexy smirk, those incredible deep brown eyes, pushed him into the killer-of-hearts category. Any woman on the planet would be putty in his hands. She took a small step back. Dangerous. Very, very dangerous.

Jarek pulled the drawer out again. "What do you call this?"

"A kitchen utensil drawer."

"Ah, yes, I see its function. And you are correct, not everything is unpleasant."

Awkward "morning-after" silence filled the air. Only problem was, they didn't have great sex that usually prompted it. Pity.

Whoa. Don't go there, girl.

She cleared her throat. "Would you like some coffee?" She maneuvered to the sink, started preparations.

"What is coffee?"

The questioning tilt of his head made her seriously consider calling a professional to help him. In most instances, mentally ill patients had some type of foothold in reality, if only a tentative one. If this was any indication of how their conversations were heading, it was going to be a very long rest of the day.

His quirked eyebrow reminded her he waited for an answer.

"You know, coffee. Most people have it first thing when they get up so they can function." She shook her head. "I'm sure you'll recognize it once you taste it. Why don't you have a seat? I'm going to grab a shower, and then we can talk."

Kelly didn't wait for a response. Being in such close proximity to him in the kitchen caused her brain to think very bad thoughts. Lusty, naughty thoughts.

David had been sexy too, her conscious reminded her.

She flew to the bathroom, locked the door with shaky hands. She'd glimpsed a brief hint of desire in Jarek's eyes before escaping. Hopefully he didn't see the same thing in hers.

Jarek sat at the table, listening to the chugging of the machine dripping liquid into a pot. The room facing him had a very large window where sun streamed in at a steep angle. A muted cacophony of noise drifted through the pane. Definitely not the familiar bird song of home. His ears pricked at the noise from behind the door Kelly went through.

The woman. When she appeared wrapped in a short robe, her well-toned bare legs stretched as long as day down to peach-colored toenails, desire flared deep and hot in his body. Whatever she was wearing beneath that robe must be a mere slip of material. He thought he saw a glimmer of desire in her eyes, but it had been so brief, he couldn't be sure.

On the other hand, her sudden departure and sharp tone spoke of barely controlled tolerance. Kelly was so different from the women on

Leisos. The challenge intrigued him. A lot.

Stop being ridiculous. Focus on what was important. Leisos. He doubted Kelly had the knowledge to send him home since she clearly didn't believe him when he spoke of being from another time. Since these modern people could create something as magnificent as a car, they might have some way of helping him. He would speak to her about it. If not, then it was up to Narena. He hoped she was all right, for both their sakes.

Running water from the "shower" ceased. Thanks to Narena's potion, he understood most of Kelly's words, but some of her language was peculiar.

Thuds and bumps echoed from the closed door down the hall. He raised a brow, tiptoed across the plush floor covering, put his hand on the knob. The door swung wide. Kelly clutched a scrap of silky-looking material in her hand. His gaze dropped to the soft curve of the top of her breast peeking out of her robe. Body parts stirred.

The sound of her gasp drew his enticing view of naked flesh to her flushed face where a lock of short, wet hair hung over her forehead. He itched to touch it. His eyes found their way back to the material in her hand, probably what she had been wearing earlier. Which meant there was nothing between her flesh and the robe. Steam from the room carried the soft fragrance of peaches. She looked good enough to eat.

"Don't you knock?" Eyes wide, she sidestepped him, and whirled around at her bedroom doorway. "I don't know how it is where you come from, but here, if you see a closed door, you knock. Understand?" She shut the door firmly behind her.

Definitely a challenge. He smothered a grin. It might actually be fun.

Chapter Six

Holy moly, she was in it big.

"In through the nose, out through the mouth." Kelly inhaled slow, deep breaths.

There had been strong, potent desire in Jarek's eyes. She tried to calm her nerves as the practical part of her brain kicked in. Hey, it was the twenty-first century, and she was a good-looking woman. Take it as a compliment a sexy guy desired her. Just keep him at arm's length. No problem. She could handle it. Yeah, right.

Therein lay the challenge. Would she be able to keep him at arm's length? Jarek was intensely hot, but she didn't want to be attracted to him. His charm and fabulous body weakened her defenses. If she let him get close, she would become vulnerable, which would only lead to heartache. And with the heartache usually came loads of guilt.

Her best bet was to nip this in the bud right now. Just think of him as a mentally unstable person. That was it. He wasn't all there. If she could focus on that, then her compassion wouldn't be overridden by her passion.

Good lord, I'm starting to rhyme.

She flopped back on the bed, stared at the ceiling. Not now. It had taken her so long to gather the fragmented pieces of her soul and start over. It wasn't fair. She had a career that could take her places. She liked living in Lackton. Having feelings for Jarek would change everything.

No. She wouldn't let that happen. Saving Jarek's life, giving him a place to rest went above the call of duty. She would go out there, be the gracious hostess, give him some coffee, a bite to eat, and show him the door. He could find someone else to help him get home.

She dressed quickly in jeans and a tee, ran a hand through her short hair, walked out to the kitchen. The setting sun haloed Jarek's silhouette in an ethereal yellow-orange glow as he looked out the patio doors. Her heart slammed into her throat, but she refused to back away from the plan.

"Hi."

"The scenery is very different here than in my land, but the sun has the same glow as it makes way for night." He turned away from the window, stared at her, as if he was lost.

Steady girl. Stay strong. "Did you help yourself to coffee?"

He shook his head.

In the kitchen, she took two mugs from a cupboard, poured black brew from the pot. "What do you take in it?"

"Since I am not sure what coffee is, I cannot tell you."

"I'll make it the same as mine, and if you don't like it, you can have something else." Her heartbeat picked up the pace. Not a good start. If only her body would obey her mind.

She poured cream and sugar into the mugs, gave them a quick stir, walked over to the dining room table.

"You need another dose of medication. Come sit down." From her purse, she retrieved the little bottles from the morgue and administered the medication into what remained in the IV bag. "I'll remove that once the bag is empty."

Kelly sat at the table, took a hefty sip of coffee, savoring that first taste before the caffeine hit her system. Heaven. She sneaked a quick peek at Jarek, who sniffed at his mug, took a tentative sip, and sighed. The mug at her mouth covered a smile tugging at her lips. He liked coffee.

"Hmm, yes we have something similar to this in Leisos, but it is called kava. Nice to know some things have not changed."

"Okay, we need to talk about that."

He waited expectantly.

"The Leisos thing. You can cut the act now. You got what you wanted. I saved your life, kept your presence a secret, even gave you a place to sleep. It's time you got straight with me."

"What is 'getting straight with you?'"

Kelly gritted her teeth. "Which hospital did you escape from?"

"I already told you. I escaped from Leisos, not some hospital." At her piercing glare, he continued. "I truly am from Leisos. I have been brought to the future because there was no time to search for the type of poison, or a way to stop it."

This was not going as planned. Jarek's unblinking, steadfast gaze was compelling. His eyes didn't flicker to the left or over her shoulder, telltale hints of lying. But that only meant he believed he was telling the truth.

"It is obvious Narena picked you to help me," he said.

"Obvious."

"Yes. You are her descendent."

"Me."

"Yes." Jarek sighed. "The birthmark on your neck, of the crescent moon and star. When I spoke of it earlier, you were very surprised. Frightened even. I gather it is not a common thing in this time."

"I wouldn't know. I don't go around looking at people's necks."

"You said you work on dead bodies. Do you prepare them for burial?"

"No, that's a funeral director. I find out how they died."

"Then, in your inspection, you would notice birthmarks, especially unusual ones." When she didn't react, he continued. "Am I also correct the birthmark runs in your ancestors? Probably the women?"

She dropped her gaze, unwilling to let him see tears building at the mention of her family. She didn't know about her extended relatives, but her mother had the mark. And Stephanie had it. They were both gone now. Even her father had died. She had no one. At least no one to ask right away.

There was an aunt she had met a long time ago as a child. What was her name again? Victoria, Tessa...No, Vanessa. Yes, Aunt Vanessa. Her aunt probably didn't even remember her. She chewed on her bottom lip, trying to figure out if she had the woman's phone number. She didn't really want to contact her aunt because that would be admitting there was a supernatural force at work.

A warm hand covered hers on the table. She didn't look up.

"I have caused you pain. I am sorry," Jarek whispered.

Kelly forced the lump down in her throat, stared at the round wooden table to gather her composure before answering. "You're not the cause. Anyway, it doesn't matter. My birthmark is not proof you are who you say you are."

"But I have nothing else to give you as evidence."

"Well, I guess you're on your own then."

"Why would I lie to you? I have nothing to gain. I have not asked for anything, only that you believe me. If I had wanted to, I could have hurt you a hundred times by now. I know you do not have the power to send me back. I only ask for your patience until I hear from Narena."

She tried to ignore the hurt and frustration in his words. "I don't like freeloaders."

"What is a freeloader?"

"It's someone who uses people, who takes advantage of them and

44

the situation," she said.

"I have no desire to take advantage of you. I will repay you."

"How? Do you have any money?"

"In Leisos, yes."

"Back to Leisos again. That doesn't help me here."

"I can hunt for you." He sat straighter, tilting his chin up.

Kelly couldn't help the grin spreading across her face. "We don't hunt for our food anymore, Jarek. We buy it in a store."

"Already prepared? What a wondrous thing."

"Some health food types don't think so. A lot of people still cook for themselves."

"I can prepare meals for you."

"You know how to cook?" A guffaw came out before she could stop it. She pictured him in an apron and laughed harder.

"Yes, I can prepare food," he defended. "One of the kitchen maiden showed me."

"And what else did she show you?"

A wicked grin tweaked his mouth before he looked away.

What harm would it do to give a guy who was down on his luck a few days of grace? Like he said, he would have hurt her already if that were his intention. Even though the poison had weakened him, he was still very fit. And strong, judging by the muscled biceps and shoulders. As for robbing her, she didn't have many material possessions, and what little she had in savings was stowed away in the bank.

Kelly couldn't hold back her laughter. "Okay. You win. It would be nice to have someone cook for me, since I'm not that great myself. But only for a couple of days. I mean it. By then we will have to find some other arrangement."

"But I have no way of contacting Narena."

That popped her lighthearted balloon. "I thought she was a

sorceress and would be able to connect with you. Weave a spell or something. She didn't tell you anything sending you a million miles into the future?"

"I am not sure if it is a million miles. She may have told me what to do, but I have either forgotten over the journey through time or was too sick to comprehend it. However, since I am well and have not heard from her, she may be unable to bring me back."

"Then I'm stuck with you?"

Kelly groaned at Jarek's shrug. Great, she just made a deal with the devil.

Later that evening, after removing the IV and placing a band-aid over a cotton ball on Jarek's hand, Kelly sat cross-legged on the couch while he reclined on the floor nearby, propped up on his elbow. A box containing a half-eaten pizza sat on the narrow coffee table between them. Earlier, she gave a short demonstration on how to use a stove. The oven would wait for another day. Take-out choices were Chinese, Mexican, or pizza. Who knew what the people in Leisos ate? She kept it simple, ordered a cheese pizza.

Kelly picked at the slice of pie on her plate. "Tell me about your family. Do you have any brothers or sisters?"

"Two brothers. No sisters."

"Are you close?"

"Rayja is my twin. At times it is like we are the same person. As children we were always getting into trouble. More his doing than mine." He flashed a cheeky smile.

"Humph. I bet. What about your other brother?"

Jarek's hand stilled momentarily as he reached for his beer. She'd explained the drink was similar to ale. He grabbed the glass, took a hefty swallow, grimaced but drank another sip before answering. "I did have another brother, Ariki, older than me."

"Did? What happened?"

"I am not sure. One day he was gone and I have not heard from him since."

"Gone, as in disappeared?"

"Perhaps. Ariki had a mind of his own. It is possible he ventured down a different path than to rule Leisos. He has been gone a few years."

"I'm sorry." She paused respectfully before continuing. "What about your parents?"

"My father, of course, is the king. My mother died in childbirth. And I have an uncle, Lord Tavarian. He is a good man." Jarek's voice softened.

"Sounds like you miss him."

"Tavarian taught me how to fish when I was young. At times we still go hunting together. I enjoy his companionship." He studied her. "What of your family?"

"I don't have one." She averted her gaze to her food.

"You are an orphan. You have no recollection of your parents?"

"I had parents. Just not anymore."

Yes, she had plenty of memories of her parents, but talking about them was really difficult. It had been years since they died, and the loss still gripped her heart. Appetite gone, she tossed the uneaten portion of dinner in the box, flipped the lid closed.

"I have caused you pain again. I am sorry."

She gathered plates, napkins from the coffee table. "I don't need your pity." Because then the guilt would come crashing in.

"That was not my intention. I merely meant to offer sympathy, as

47

speaking of your family causes you heartache. I will not bring up the subject again, but if you wish to speak of it, I will listen."

"Now it's my turn to apologize," she said with a rueful wince. Jarek had only been making conversation. How would he know her family was a touchy subject. "They died some time ago, and parts of the memory are still raw. I didn't mean to snap. I'm sorry."

He accepted her apology with a nod, carried the empty beer bottles to the kitchen, and leaned against the doorframe while she cleaned up in silence.

Kelly gave the counter a final wipe. "We should try and get some sleep. Tomorrow, we'll see about getting you a few clothes."

"I have no means of payment and do not want you to think I am 'freeloading.' I will continue to wear what I have."

"Then you can cook tomorrow to pay me back. And you can't wear that any more because it's starting to smell. Once we get you some clothes, I'll show you how to use the shower."

Jarek pulled the corner of his tunic to his nose, inhaled. A frown followed a quirk of an eyebrow.

He snapped his head around at the ringing of the phone, his eyes darting this way and that, as if trying to locate the noise.

"It's just the phone, Jarek. Remember, I got a call at the morgue. This one rings differently, that's all. Wow, it's late." Who would be calling her at this hour? She brushed past him and answered it. "Hello."

"Kelly? It's Calvin McDonald."

Her boss. Why would her boss be calling her at home? She didn't have to work tonight. Maybe a coworker couldn't make it and she would have to go in for the graveyard shift. She stifled a groan, tried not to sound annoyed. "Yes, Mr. McDonald."

"Er, Kelly. How was your shift last night?"

Weird. He never asked her that before, let alone called her at home.

48

And her probationary period wasn't up for a while yet.

"Fine. Why?"

"Well, there seems to be a little bit of a problem."

A ball of apprehension formed in her stomach. "What kind of problem? Did I make a mistake or forget to run a test?"

There was no response for a moment. She had the sensation of the rug being yanked from under her feet.

"No. The autopsy you performed was fine."

Phew. For a minute he had her going.

"It's the one you were supposed to perform that I'm calling about."

"Pardon?"

"There seems to be a body missing."

Chapter Seven

A body was missing?

Holy crap. Sweat beaded on her upper lip. Her mind raced through instructions her co-worker gave. There were five bodies in the cooler yesterday afternoon when she started. She finished one autopsy, was about to start another when...Oh God. Jarek. He was on the slab instead of the drug-overdose victim.

Her eyes shifted to Jarek, sitting at her stereo receiver, watching the numbers as he turned the dial.

"Kelly...Kelly."

"Yes." Her voice cracked, and she cleared her throat. "Yes, Mr. McDonald."

"Is there anything you can tell me about this?"

She was screwed. Unless she came up with an excuse, she was going to lose her job.

"I see by the log you had a body pick up." Her boss's voice faded for a moment, the sound of flipping pages came across the line.

"Yes, that's right." She even sounded guilty.

"I presume you remembered to lock up. There are people out there who have been known to steal bodies, whether to sell to medical schools or even for necrophilia."

Kelly tamped down the desire to gag. Jarek gave her a wide eyed look of concern. If she told Mr. McDonald about Jarek, he'd either think she was nuts, or would haul Jarek away. While the thought of not having to deal with her guest was momentarily appealing, she couldn't do that to him. She wanted to know the truth about her birthmark.

But what to say to her boss?

"Kelly?"

"Sorry, Mr. McDonald. I was just shuddering at the necrophilia comment."

"There are some strange people in the world."

"Yes. Anyway, when I came back from the pick up, there were definitely five bodies in the morgue." It was the truth—only one of them was still alive.

"Hmm. Okay. I'm sure we can get to the bottom of this. It's probably an administrative error. This was brought to my attention late today, and I haven't had a chance to contact the rest of the staff. I'm sorry for disturbing you at home so late. Have a good night."

"Okay, Mr. McDonald. You too." Kelly hung up the phone with shaking hands.

"Is something the matter?"

She couldn't talk to Jarek about it right now. The painful feelings about her family and this curve ball from work constricted her throat.

"Nothing is wrong." The words rasped out in flat monotone syllables. "I'm going to bed. Good night, Jarek."

She went to the safe haven of her bedroom to compartmentalize the phone call and prioritize the steps needed to deal with the problem. She shut the door, sat on the bed. Darkness enveloped her.

The missing body. Where in the hell could it have gone? Maybe there weren't five bodies to begin with. She didn't actually count them; she just took her co-worker's word for it. Had the error merely been a miscount, her boss wouldn't have called to ask about it. If this was a joke, it wasn't very funny. In the event the mistake wasn't rectified, she could be out of a job by week's end.

She got undressed in the darkness, slipped into her teddy, crawled beneath the bed covers. At this point in time, her choices were to come clean or wait, and since the first option would certainly lead to her being fired, she'd wait and see what her boss found out.

Her head settled deeper into the feather pillow in preparation for sleep, but a nagging thought refused to let her relax entirely. She had lied for Jarek, to the police and her boss. If she wasn't careful, she could be lying to herself next.

This was not turning out to be one of Jarek's better days. Kelly refused to talk to him about the phone call. She'd stared at him for the longest time, said everything was fine and went to bed. But she couldn't hide the tenseness in her voice or the look of desperation in her eyes. Something was definitely wrong.

There was also the conversation they had about their families. Her eyes had been filled with so much pain. Something bad must have happened. He was startled by the desire to let her cry away her grief in his arms.

Should he go to her, offer comfort? She was probably in bed right now, which brought up visions of her wearing the scrap of peach-colored clothing, its material clinging to her breasts, his fingers tingling as he reached to slide it off her shoulder...

Enough. Being so near Kelly but not touching her made it harder and harder to focus on what was important. If Narena didn't contact him, he would have to find another way back. He should be concentrating on that, not the woman in the other room.

But he got a kick when Kelly's eyes snapped with fire. Her independence marveled him, but men in Leisos would never approve of a woman like her.

Leisos. Thoughts of home brought Narena and his return journey to mind. When the ritual began to send him through time, Narena gave him the small blue crystal resting safely under his tunic and also the armlet. The melded intricate design of crescent moon and stars intrigued him because he'd never seen anything like it before. It was beautiful, mystical, and since it came from the sorceress, probably magical. Did the armlet and crystal have powers to help him get home? Why else would Narena have given them to him? He pulled out the thin strip of leather, inspected the multi-faceted stone for etchings or markings but found nothing.

All he could do was sit and wait to hear from his friend. He wasn't accustomed to waiting and patience had never been his strong suit. He sprang up, paced the room, went down the hallway and stood outside Kelly's door.

Narena and Kelly. Two very different women, yet so much alike. They were both independent, smart, beautiful. Narena had thought nothing of putting herself in danger to help him. And now, her descendent, Kelly, was helping him in this time. No wonder he was starting to have feelings for her.

His fellow countrymen would laugh at the idea of caring for a woman other than to curb one's sexual desire. Though he was well known for bedding many women who offered themselves to him, he always respected them. Kelly would not allow Jarek to walk away after sex, if she slept with him at all.

Bed. Kelly. The two would make a pleasing combination, but it wasn't to be. At least not yet. With a muffled oath, he stalked back to the living room, picked up the pillow that had fallen to the floor and tossed it onto the too-small couch. This would do. For now. But the fire burning for her in his veins wouldn't be held back much longer.

"No, Stephanie, you can't come with me. Now go back." Kelly headed down the sidewalk toward the car.

Her younger sister ran down the front steps, stood in front of Kelly, her big blue eyes pleading, her hands clasped as she begged. "Aw, come on Kel, please. Please. I won't be in the way, I promise."

"I told you already. You can't come. It's a school night, and the concert won't be over until late."

"But it's 'Righteous,' my favorite band. I'll never be able to see them again. Please, Kelly. Please."

"Steph, I'm going to say this once more before I ground you until you're eighty. Get back in the house. You know the rules. I'll be home by midnight." She slid into the car waiting at the curb and called out the window, "And don't forget to do your homework."

The scene changed. A police officer stood on the steps where Stephanie had been earlier. Rain danced off the roof of the black-and-white parked curbside. The summer shower couldn't wash away the odor of fear surrounding Kelly as she listened to what the officer said. His words echoed as if speaking from down a deep tunnel. For some reason, it was raining inside the house and getting in her eyes because she couldn't see. The officer was trying to tell her something, but she couldn't hear because someone was screaming. Who was screaming? Where was Stephanie? Stephanie! Stephanie!

"Stephanie!" Kelly wailed, bolting upright as the nightmare lost its grip. Tears streamed down her cheeks. Her chest heaved for oxygen. She buried her face while sobs wracked her body.

The crash of the door smacking the wall snapped Kelly's head up. In her sleep-clogged brain, the form silhouetted in the doorway was a police officer and the nightmare became life.

"No, not again. I can't go through it again." She whimpered through trembling lips.

Jarek rushed to the bed, turned on the lamp, sat down. He pulled Kelly into his lap, enveloped her in strong arms. She didn't protest, buried her face in his chest and let the nightmare slide away with the tears as his hand rubbed her back in gentle strokes.

When the sobs turned into dry hiccups, he eased her against the pillows.

"Are you all right?" he asked, concern mirrored in his eyes.

Kelly nodded, not trusting herself to speak. Most of the time, the nightmare was vague, with only the sense of loss and emptiness. But on occasion, images of that fateful night returned and each time she felt her heart rip in two.

She pushed a hand through sweat-soaked hair, accepted the tissue Jarek held out, blew her nose. "Thank you," she whispered.

He nodded, brushed a lock of hair from her forehead. His hand trailed down her cheek. He rose and moved to the door.

"Don't go." The words were a quiet plea. "Would you sit with me for a while?" She hated how the nightmares turned her into a little girl afraid of the dark.

"I will stay until you fall asleep." Jarek sat, took her hand.

The soft glow from the bedside lamp against the darkness of the room put part of his handsome face into shadow. Tense lines around his eyes relaxed when she nodded her thanks. She slid under the sheet, closed her eyes. Sometimes demons from her nightmares returned, and a part of her hated she wanted — *needed* him here in case they did.

Chapter Eight

When Kelly woke the next morning, the bedside light was still on, and something warm clutched her fingers. Jarek's hand. His sleeping head rested on sheets beside her, the rest of him disappeared off the side of the bed.

She was so touched by this tiny act of kindness a lump formed in her throat. He'd stayed the whole night, ready to chase her phantoms away.

Lips that had been pressed into a thin line for most of the past day were slightly parted as he took a deep, sleepy breath. Long, dark lashes lay against high cheekbones. Beard stubble covered light bronzed skin. A soft moan brought her attention back to his mouth. Visions of his lips trailing a path of fire across her skin bloomed in her mind. She drew forward, compelled to find out how soft those lips were.

And shook herself out of her daydream. What the bloody hell was she thinking? Letting Jarek kiss her lips or any other part of her body was out of the question. Arm's length. Just because he'd come in, held her after one of her nightmares, didn't mean she should invite him into her bed, or into her heart. He was a nut case. Narena, Leisos, La-La Land...

Besides, casual sex wasn't her thing. She wanted it to mean something.

Even so, she was still a warm-blooded female who could appreciate a hot, sexy guy in her room, even if he was beside her bed and not in it.

Jarek gave another soft moan as he stirred from sleep.

Then she remembered the late-night phone call, which quelled any thoughts of sex.

The *surduta's* chirping caressed Jarek's ears. A slow smile crept up at the thought of the coming day. He was to meet Larennia this morning by the wading pool. She promised to wash clothes away from the others, so it would be easier to slip into the trees where they could be alone. Smile turned into wolfish grin. The humming of his blood stirred other parts of his body. He spotted her, bending down by water's edge, silky hair shimmering in sunlight. She turned to him, but it was not Larennia waiting for him. It was Kelly. The tip of her tongue peeked out from between crimson lips. Sun haloed her golden hair. She looked so much like a goddess, his heart constricted.

"It must be one hell of a dream," she said. "Do you always wake up with that kind of look on your face?"

His eyes snapped wide. The vision in his dreams sat before him, propped up by pillows. Wincing at the ache in his neck from sleeping beside the bed, he lifted his head from a butter-yellow quilt with tiny pale pink roses. His gaze crossed the blanket to white fingers enclosed in his palm and onward to the lopsided smirk on Kelly's face. He withdrew his hand. The pleasure of seeing Kelly in his dream instead of Larennia troubled him.

"Not fair waking up from such a nice dream to the harshness of reality, is it?"

He rubbed sleep from his eyes, cleared his throat, and mumbled, "Good morning."

She focused on smoothing unseen wrinkles from the bed covers.

"You didn't have to stay the whole night, you know."

He didn't understand why she felt the need to defend her reaction to the nightmare, like a child refusing to accept any comfort. "It was of no consequence. You had a bad dream, so I offered solace."

She stared as if searching for some other hidden meaning. "Well, don't make a habit out of it." She flipped back covers, dismounted from the bed, and stepped over his outstretched legs.

He grinned as she left the room. Kelly's tough, no-nonsense exterior was beginning to show a few cracks.

Kelly forced herself to eat regardless that the toast tasted like cardboard. Her stomach was tied in knots, but at least the bread would help mop up three cups of coffee already sloshing around in her belly. No word yet if her boss found the body of the overdose victim.

She didn't want to go out, but in another day, the odor emanating from Jarek would be too strong to live with. And getting out would be a hell of a lot better than sitting by the phone, waiting to hear from Mr. McDonald. Besides, she couldn't help her supervisor. She had no clue where the body was.

Across the kitchen table, Jarek sat happily munching bread, oblivious to her inner turmoil.

"Jarek?"

"Yes." Brown gaze connected with hers. Bedroom eyes. Yikes. She blinked herself free of his spell.

"Ah, when you woke up in the morgue, did you notice anyone else on the slab with you?"

Eyebrows shot to his hairline. "I awoke when you pulled the drawer out and the instrument began to ring."

"The phone."

"Until then I must have been in a deep sleep. I do not recall another person there. Why?"

"Nothing. Nothing." Great. A lot of help he was. She sighed, pushed her plate away. Since she couldn't do anything about the work situation, might as well get it over with and take Jarek shopping.

As much as she would have liked to throw him in the shower before they left, it was pointless. He'd have to put on dirty clothes again anyway. Despite the tinge of manhood wafting around him, she hustled him out the door. Jarek insisted on taking the stairs down to the car. His wary expression when they neared the elevators told her it would be fruitless to argue. He did, however, keep his eyes open as they drove to the shopping mall about a mile away.

On the way, Jarek's head swiveled left and right at the marvels of modern society — neon signs, traffic lights, the way people were dressed. His jaw dropped at the sight of a middle-aged woman squeezed into a gold spandex dress with black tights. The questions he bombarded Kelly with seemed genuine enough.

"Why is that man speaking so loudly and moving strangely in his car?"

She glanced past her passenger to the young man in the vehicle beside them, stereo playing rap music at a hundred decibels. She shrugged. It was beyond her comprehension as well.

"What is that mode of transportation called?" He pointed to a heavyset man astride a Harley in front.

"It's a motorcycle. Basically the same concept as a car, but has two wheels instead of four, and there is nothing between you and nature's elements."

"Similar to riding a horse."

"Yes, only much faster."

"I see the attraction, and I like the sound it makes."

"Most men do." She smiled. Apparently, some parts of the male psyche hadn't changed in two thousand years.

"What does the man's clothing say?" He strained against the seat belt as if getting closer would help him understand.

At the stop light, Kelly squinted through the windshield at the shirt. "It says, 'if you can read this, the bitch fell off.'"

"Explain."

"Not in this lifetime."

And the questions continued during the drive.

Whereas a kid would ask why, Jarek wanted to know how, for what purpose, and when. A part of her wanted to stick his nose in a set of encyclopedias or tell him to shut up, but it was as if seeing modern man for the first time, through his eyes.

She pulled into a strip-mall parking lot on the right, found a spot a short distance away from the doors, and killed the engine. "We'll get you clothes first and head a few doors down to the drugstore for some toiletries."

He gazed at the throng of people milling about, carrying bags or parcels to and from their vehicles. "I did not realize there were so many people living in this land."

"This is nothing. You should see New York." Out of the car, she waited for Jarek to join her, and pushed the button on her key fob. The car chirped three times.

"What does that do?" he asked.

"Locks the doors to the car."

"Why do you feel the need to secure your mode of transportation? Will we not be using it again?" Jarek frowned.

"To prevent someone from stealing it. Unfortunately, with modern society comes modern crime."

"Why would anyone wish to take something that is not theirs when there is so much abundance in this world?"

"An age old question. Come on. We need to get groceries later, too."

Kelly led Jarek through doors of the clothing store and headed to the men's section. Soft rock music played from hidden speakers. She went to a rack of jeans, flipped through the selection. Other shoppers glanced in their direction. They must have noticed his odd clothes. Or smell. Or both.

"What's your size?"

"Am I supposed to know the answer to that question?"

Who needed children when you have someone pretending to be from the past? This was going to take a long time. She scanned Jarek up and down, gauging his size, grabbed a pair of dark blue denims and held them up to his waist, checking the leg length. Too big. She repeated the procedure with another pair from a different rack. Much better. Maybe some black jeans in the same size.

"You can try these on." Men's shirts next. When he didn't follow, she turned around and her mouth dropped seeing Jarek fiddling with a tie at his waist, about to lower the pants he was wearing.

She ran up to him, hoping no one saw his attempted strip tease. "Not here," she hissed. "Wait until we have all the clothes you want to try on and then head to the change room." The last was ground out between clenched teeth as she pivoted and marched down the aisle.

And that, Your Honor, is why I killed him. The plea and imagery of a courtroom danced through Kelly's brain. She wasn't going to make it. The man had only been with her a couple of days, and she was ready to leave him in the store. Maybe someone else would find the lost puppy and take him home.

She said nothing while flipping through the shirts. Metal grated against metal, screeching in protest.

"You are angry." A hint of sadness threaded through in his words.

She sucked in a deep breath. "No, I'm not angry. I'm frustrated. It's very difficult having to explain everything and keep an eye on you. It's like having a three-year-old."

"Children are meant to make one smile."

His words, spoken with warmth, whisked her into a daydream but she wiped the notion of white picket fences and children away. He's a lunatic, she reminded herself.

"Here." She thrust four cloth-laden hangers into his waiting hands and led him to changing rooms behind them. "Go into one of those little cubicles, lock the door, and try these things on. I'll wait right here."

Jarek hung up the items on a wall peg, poked his head around the corner. "You could come in and help me." His eyebrows wiggled suggestively.

"In your dreams." Her hand snaked out and closed the door.

And yours, her conscious teased.

Kelly crossed her arms, glanced around the store while Jarek tried on the clothes. The other customers had lost interest in them and continued browsing. She couldn't help but peek under the partial door when his pants hit the floor. No, no, no. Her eyes darted away as provocative thoughts taunted her brain.

This was not good at all. One minute she wanted to strangle Jarek and the next she couldn't wait to see him naked. She either needed to have her head examined or get drunk. Maybe both. She could always disregard her morals and have hot-blooded sex with the man.

"The metal mechanism on the leggings is amazing." Jarek's words floated from the change room.

She was about to warn him on the hazards of first-time zipper use when he strode out wearing the black tee shirt and black jeans.

"The leggings are a bit constricting. It will take some getting used to."

Oh, lordy, lordy. Kelly sighed at six-foot plus delectable male package. Saliva pooled in her mouth. Her eyes moved from chestnut-colored hair, down wide shoulders, to what could only be a rock-hard chest. The shirt fit over his torso like a second skin. Her gaze traveled down to hip-hugging, snug fitting jeans, then continued along the length of his legs and ended on bare feet. It took all her resolve not to check out his butt.

"Clothes look good." Her voice squeaked. She turned slightly away so he couldn't see the heated blush rising in her face. "Go try the others. And we'll need to get you shoes as well." She gazed heavenward, looking for some type of divine intervention in getting this man out of her life before she did something she would regret.

As Jarek returned to the change room, Kelly followed the line of his butt until the door closed behind him, and she groaned. Shouldn't have done that.

Needing to put space between herself and the sight of garments hitting the floor, she turned away in search of a distraction. A display of packaged items for sale. Perfect.

"I, uh, I'm going to get you some socks and stuff. Put whatever doesn't fit on the rack outside."

Selecting underwear for a man was both embarrassing and very intimate. Thank goodness they didn't have a huge selection—just boxers and briefs. She couldn't picture Jarek in anything but briefs. She snagged a few pairs, along with socks, and met him as he carried two pairs of pants and four men's tees. Part of her was relieved he put his old clothes back on. She didn't have the energy to run interference once the female population spotted him in those black jeans and shirt.

"That's it for here. We'll need to get you something for your feet. I think there's a shoe store in this mall."

"I do not like you having to pay for these purchases." He pursed his lips.

"Don't worry about it. You can't very well wear the same clothes day after day. And you need shoes."

"I will repay you, Kelly." Shoulders flexed back while his chest puffed out slightly.

His pride touched her. She continued onward to the cashier. True, the clothes and shoes would set her back a bit, but what other choice was there? He would be staying with her for only a couple of days until she found someone who could help him. He obviously didn't have the mental or physical means to live in reality. When the time came for her to say goodbye, she would do it with a clear conscience, knowing she had helped another individual. When they did take him away, he'd have some of his own clothes to wear instead of a mental health facility gown.

She handed over a debit card to the sales clerk.

"What is that?"

The curiosity reprieve had been short and sweet.

"It's called a debit card," she whispered so as not to be overheard by the staff. "It's a form of payment for items when we don't have cash. I'll explain later." The clerk arched her well-plucked eyebrow, handed back her card. Kelly gave the bag of clothes to Jarek and headed to the exit.

Once outside, she walked toward the shoe store two buildings down.

"Will you explain how money is used in this time?"

He was a persistent one. "We still use cash, but some people prefer not to carry it, so the card I paid with uses my money that is held in a bank. I can access it whenever I like. There is also credit if we want to pay later."

"You do not carry money or coins as a rule?"

"It's safer not to."

"Why?"

"There is a lot of crime. People get mugged every day for their wallets, jewelry, sometimes even for the clothes they are wearing."

Jarek's brows knitted together as they entered the store. "I would have thought, with the passing of so much time, we would have become more civilized. I see in some cases, we have not."

Kelly let the passage of time comment slide. This wasn't the place to bring up the subject of his fantastic story about time travel. It just reinforced her decision to get him the help he needed.

Glancing at his sandal-like footwear, she guessed his feet were not accustomed to being squeezed together. Aisles and walls were filled with hundreds of shoeboxes. Jarek would probably be most comfortable in boots. Sneakers might feel strange, and he wasn't a loafer kind of guy.

She led him to a rack of cowboy boots, grabbed a pair with a square toe. She motioned for him to sit and picked up the foot-sizing plate from the seat next to him. If the man didn't know his waist size, it was a sure bet he didn't know his shoe size either. She slipped it under his foot. Twelve and a half. What was it people said about shoe size in relation to other body parts? She shook her head. This was truly getting out of hand.

Kelly rose from her squat, scanned the rows of boxes. She selected three and opened their lids.

"You need to try these on, make sure they're comfortable enough. Put on a pair of socks first," she instructed him.

Jarek remained quiet. He donned socks, and wiggled his toes as if experiencing the sensation of cloth on his feet for the first time. After pulling on each set of boots, he walked up and down the aisle.

When all was said and done, he sat, pulled off the last pair. He inspected them, running his hands along the upper seam, tapped his fingers on the heel, and plopped them down beside Kelly.

"Well, which ones would you prefer?" She looked up from her vantage point kneeling on the floor.

"I would prefer not to wear any, as I am not accustomed to so much covering my feet. However, I see people here wear a variety of different things. And I noticed you appreciated these more." He motioned to the motorcycle-style black square-toed boots. "Since they seem to please you, I will select them."

Kelly averted her attention, scooped up the other boots, and put them in appropriate boxes before returning them to the shelf.

Her opinion mattered to him. Guilt over her decision to get him psychiatric help made her feel like a heel for what she had to do.

"This isn't about what I like. It's about what is best for you. If you like the pair, then we'll buy them." She took the box while he laced up the bindings of his sandals.

"What of yourself? Are we not going to look for a pair of shoes for you?"

"I don't need any." She had a hard time spending money on herself and a new pair of shoes would be a luxury she couldn't afford.

"When was the last time someone bought something for you?" he asked quietly while waiting in line to pay.

"It's not important."

Kelly disregarded the quizzical look from the sales staff, paid for their purchase, thrust the bag at him, and walked straight out the door, not waiting to see if he followed. Once outside, she continued to the drugstore.

Jarek's long stride brought him up to Kelly. He turned her to face him. Even through her shirt, the gentle rub of his thumb felt comforting.

"If we were in Leisos, I would shower you with gifts."

A line from a famous movie about not being in Kansas anymore was on the tip of her tongue, but she knew the point would be lost. Besides, her objective was to aid this man, get him the help he needed, not to refute his notion of lost lands.

He waited outside while she stalked through the drugstore aisles, grabbing items and throwing them into the basket in her hand. Guilt settled over her like a heavy cloud. He wouldn't shower her with gifts if he knew what she planned. He trusted her. When she handed him over to the psychiatric doctors, her betrayal would probably push him farther into insanity. The thought almost made her want to cry.

Chapter Nine

Jarek closed his eyes in blissful indulgence. Warm water, captured from a far-away lake and transported to Kelly's apartment, pelted down upon him. He was fascinated by the varying degrees of temperature. Kelly had placed assorted items on the counter: some soap, an ingenious disposable razor to shave bristle from his face, a toothbrush, a sweet mint-tasting paste.

Although the soap was similar to what he used at home, this one had a strong floral smell. He lathered up his skin, let water wash bubbles down the drain. The forceful spray on his back was erotic. He imagined Kelly's naked body, water streaming across her breasts, trickling down to secret passages. Soft. Supple. Desire pulsed, heated his blood. He licked his lips in anticipation of how she would taste. Hands itched to have her body pliant beneath them.

He took in a strangled breath, turned the knob from warm to icy cold. The desired effect was temporary. He wanted Kelly, and with each passing hour, his desire for her grew. But the signals she gave off were very different. Since this morning, her tone was clipped.

In fact, their conversation was almost strained since his question about the last time a person had bought her anything. She possessed such a pure, generous spirit he found it hard to believe she had not been given gifts or tokens of appreciation.

After cleaning up and donning new clothes, he inspected himself in the mirror. Fingers plucked at the shirt. Although the clothing fit tighter than he was accustomed to, it was made of lighter material and allowed his skin to breathe.

The tee also defined his muscles more. He noticed the desire flash in Kelly's eyes when he first walked out of the little room in the store, but she'd been quick to tamp it down. Which made her current aloofness all the more confusing. Was she struggling with something? He doubted she'd tell him if he asked.

When he opened the bathroom door, the whiff of heated olive oil wafted from the kitchen, beckoning his growling stomach. The chopping of a knife hitting wood accompanied the aroma. It seemed Kelly was preparing a meal, a task he had promised to do.

After their stop at the pharm...phaam—he couldn't remember the word Kelly had used—they bought food. In this time, one could find enough food to feed an entire family in one place. In Leisos, the staff would have had to travel a great distance to market for the same things.

He poked his head around the corner of the kitchen. "Do you wish to make a liar out of me?"

She jumped, shrugged and continued slicing up the meat.

"Do you think I will poison you?" He raised a hand to cover his heart in mock indignation.

Corners of her lips twitched. He liked to see her smile.

"I, uh...thought I would get started since you were in the shower."

"It is nice to be clean again. I will continue creating the meal. It is the least I can do for your generosity today. Thank you for the clothing."

Kelly nodded, pulled out two plates from a cupboard, set them on the table. Jarek took her vacated position at the stove, grabbed a wooden spoon, and stirred the sizzling meat in the pan. This unit made cooking easy. No fires to contend with, no flint, no wood. And the room was without the blistering heat of open flame. As the meat cooked, he sliced the vegetables. Neither he nor Kelly spoke.

Jarek couldn't abide the silence any longer. Since entering the kitchen, his questions were answered with either "yes" or "no." And she still wouldn't look him in the eye. The air had grown thick with tension. "Have I said something to offend you?"

"No."

"Then why do we not talk?"

Kelly flicked him a glance, stared at her plate. "What do you want to talk about?"

"Are you not curious about Leisos? I thought you would ask as many questions about my homeland as I have asked about yours."

She laid her fork on the table, pushed away half-eaten food. "I guess there's no getting around it. I think you're a really nice guy, but it's obvious I can't help you. I know you think you're from Leisos, but I don't.

"And as much as you want me to believe you've come from the past, lived in a far and distant land, it's not possible. There is no such thing as time travel. The sooner you understand it, the better off you'll be. Since I haven't been able to convince you, the only other option left for me is to get you to someone who can. So, tomorrow before I go to work, I'll contact some people, and we'll take it from there."

His temper flared as frustration wrangled with fear. She doubted him. He was telling her the truth. He had no reason to lie, a fact he mentioned to her already, repeatedly. Why would she not believe him?

He scrunched his napkin into a ball, jerked up, sending the chair toppling with a shove. A part of him wanted to shake her so she would understand. The napkin flew from his hand to land on the unfinished meal. He stalked to the patio doors to gather his thoughts. The corner of his mouth turned up in a sneer.

At home, stars had always given him solace. Here, he couldn't see them due to the city's lights. They probably wouldn't even be the same. He spun away from the darkness, fisted his hands in frustration, and gathered air into his lungs in an effort to calm his ire.

"Do you believe in a God?"

"What?"

"God, a god, any god. Do you believe in it?"

"What does religion have to do with this?"

"Just answer the question!"

Kelly snapped back in the chair, arms folded, closed-off, unyielding. "Yes, okay. I believe in God. What about it?"

"Why?"

"What do you mean, why?"she shot back, glaring daggers at him. "You asked me a question, I answered it. Now you want to know why I answered?"

"Why do you believe?"

"I dunno. Faith, I guess."

"Faith. You believe in something you cannot see, hear, taste, feel, or smell, yet when pressed to reply, you answered honestly. But when I ask for belief in Leisos, a place you also cannot see, you do not believe me. I stand here as living proof Leisos exists. Why? Why can you not believe me?"

Hugging herself, she surveyed the room, squirmed in her chair. "Because if I do believe you, it goes against science," she whispered.

"So does God."

Jarek crossed to the table, her wide eyes softening his heart. He touched her chin, tilted her head up. "Just because it has not happened does not mean it cannot happen. Please, Kelly. I would not lie to you."

"Science is my life. It keeps me sane." She clasped his hand in hers. "I need more proof than just you. I'm sorry."

With dismay, he withdrew his hand, turned away to hide the

helplessness and hurt building within him.

No matter what he said, she wouldn't believe him. She would call the authorities, and they would come to take him away — undoubtedly, to a place not as nice as this.

"Since you are unwilling to help me, take me to someone who can. Who is your leader? Your king?"

"It's not like that here. We don't have a king. And there's no way you're going to get in to see our 'leader.' Besides, it doesn't matter. No one else will believe you either, Jarek."

Anger seethed to the surface again. He straightened to his full height, stared icily down at her. "If my brother dies because you were not willing to help me, his blood will be on your hands."

Jarek's words stung like a slap across Kelly's face.

"It can wait," she said, holding a palm up. "It's been an emotional day for both of us. Let's get some rest." Although she said the words to placate him, his rigid stance and demeanor remained the same. He wasn't about to let her off the hook. She went to her room without saying good night.

He had no right blaming her for something out of her control. What the hell did he expect? He waltzed into her life, demanded she believe his story, and turned her belief-system inside out.

After Stephanie's death, she'd immersed herself in work to hide from life, from herself. Science was her sanctuary — a peaceful, idyllic world where everything had a place, an answer, and a purpose. Until now.

As of a few hours ago, Jarek occupied a compartment in her mind labeled "mentally unstable." She accepted it, dealt with it, and was comfortable with her assessment. Then he'd thrown her a curve ball — doubt. He came up with an argument, albeit a flimsy one, which planted a kernel of uncertainty in her view about time travel.

Now what? Her solution to the problem of what to do with him was evaporating. She could readily accept the presence of a deity — although there were still some questions about that one — but the scientist in her had a hard time believing he was from the past. But maybe that was the problem? Perhaps she was too busy scrutinizing the situation instead of taking a leap of faith.

Wait a minute. She launched herself across the bed, grabbed her laptop, and turned in on. Her impatient fingers tapped while the machine booted up.

Google. Why hadn't she thought of this before? Because before, she figured Jarek was crazy. After the computer sang its usual wake-up song, she navigated to the Google page and typed in "Leisos." Her index finger hesitated over the enter button. If he was right, she had to be prepared to face the fact that science wasn't everything. Could she? Maybe a part of her wanted to believe him. But would her belief—and ultimately, her trust in him—be for his sake, or for hers?

Chapter Ten

Kelly dreamt of a room, dark save the radiance from a single candle on a table. The rustic chair had no partner and held a woman clothed in gossamer layered fabric shimmering in soft muted light. Ebony hair cascaded down her back, obscuring part of her face as she bowed over clasped hands. Hanging from her grasp on a piece of leather, a stone radiated a tiny glow from within its core. She repeated a mantra in an unfamiliar language.

Eventually, the woman stopped chanting, seized the stone, and turned. The candlelight enhanced her olive complexion, sparked fire in her violet eyes. A star and the tip of something else on her neck peeked from under the veil of hair. Time stilled. Walls of the room faded. As the dream receded, the woman said, "Believe, Kelly."

Kelly jolted awake. Her heart deflated when she gazed around the room and found she was alone. It was pathetic she felt disappointed. The moon shone through the window, spreading its silver halo across the bed and onto her nightstand. Annoying numbers on her clock radio taunted two-fifteen. Lovely.

Although the woman in the weird dream was a stranger, she felt a connection. It was even weirder when the woman's violet eyes stared right at her, as if Kelly was there with her.

Something from the dream refused to let go. She struggled to recall the scene before it faded. Mentally hitting the replay button, she squeezed her eyes shut, concentrated on the image from her dream until it became clear. There. On the woman's neck. A tattoo. No, a birthmark. A star and the edge of something else.

"Coincidence," she muttered.

Last night, she'd found one very short notation on the Net regarding Leisos, supposedly located somewhere around ancient Persia, but there was no factual evidence for verification. That, and Jarek's repeated comments about Narena made her dream about the woman.

Yet as a scientist, she knew there were no such things as coincidences.

Jarek could easily have gotten the same information and deluded himself into believing he was from Leisos. It didn't substantiate his claim.

She stared at the ceiling.

"Believe, Kelly," replayed on a loop inside her head.

Surprisingly refreshed after only four hours of sleep, Kelly woke the next morning with a renewed desire to contact her Aunt Vanessa. The woman was the only female relative alive who might be able to provide information about her birthmark.

She sat up in bed, hugged her knees. Reconnecting with Vanessa would bring up parts of the past best left undisturbed. A blurry mental image of her mother's sister, a beautiful woman wearing a long multi-colored skirt and flowing top, rose up in her memory. The relationship between her mother and Vanessa had been strained, for reasons Kelly's mother never revealed. If she were lucky, whatever transpired between the two of them wouldn't be an issue now. This might be the only way to correlate what she saw in her dream with Jarek's claim she was related to a sorceress.

It was time to chat with Jarek and find out just what he knew about her family trademark.

Jarek picked up the bowl of eggs and beat them a little more than necessary. He dumped the mixture into the pan, where it sizzled in a dollop of butter. Hopefully, the offering of breakfast would smooth things over so he and Kelly could talk.

His ears perked at the sound of water in the bathroom. Images of Kelly in the shower invaded his thoughts. Fire heated his belly, thickened his blood.

Stop it. Kelly needed time to sort out his presence here, and having him panting over her would not help matters.

Since the moment he awakened in this time, lying in the cold tomb, he'd never felt so vulnerable. The emotion was alien and he didn't like it. Kelly demanded proof, which he didn't have. He could offer nothing but his word, yet it wasn't enough. Unless she came around, his family and the people of Leisos were doomed.

The object of his thoughts entered the kitchen wearing a form-fitting short-sleeved top that hugged her breasts. His eyes zeroed in on her slightly pointed nipples. Jarek inwardly groaned. She was driving him crazy. He blinked in an attempt to clear lusty thoughts clouding his brain, turned back to the stove and portioned the eggs onto two plates.

"Good morning." He smiled, handed her a cup of coffee. He remembered how to make the brew by watching the previous day. She accepted the cup and followed him to the table to sit down.

As he picked at his food, she stared into the depths of her mug.

"Did you sleep well?"

No reply.

Jarek sighed. She wouldn't even speak with him.

"How did you know about my birthmark?"

Gathering his thoughts, he leaned in, braced elbows on the table. At least she was partly curious. Hopefully, it was a good sign.

"You said you knew where I got it. How did you know it was a birthmark and not a tattoo?" Her blue eyes pierced his.

He took a deep breath, let it out. "As I told you in your place of work, the birthmark on your neck is the same as Narena's. You never told me whether the other members in your family have one."

Kelly chewed the bottom of her lip. "My sister and my mother both had it."

"Is there another female family member you can contact who might have this birthmark as well?" She was talking. This was good. Perhaps she was willing to at least investigate the possibility.

"Maybe. But I need to find out a few more things before I dredge up painful family history. Tell me about Narena. What does she look like?"

His brows knitted together, not expecting Kelly to care how Narena appeared. "She is quite beautiful."

"What color is her hair?"

"Ebony. It is very long and hangs down her back. She has smooth skin, like you, but the shade is more like mine."

"What about her eyes?"

"They are the color of violets in spring."

A small line furrowed between her brows. "The birthmark you claim we share. Where was it on her?"

When they were growing up, he'd teased Narena about the mark, asked her if all healers or sorcerers had them, but she never answered. He pointed to his neck. "It sits there. At times the birthmark is covered by her hair, but not always."

Kelly walked to the patio doors and stared silently out. After a moment, she turned from the waist and her hand touched the curtain gathered at the end of the window, studying it before she let it go.

"In a dream last night, I saw a woman I've never met sitting alone at a table. She had very long black hair, violet-colored eyes, and a birthmark here," she indicated the exact spot Jarek had pointed out, "of a star and the edge of something else. I couldn't see what the other shape was because her hair partially covered it."

Yes! Narena! Had the sorceress come to Kelly in a dream with a message? "Did she speak to you?"

"She only said, 'Believe, Kelly.' Now, how could I dream about someone I never met?"

"She is a sorceress. She was trying to communicate with you."

"From a couple thousand years ago? I don't think so."

He stared pointedly at her. "Do you have another explanation?"

"No, I don't. But I'm still not willing to accept it. Yet. I'm going to try and contact my Aunt Vanessa, my mother's sister. Since my mom had the birthmark, I think Aunt Vanessa might too. I don't have any other family members I can call, so you better hope she has one."

For the first time since yesterday morning, he felt like he was making progress. "And if she does?"

"Then we go on a genealogy quest."

A worn green address book lay nestled in a box of old papers. Kelly's trembling fingers flipped pages until she spied Aunt Vanessa's phone number. Praying it hadn't changed, she punched in the sequence and listened to the *brrring* on the other end.

"Hello?" The similarity to her mother's voice unsettled her.

"A-Aunt Vanessa?"

"Kelly? Oh my goodness, I can't believe it. How are you?"

Vanessa's excited response brought a lump to Kelly's throat. Here she was worried her aunt wouldn't even remember her, and after all this time, there was instant acceptance. It would have been great to see her face-to-face.

"I'm doing really well. How about you?" Unshed tears threatened to overspill.

"Oh, I'm fine, just fine. My goodness. This is such a shock. I almost don't know what to say. Are you here in town?"

"No. I live in North Carolina now."

"How have you been keeping since Stephanie died, sweetie? It must have been so hard on you."

Kelly's composure threatened to crumble. She gripped the phone tighter in her hand. "I won't lie. It's been really hard. But I have my work, and it helps a lot. Umm, how...how did you know? I mean, uh, who told you?"

"Oh, I have my ways, honey." The reply was like a warm hug across the miles. "And yes, I know about Lucille as well. You don't have to explain. Some things are better left alone. But, the death of your parents is not the reason you called, is it?"

Kelly said a silent prayer of thanks. Someone must have had told her aunt about Lucille and Martin's car accident. If Aunt Vanessa had already known, why hadn't she contacted Kelly? It was a subject best broached in company, not over the phone.

"Ah, no. Aunt Vanessa, I... I was wondering if you could give me some information."

"I'll do the best I can, dear. What about?"

"Well, ah..." Kelly pulled at a strand of hair. "How much do you know about our family history?"

"A fair bit. Are you researching our family tree?"

"You could say that. How far back has our family been traced?"

"Oh my," Vanessa said. "Quite a ways. I don't have all the documentation, mind you, but I know where a lot of it is. Do you have a computer, Kelly?"

"Yes, of course. Why?"

"Well, give me your email address. We can stay in touch, and I'll also send you a link to some information."

"That would be great. I'm a bit lax at sending emails or letters, but I'll do the best I can. Um, there is something else you might be able to help me with."

"What's that?"

She paused, getting her words in order. "Do you have a birthmark?"

"Yes, as I'm sure you do too."

"So, you... you know..."

"About the birthmark on the neck, shaped in a star with what looks like a crescent moon? Yes, I know about it, because it runs in our family. At least on the women's side."

"But don't you find it a bit odd?" Kelly stammered. "I mean, it is a bit peculiar only the women have it."

"Well, it does have to do with genetics. When you go to the website, it will explain a lot of things."

Kelly rattled off her contact information in a daze. Even though she had met her aunt only once, there was no awkwardness, no accusation or hidden agenda. She didn't know what to make of it.

Aunt Vanessa's words severed Kelly's train of thought. "When am I going to see you? It would be so nice to catch up. Goodness, I don't even know what you look like now."

"I'll try and send a picture with an email soon. And as for getting together, I'm not sure. Things are a bit hectic for me at the moment. But I'll let you know. Anyway, I'm going to have to let you go, Aunt Vanessa. I have to get ready for work. Thank you so much for everything."

"Nonsense, girl." Her aunt smiled through the phone. "You're family. There is nothing more important. Take care and drop me a line when you can. And Kelly, I'm so glad you called."

Kelly held the phone, the dial tone blaring in her ear before she replaced the unit in its holder. A strange mixture of emotions seeped into her heart — happiness, confusion, loneliness, a touch of guilt for never taking the initiative to reach out to her aunt. Maybe it was time to change that.

She sat on the edge of her bed in stunned silence as the information sank in. The birthmark was a family trait going back for centuries. All the women had it. It could mean she was related to this sorceress Jarek kept mentioning. If so, maybe Narena had really been trying to contact her.

She was just about to go to the living room and relay some of the information to Jarek when the phone rang. Probably Vanessa calling back about something. "Hello."

"Kelly? It's Mr. McDonald. Please come in and see me before you start your shift today." His voice was tight, clipped.

She was so screwed.

Chapter Eleven

Bikinied beauties danced across the screen. Jarek gaped at the scantily clad female bodies advertising suntan lotion on the television. He gave Kelly a few sideways glances before leaning in for closer inspection. After the call from her boss, informing her he wanted to see her before she started work, Jarek's antics were a welcome distraction. She had to bite the inside of her cheek to keep from laughing.

Kelly thought about her conversation with her aunt. Although the information Vanessa gave her was sketchy, it opened up the *possibility* Jarek could be telling the truth about the whole Leisos and sorceress thing. Either that or it was the most elaborate ruse she'd ever seen.

Jarek could have seen Kelly somewhere before, noticed the birthmark, done some research, and come up with this preposterous story. But why? There was nothing to gain. He hadn't asked for money, although so far, he'd gotten some clothes, free meals, and a place to stay.

He only asked that she believe him.

With the promise from Jarek to stay in the apartment and not answer the phone, Kelly closed the door and made her way to her car. Outside, thick steely-grey clouds hung low in the late afternoon sky. The threat of rain permeated the air. She paused, considered going back for her umbrella but decided against it.

She slipped into her car, tapped her fingers against the wheel.

Uneasiness filtered through her body. She wasn't looking forward to going to work, which was totally the opposite of the norm. The meeting with her boss filled her with dread. She gripped the steering wheel tighter, turned the ignition.

"I've been through worse," she said, partly in affirmation and partly to bolster her courage. Compared to the deaths of her parents and sister, facing Mr. McDonald would be a piece of cake.

The first droplets of rain began to fall when she pulled into the parking lot at work, making her trot quickly toward the building. It seemed like fate was pushing her to the meeting faster than she wanted to go.

Kelly straightened her shoulders and walked to her boss's office. Three quick raps on the door went unanswered. She frowned, knocked again, but silence reigned. Odd. She turned on her heel and headed to the morgue where her co-worker sat at the desk, writing in a file.

"Hey, Simon. How goes it?"

"Hi, Kelly." He glanced at the clock on the wall. "You're a bit early."

"Mr. McDonald wanted to see me before my shift. I went to his office, but he wasn't there."

"Oh, yeah. He got called out for an emergency meeting. Didn't say what for or when he'd be back. He did say he would speak to you tomorrow, though."

Great. Another day of stewing. "Okay." Avoiding Simon's gaze, she put her purse in the desk drawer. "Did he mention what he wanted to talk to me about?"

"No. Could be about the missing body. I had a chat with him about it."

Kelly almost slammed her fingers in the drawer. She cleared her throat, kept her voice as calm as possible.

"What do you think about that?"

Simon lay down his pen. "Weirdest thing I've ever seen. I've heard stories about bodies going missing. Not saying it can't happen, but it's never occurred in the ten years I've been here."

"Maybe there was a miscount."

He shrugged, looking over the top of his glasses. "I wasn't here that day. I can't see Marcus making a mistake like that. Didn't you do a count?"

"No. Am I supposed to?"

"Never hurts."

"I'll keep it in mind." She crossed to the closet where the lab coats were kept. "What does Marcus have to say?"

"McDonald hasn't spoken to him yet. Marcus is out of town until tomorrow."

Some of the tension left her shoulders. There was still a possibility the mistake wasn't Jarek but an actual administrative error. A sigh of relief escaped her lips and she shoved her arms through the sleeves of the white smock.

"Since I'm here already, you might as well take off early." She came to the desk. "Do I need to do a head count?"

Her shift went smoothly with no visit from her boss. When it was over, she grabbed her handbag and headed to her car. The rain had stopped and the scent of wet pavement drifted in the air as she jumped a few puddles in her haste to get to her vehicle. She fumbled for her keys, distracted, impatient to get back home. Once in the driver's seat, something shiny on the passenger side of the windshield caught her eye. A frown creased her forehead, and she got out. Pinned beneath the wiper was a single blue rose wrapped in cellophane. Her world spun, the breath left her lungs and she leaned against the car door.

Only one person knew blue roses were her favorite flowers.

The man she never wanted to see again.

Chapter Twelve

Apparently she made it home from work, since she was sitting in her apartment parking lot, but Kelly had no recollection of driving. Her eyes zeroed in on the blue rose lying on the passenger seat.

He was here.

She stumbled out of the vehicle and ran to the entrance of her building, her heart thumping in tandem with her racing feet. David had found her. Did he want to resume their relationship? Maybe the flower was only a token to say hello. If so, wouldn't he have left a note?

Her hand shook so much she dropped her keys in front of her door. She retrieved them from the carpet, cupped her right hand with her left to slide the key into the lock. With a heavenly snick, the lock gave. She zipped inside.

And collided with a compact wall of muscle. Shrieking, Kelly backed against the closed door. Terror clogged her throat.

"Kelly, Kelly." The hall light flicked on. Jarek stood there, hand outstretched, as if trying to calm a trapped animal.

She stepped forward, slid into his embrace and held on tight. Since her parents died, she'd relied on no one. Hadn't wanted to. But she needed Jarek now. As his powerful arms held her close, the steady beat of his heart calmed her, and the adrenaline burst ebbed.

He tucked her head beneath his chin, caressing her back in slow, soothing strokes. When she broke their embrace, he held a moment longer, gave her a final squeeze. A tremor danced through her when he stepped away and framed her face with his hands. Craving more of his touch, she started to close the gap between them, but changed her mind. Best to keep her distance.

"Are you all right?" His eyes traced over her face.

She glanced away, not wanting him to see vulnerability in her face. A grown woman shouldn't be running to the nearest person for comfort—especially a man who claimed to be a time traveler, but in all likelihood was from the loony bin.

He led her to the living room, pulled her down to sit on the couch, and tilted her chin so she would look into his eyes. "What is wrong?" His lips pursed into a thin line. "Something frightened you. Tell me. Perhaps I can help."

His old world charm pulled a smile at the edges of her mouth. Whether he was crazy or not, his concern warmed the iciness in her veins. It might be good to tell another person of the guilt she lived with every day, the pain invading her soul.

Kelly plucked at an unseen fiber on the couch, stalling, knowing she should unleash her burden but at the same time scared to relive it as well. Jarek took her hand, caressed it with his thumb.

"After my sister died, I was in a really dark place. I broke off my relationship with David, the man I was seeing at the time. Naturally, he was disappointed, upset. He didn't understand why I wouldn't want him to help me through a difficult period of my life. But I needed to be by myself. And I needed time to heal, away from everyone, everything. The best way for me to deal was *not* to deal.

"I threw myself into my studies, doubled up on courses. When I wasn't at school, I took whatever extra shifts I could at work. David thought once I finished grieving, we could get back together. And maybe, unconsciously, I sent that message, but it wasn't intentional. He said I was avoiding him, but in essence, I was avoiding life. Instead of giving me the space I wanted, he became persistent, waiting for me after work or wanting to help with my studies."

She walked through memories of those dark days in her mind, seeing shadows of her existence. School. Work. The fitful sleep. Not eating for days. The endless numbness.

Jarek's deep, soft timber broke into her reverie. "Perhaps it was the only way he knew to aid you."

"Maybe." But every time she saw him, she saw Stephanie. She couldn't tell Jarek that. Not now. Not yet. "I asked him not to contact me again. He became angry, defensive, accused me of playing him. It got to the point where I thought it best to break off all contact. So I left, packed up everything I could take with me in a weekend and drove away."

She leaned back against the couch. Memories sliced her heart into jagged pieces.

When she felt she could talk again, she continued. "Tonight, when I finished work, I found a single blue rose on the windshield of my car. David knows my favorite flower is a blue rose."

"You believe this man, David, has returned?"

"I haven't dated since I moved here a year ago. No one else knows what my favorite flower is, and a blue rose is not that common. He's here. I know it."

"What are you going to do?"

"I'm not sure."

"Do you wish to resume a relationship with this man?" His hand tensed around hers.

"No."

"Why not? He has taken the time to find you, so he must care for you. Did you not enjoy his company when you were together?"

"Oh, I know David cares for me, but there is such a thing as caring

88

too much."

He frowned, shaking his head. "I do not understand."

"In my time, it's called stalking." Kelly blinked. *In my time*. Now why would she say it like that, as if she were explaining it to someone who wasn't from this era? Must have been a slip of the tongue.

"Explain 'stalking.'"

"It's when a person doesn't take 'no' for an answer. They believe they're meant to be with you, no matter what. There are different degrees. David was persistent, but I'm pretty sure he would never hurt me. I just don't want to see him again. I don't have those types of feelings for him anymore."

A spark flickered in Jarek's expression. "What do you mean?"

"You know, when you can't wait to see the other person. When they look at you, and your whole world lights up. The soft butterfly tingling in your stomach when they gaze into your eyes..."

Her cheeks reddened and she turned away. Why the embarrassment? It wasn't like she felt that way with Jarek. Hell, she didn't even know him. "Haven't you had those feelings before?"

His expression was inscrutable. He didn't comment but she could sense him staring. Deep, steady, unblinking, like he was trying to see into her heart. The silence dragged on for an eternity. There was only so much of her soul she was willing to reveal. The agony of that fateful night was still too painful and raw to expose to a virtual stranger.

She rested back with a sigh, the weight on her heart easing a bit. The couch shifted as Jarek rose.

A series of four sharp pops split the silence.

Jarek flexed his hands after cracking his knuckles. They tingled with the urge to hit something. His chest tightened. He was getting attached to a woman he barely knew. Granted, he wanted to get to know Kelly better, preferably in bed, but that yearning took second place to his desire to help her. It was very confusing.

He studied a picture of a moonlit scene on Kelly's wall, putting some space between himself and the woman who had bewitched him. Since she was a descendent of Narena, maybe she wielded power over men. What other reason could there be for his increasing protective feelings toward her?

"No, I have never felt those things for another person," he answered finally. He gazed at the muted colors within the frame, searching for answers to questions he was too afraid to ask. The scene depicted a couple in a small boat on a lake. A full moon hovered low in the sky, images of stars glimmered in the water's inky reflection. He glanced out the large glass doors on his right. "I wish I could see the stars."

"Uh, the lights from the city block them out. If you go out to the country, you can see all the stars."

"I have not seen them since I left Leisos. I miss them." He faced her. "What will you do if you encounter David?"

"I'm not sure. It depends on him. He may want to just say hello or have a drink for old times' sake."

They settled into silence for a bit before she rose from the couch. "I'll be right back."

Kelly returned with two glasses of wine and a slim black rectangle under her arm. She placed the glasses on the coffee table, flipped the thin, black rectangle's top open, and pressed a button. A snippet of music filled the air. Her fingers tapped on the unit while her rapt fixation on the box piqued his curiosity. He sat beside her on the couch, took a sip of wine. Hmmmm, nice.

"What is this object?"

"It's called a computer. A laptop, actually. It allows me to search the Web. And don't ask me to explain it because I'll get a brain aneurism."

"What are you doing?"

"I'm hoping to settle an inner argument."

She tapped more letters and dragged one of her fingers across a square patch of gray at the bottom. An arrow on the screen moved and stopped over the letter "e." She hit the small pad twice. Images of people and words filled the screen. Fascinating. Each click replaced the images and words with new ones.

"This is really bizarre. Why would Aunt Vanessa send me to a website requiring password access?"

He inspected a long list of names, all of them unfamiliar. Kelly gasped. Her fingers shook as she hit the keys again and clicked on a button. A black box appeared on the screen with a tiny hourglass, replaced by an image of a striking woman. She inhaled sharply, tapped the pad, and the image came to life.

"Hello, Kelly. If you are viewing this message, it is because you have contacted me and are looking for answers to who you are. Your carefully constructed world of science is in for a shock. Yes, my dear, I know you are a scientist—a seeker of truth. This website, our family tree, so to speak, will show you where you come from, and possibly where you will go."

Jarek's eyes widened. It was as if the lovely woman sat across from them, speaking directly to Kelly. But that was impossible because there was only he and Kelly in the room.

"The women in our family come from one great line. Although we are all different, we share the same birthmark—a star and a crescent moon. It usually is located on the neck, but not always. This birthmark is on every female in our line, inherited from a highly regarded and wise sorceress named Narena. She lived in a land called Leisos two thousand years ago and was held in the highest esteem by kings and lords in her time. She had incredible powers. Some of her gifts have been passed down through generations, and all the women in our line possess a power from the sorceress."

Narena! This woman knew of her. He felt vindicated. Kelly had no choice but to believe him now.

"I know you must be reeling with this information. Please keep an open mind and consider what I have said. I am a phone call away when you wish to talk. Remember, I love you very much." The image faded to black.

The women in Narena's line had gifts. He wouldn't have to wait for the sorceress to contact him because they could send him home. He wanted yell with joy.

A soft whisper beside him pulled his attention away from the screen.

"Holy shit."

Chapter Thirteen

Maniacal, hysterical laughter filled her ears. Who was that? It was getting on her nerves. A hand gripped her wrist. Silence filled the air. She had been the one laughing. She was going insane. There was no other reason for feeling like the world was spinning and she couldn't jump off.

Her gaze shifted to Jarek beside her. Tense lines edged the corners of his mouth.

"Kelly, are you all right?" His words broke into her inner rant.

Her eyes snapped into focus.

Good question. Her precise, carefully constructed world, one that had taken time and energy to build, shook on its foundation. Should she hang on, or let it fall down on top of her?

"Yeah, I'm just peachy. In the past forty-eight hours, I brought home a guy who claims he's a time traveler, my ex-boyfriend started stalking me, and now I've found out I'm descended from a sorceress who supposedly passed on her gifts to others. Hey, it's another boring, average day for me." Escaping Jarek's grasp, she vaulted off the couch and ran a hand though her short hair.

He frowned and rose. "I do not understand. This is the proof you asked for. You should be happy."

"No. You're happy," she shot back, glaring. "Don't you see? I can't deal with this. What I've learned throws science out the window. Hell, the only thing I could rely on is obliterated, and you want me to be happy."

He closed the gap between them until inches separated their bodies. He reached for her cheek, but dropped his hand before touching her. "You can rely on me."

Kelly gnawed on her lower lip, her composure on the brink of crumbling. "I don't rely on people. I don't want to."

He hesitated before pulling her close. "Why?"

"Because people end up hurting me and then leave me to pick up the pieces."

She rested her head on his chest, listening to the steady rhythm of his heart. Strong. Sure. Safe. She let down her guard, allowed his warmth to permeate the shell around her heart. It felt good but forced herself to step away before she got too comfortable in his arms.

"I need some time to deal with this and try and get some perspective. I'm going to bed."

"I can help you deal with it, Kelly." He reached for her hand, but she shied away.

"How? How are you going to help me?"

"We can talk."

"About what? You were right, and I was wrong—at least about Narena—so what's there to discuss? And since you know Narena, and she lived around two thousand years ago, the obvious conclusion is you are from the past. Talking about it won't change that. I have to learn to live with it." Arms folded across her chest.

"You make it sound like it is a bad thing."

"Yeah, well, it's not the greatest." Because now she didn't know what was true or not.

Anger sparked from Jarek's eyes. "I did not wish to disrupt your perfect little world. It was either find someone to help me or die, and put in my position, I am sure you would have chosen the same. There are others who are suffering besides you, Kelly. Narena took a tremendous risk sending me here, and I have no idea whether she survived. If she did not, I am unable to go back to my homeland or my time. But I am learning to 'deal' as you say." He grabbed his wine glass, took a hefty swallow.

Loud ringing broke the tension in the room. Kelly started, snapped her gaze to the phone, then back to Jarek. She glowered at the noisy intrusion and picked up the phone.

"Hello."

Silence.

"Hello, is anyone there?"

No heavy breathing, no dial tone, no background noise. An ominous soft click signaled the caller had hung up.

Kelly's thoughts whirled as she replaced the receiver and checked her watch. After one a.m. Who in their right mind would be calling at this time of night? It could have been a wrong phone number, but she didn't think so. First the blue rose, now a silent phone call. Coincidence? Unlikely. Her hands shook as she turned and went to her bedroom, leaving Jarek standing in the middle of the living room.

She closed the door, sat on the bed. Information overload screamed through her mind. She couldn't deal with this. It was too much at once. There must be a hole somewhere to crawl into and wait until everything went away. No more babysitting, no more talk about time travel, sorcery, and men who couldn't let go.

She'd been happy with her structured, predictable, and calm life. No waves, nothing unexpected. Then Jarek arrived. And because of him, feelings she'd locked away for good were reawakening. Kelly gripped the edge of the bed as tears threatened to flow. She had to deal with the events of the past forty-eight hours the only way she knew how—analytically.

The other side of the argument needed to be considered. Aunt Vanessa provided fascinating news about her heritage, which, when thought about it, could be kind of cool. A spark of hope ignited.

If she were honest with herself, she'd admit Jarek caused her head and heart to spin. As much as she wanted to believe he was a loony-bin escapee, the truth wormed its way under her skin.

Skin. That was another issue. His skin, his touch, his eyes, his body. They all called to her. At times, the look of wanting in his eyes sent her blood humming, flushing heat through her body. Intimate parts came alive. These reactions were entirely different from what she experienced with David. Deeper, more intense.

Maybe it was time to release these feelings. Let them live. Allow her body and mind to experience what the sensations had to offer. If she believed what Jarek said, he wouldn't stay. It wouldn't be a bad thing to bring her body and soul back to life, if only for a brief time. She should take whatever he offered, and when the time came, let him go with no regrets.

Her thought process screeched to a halt. Regardless of where her body wanted the relationship to go, her conscience said she needed to apologize. She'd snapped at Jarek — damn near ripped his head off — when he offered comfort. He had done nothing to harm her and didn't deserve her tirade. It was time to make amends.

In the living room, he stood in the darkness, staring up at the sky, his body in silhouette. One arm leaned on the patio door. Probably looking for stars, she thought. She placed a tentative hand on his back.

"Jarek." Regret washed over her when he didn't respond. "Jarek." She pulled lightly on his arm. "I'm sorry. What I said was uncalled for. I never meant to hurt you. The past two days have been unexpected, to say the least, and I'm not dealing well with it."

He turned his head, his face in partial shadow as he gazed into her eyes. Pain reflected there, a mirror image of her own. "I too, am having a difficult time dealing with things, Kelly."

"I know. I should have given your feelings some consideration." Her hand squeezed.   "Please forgive me."

He pulled her close and rested his chin on her hair. "We will manage what is to come together."

"Yes."

She rested her head against his chest. The strong, steady beat of his heart soothed her anxiety, giving her strength.

"What do we do now?" His deep voice reverberated under her ear. A shiver ran through her body. *Take it slow,* she reminded herself. She stepped away, but her hands lingered on his arms. With a delicate touch, her fingers traced the bronze armlet around his bicep while she contemplated her next step.

"I think the first thing we should do is have a talk with my aunt, face-to-face. I need some clarification, and I can't talk about this over the phone. I guess we go on a short road trip."

Jarek's mouth broke into a sexy grin, and he raised his eyebrow. "Does this mean you believe that I come from another time?"

"Let's just say I'm one step closer to believing you."

"When do you wish to leave?"

"The sooner, the better. I'll have to call into work and let them know I need a few days off. Barring any problems, we can leave in the morning."

Hopefully. She hadn't had the meeting with her boss yet. He might not give her the time off.

"Are you going to tell me about the call you had earlier?"

"It was nothing. There was no one there."

"From what you explained to me the other day, someone must dial numbers to reach you. Therefore someone had to have been there.

And it was something. You were upset after the call. Even now, I see fear in your eyes."

Kelly cast her gaze downward. She didn't have proof, only speculation.

He turned her face back to him. "You are afraid."

"I'm not sure. It could be nothing, but it *might* be David. I can't think of anyone else who would call me so late at night. Then again, it could have been a wrong number."

"Anyone who wishes you harm will have to deal with me first."

The certainty in his voice was like a soothing balm on her raw nerves. She thought it kind of sweet Jarek would want to protect her, considering they didn't know one another very well. But she didn't want him to get hurt.

"David is not someone to turn your back on, Jarek. Don't worry about it. I'm sure it's nothing."

He grabbed her hand, held it tight. "I will not let any harm come to you, I promise." The harsh, steely tone of his words was unmistakable.

Her pulse stuttered at their clasped hands over his heart. "Why? You've only known me a few days. Why would you put yourself at risk? Not saying there is any, but still..."

He cut her words off with a gentle kiss. Kelly was so surprised, she held her breath until tenderness washed away her shock, allowing her to give in to the slow flicker of wanting. She closed her eyes for a couple of heartbeats before he finally pulled away. His eyes burned for an instant and he gave her a quick kiss on the forehead.

"You mentioned getting some sleep, and I wish to indulge in a shower. I will see you in the morning, Kelly." He walked to the bathroom and closed the door with a soft click behind him.

Her fingers touched her tingling lips. Sleep? Who was he kidding?

Standing under the cool stream of water, Jarek gritted his teeth. He seemed destined to torture himself, and this was the price he had to pay. He thrust his head beneath the spray one last time before shutting off the taps.

As soon as he'd gathered Kelly in his arms, he didn't want to let her go. Her doubt that he would stand up to anyone who tried to hurt her felt like a punch in his stomach. All he could think about was kissing her, tasting those luscious lips, and devouring her mouth. At least he showed some restraint and kept the kiss short.

Now, more than ever, he wanted her. But bedding Kelly in her vulnerable state would be foolish. He had to get back to Leisos, where his heart should be, not here with steamy images still plaguing his mind.

Jarek toweled himself dry. He was behaving like a lovesick lad thinking with his heart. When he bedded other women, he had never given his heart — or theirs — any consideration. He didn't understand why his thoughts traveled down such a path when the end seemed so obvious. He would go back to Leisos, find the person who had tried to kill him, and forget about Kelly and this time.

Or would he? Would he be able to leave and not have any regrets?

He hoped this trip to visit her aunt would provide information on how he might be able to contact the sorceress since he hadn't heard from her. Worry nibbled at his brain. It was frustrating being so far away and not knowing what was going on. Patience was not one of his virtues.

He inched open the bathroom door and peered across the hall to Kelly's closed door. She must have already gone to bed. He padded naked down the hall. He was pretty sure seeing his unclothed body might be a surprise, but he doubted she would take advantage of the situation. If the roles were reversed, he wouldn't be able to keep his hands off her, even after the cold shower.

Chapter Fourteen

Sweat pooled beneath Kelly's armpits and her entire body trembled.

"Do you mind explaining this?" Her boss pointed to the frozen television image of her and Jarek in the back hallway leading out of the morgue.

Busted.

"I'm waiting, Ms. Richards."

The television and video recorder sat against the far wall of Mr. McDonald's office. She peered at the tiled floor beneath her feet, fully expecting a trap door to open and drop her into a dungeon.

She would have to lie. Again.

"It's my cousin, Jarek."

"You know the rules. No member of the public is allowed in the morgue except for the reception area. Was he here to identify a body?"

"Not yet." She inwardly cringed. *I am so going to hell with all this lying.*

"I beg your pardon."

Time to lay it on. She prayed her excuse would be convincing enough.

"It's my aunt, sir. She's not well, and he drove all night from Virginia to pick me up so I could go back with him."

Mr. McDonald cast a disbelieving glance at her. "Why did you wait two days to ask for the time off?"

Oops. She clenched her legs to keep her knees from knocking together. "Because I knew that Marcus would be away until today, and

I didn't want to leave you short-handed."

The Head Coroner's eyes shifted down to his desk, and he shuffled some papers. "Yes, that reminds me. I still need to speak with him."

Uh-oh. Probably about the missing body. She twisted her hands in an effort to look contrite.

"I'm really sorry. I know I should have told him to go to my place or wait in the car, but he was so tired. I didn't think anyone would mind. It won't happen again, Mr. McDonald."

"And you're asking for a few days off now, is that correct?"

"Yes." *Look him straight in the eye. Don't waver.* "Short notice, I know, but Aunt Vanessa is my only relative. Please, it's only for a couple of days."

The Head Coroner waited a full minute before responding. "I guess it would be all right."

She almost sagged with relief. Schooling her features to be as serious as possible, she started to stretch out her hand to shake his, then covered up the action by pushing herself out of the chair.

"Thank you very much, Mr. McDonald. I really appreciate it. I'll be back by Saturday."

She walked to the door, opened it. Freedom was one step away—

"Ms. Richards?"

She stilled, turned back to the man behind the desk. "Yes, sir?"

"No more visitors. Is that understood?"

"Yes, sir."

Smothering the desire to run out of the building, her quick pace echoed as she strode down the hall and escaped outside. Her car never looked so inviting. She hurried over and climbed in.

The cellophane package still lay on the passenger seat. She drove to the dumpster at the far end of the blacktop, and parked the car.

Out of the vehicle, her body shuddered as she clasped the blue rose, now wilted and dead, and threw the offensive flower into the bin's depths. She glanced at her watch. If traffic was light, she might make it to her aunt's house by mid-afternoon.

The five-hour drive to Virginia was filled with new experiences and old recollections. Jarek's incessant questions brought back memories of road trips with her family when she was a kid. Her little sister had a knack for getting on her nerves. Just when Kelly felt like thumping her, Stephanie would discover some new fact or point out something wonderful in the countryside. She wasn't sure if Stephanie figured out the best way of staving off a back seat scuffle, or if it was pure luck. Too bad she would never find out.

With all that had been going on the past few days, the painful memories associated with her sister hung close to the surface. Kelly kept a tight rein on her emotions, at times becoming very quiet while she worked through the pain.

Ranch-style houses alternated with larger homes on the main road into Petersburg, Virginia. Two blocks before her aunt's street, they passed a bakery. Fresh bread aroma wafted into the open car window with the early summer breeze.

A couple of minutes later, they turned into Vanessa's neighborhood. Sunshine sparkled through trees in front of the stately home of Kelly's next of kin. A well-manicured lawn edged the long driveway. Kelly put the car in park, turned off the ignition and peered through the windshield at the house.

It was mid-afternoon. They had made good time. Jarek grasped her hand and gave it a gentle squeeze. With butterflies dancing in her stomach, Kelly stepped into the fresh air. She filled her lungs with the sweet scent of roses. Her back straightened, but her insides turned to jelly. This first step on the quest to find her heritage was very unfamiliar territory.

"You look as if you are about to enter the house of the damned," Jarek said with a wink.

Her stomach flip-flopped.

"From the mouths of mortal men," she murmured. A striking middle-aged woman with auburn hair opened the door. As Kelly and Jarek drew closer, the woman held out her arms, and without a word, enveloped her in a hug. Kelly couldn't speak past the tightness in her throat.

"Welcome home," her aunt whispered. She escorted them into the house, an arm draped around Kelly's shoulder.

Once inside, Vanessa drew away and stepped back. "Let me have a look at you. Oh my, you do have your father's eyes. And I see you have inherited your Aunt Cecilia's nose." She gave Kelly another hug. "It is so good to see you at last. I'm glad you came for a visit."

Out of the corner of her eye, Kelly glimpsed Jarek take a few steps back, giving the women a moment of privacy. She fought the tide of tenderness threatening to undo her calm resolve. "Hi, Aunt Vanessa. It's good to see you too, although I have to admit, I don't remember you."

Vanessa laughed. "Of course not, dear. You were only a child and had other things on your mind. Like garnering the attention of the boy next door who always peered through the fence into the garden."

She reddened. "Aunt Vanessa, I want you to meet a friend of mine. Jarek, this is my Aunt Vanessa, on my mother's side."

Jarek took the older woman's hand, bent forward in a short, courtly bow. "It is a pleasure to meet you, madam."

"Nice to meet you as well." The woman raised an elegant eyebrow.

"Where did you find someone with such impeccable manners, dear girl?"

Laughing at her aunt's bemused expression, she rested her gaze on Jarek. "It's a very long story, and one I don't think you would believe anyway."

"Oh, you would be surprised." Her hostess led Kelly and Jarek from the ceramic-tiled entranceway down the hall. A set of white French doors on the right opened to a large room with deep burgundy carpet and antique furniture. Kelly's breath caught at the grandfather clock marking time at the foot of the staircase leading to the second floor.

A bright, airy room lay beyond another pair of French doors. Her aunt stopped before them. "Let's go out onto the sun porch for a nice cup of coffee and have a chat. I want to hear all about what you've been doing with your life for the past twenty-odd years."

An hour later, the compulsory necessities of getting reacquainted were finished. Kelly laid her napkin beside the remnants of coffee and pastries on the wicker table. Jarek occupied the matching chair on her right. He had kept silent through most of the conversation, giving vague responses when her aunt asked about his life.

She moved to the edge of her seat, braced elbows on her knees. "Aunt Vanessa, I need to ask you something about our family."

"What would you like to know?"

She faltered. How was she going to phrase the question without sounding like she'd lost her mind?

"Kelly, really. Don't be afraid. Although we've only gotten to know each other today, there is nothing you can't talk to me about."

Well, here goes. "May I see the birthmark?"

Vanessa swept back her hair to reveal the telltale mark on the right side of her neck. Kelly knelt beside her aunt's chair and touched the symbol of their heritage. Her fingers caressed the familiar spot where her birthmark lay. Vanessa's eyes sparkled as she inspected it, her hand resting for a moment on the side of Kelly's face.

"What do you know about the birthmark and its significance?" Kelly returned to her chair.

Vanessa crossed the glassed-in room to a white wrought-iron bistro table holding a leather-bound book, retrieved the volume and placed it in Kelly's hands. The intricate gold lettering and scrollwork on the front swirled in scuffed ancient script. Edges of the worn leather cover curled slightly upwards.

"The easiest place to start is at the beginning, I guess," she said, returning to her chair. "In the first couple of pages are handwritten notes from one of our ancestors, similar to a dedication. A few pages after are the beginnings of our family line, namely the females. No offense to the male population." She smiled at Jarek.

He nodded in quiet response.

Kelly caressed the soft covering, her fingers tracing delicate symbols etched into the surface. Her eyes widened. "What are these?" The indentations captured her imagination. Archaic cultures. Lost worlds. Mythical realms.

"They are ancient runes. I haven't found out what they say or represent yet."

She carefully opened the book, scanned pages filled with phrases from a long-forgotten time. Her fingers stilled on the words of her forebearers. Names on the yellowed paper pulled at a thread deep inside her soul, like a connection.

"According to research, the first known person to possess our family birthmark was a woman named Narena. I'm sure you went to the website and listened to the message I left for you there. Narena was a great and highly respected sorceress, as were others of her kind. Kings, emperors, and rulers alike were in awe of our family's talent. In some cases, sorceresses wielded more power than the rulers themselves. Some took advantage of their powers.

"Every female in our history has a birthmark, although not always in the same place and not all the same size. The records are sketchy, to say the least, but most of our line is presented in that book."

Kelly tracked the black ink through dozens of names. "In the message you left for me, you mentioned something about gifts that may have been passed onto Narena's descendents. Are you talking powers here?" Surely not casting spells and flying on brooms.

"That's the glorified perception of the abilities we have. In reality, the powers you speak of are more like gifts."

"Care to elaborate?"

An enigmatic smile crept onto Vanessa's face. "That depends on how open-minded you are."

Kelly quirked an eyebrow.

Her aunt chuckled. "Come now. You are a scientist who requires tangible proof. I can't give you that. What I can tell you is there are people who are able to do things that cannot be explained by modern science."

"Like psychic stuff?" As a teen, she'd laid her hands on a Ouija board once. Her mother found out, and it went into the trash the next day. Kelly never saw it again.

"For lack of a better term. Now, don't go rolling your eyes just yet. You can't tell me there hasn't been a time in your life where you swear you've been somewhere before but have no memory of it."

"I guess so. It's called déja-vu."

"To the common man, yes. More open-minded people call it astral travel to another dimension."

"Give me a break, Aunt Vanessa." She glanced at Jarek for his reaction.

An inscrutable mask looked back at her.

"There are people who know things before they happen or see things from the past."

"I'm sorry. I just don't believe in any of that."

Vanessa sighed. "You have a right to your beliefs, however, you cannot deny your heritage. You *are* a descendant of a sorceress. Whether you accept it is up to you. Denying it will not change history."

The weight of the information smothered her, driving out all lucid thoughts. Everything she had seen, heard, and read collided inside her brain. Her head felt like it was going to explode.

Kelly bolted from her chair, paced to the window and back again. This can't be right. Science is the only truth.

"I...I'm sorry, Aunt Vanessa. This is too much." She swallowed to calm her quavering voice. "I need time to think." Oh God, she needed to hang on. She couldn't lose it here in front of Vanessa.

She didn't spare Jarek a glance as she walked out the front door.

Chapter Fifteen

Jarek stared at Kelly's retreating back, fighting the urge to run after her. He sat helpless, as if someone had tied his legs together. Back home, he had experienced something similar when a young deer got caught in the rapids of a river. Floundering, splashing, desperate to get to shore. He'd been unable to save the animal.

Kelly reminded him of the deer.

She couldn't fight the overwhelming facts her aunt revealed, so she let their weight consume her.

He half-rose from the chair.

"Let her go, Jarek. She will be fine."

He slowly sank back down and shook his head.

"Kelly's had her world turned upside down and needs to cope with it. She's strong. Capable. Sometimes we need to figure things out by ourselves. I'm sure she'll be back."

He didn't share her confidence.

"So, Jarek, where are you from?"

Her tone of voice and sudden segue to focus on him caught him by surprise He thought it best to be as vague as possible in his reply. Although this woman seemed to have an open mind, he didn't need to reveal everything about himself—especially not that he was from the past. "Not from here."

"I gathered as much. You speak too precisely to be from the United States. Your English is grammatically correct, and you have an accent I cannot place."

"You are very observant."

"I'm curious what you think about what I have told Kelly."

"It is none of my concern."

"Really? From the way you look at my niece, I think you are very concerned."

"What way is that, madam?" He leaned back in the chair, hoping the relaxed gesture covered his nervousness.

"You care for Kelly. I can see it in your eyes—how you gauged her reaction to our discussion." Vanessa scanned him, as if inspecting his body and soul. "Does she know?"

"Know what?"

"That you are from another time."

The breath left his lungs. He was sure he gave no indication he was from the past. Yet she thought he was. "I...I beg your pardon."

That same secret smile Vanessa gave Kelly earlier spread across her face. "There is no need to hide from me, Jarek. I, of all people, don't have to be convinced of things that are hard to explain. Don't worry. Your secret is safe with me. I wish you no harm, and I won't tell a soul, I promise. Besides, who would believe me?"

Proceed with caution, his conscious warned.

"The things I had mentioned—the way you speak and how you carry yourself were my first indicators. And the armlet gave you away. It has Narena's symbols in its design."

Jarek snapped his gaze to the ornate, bronzed band encircling his bicep. He brushed a hand across the stars and moons. He fingered the catch and prayed the sorceress was all right. "She must have slipped it onto my arm before I left."

"No!"

His hand stilled on the clasp.

"Don't take it off. Doing so could be dangerous. She would not have given it to you unless it was important. Has she contacted you?" Vanessa leaned forward eagerly.

"No, and I am very worried."

Flowering bushes and lush green grass called to him from the other side of the windows. The landscape pulled him from his chair. "You do not seem surprised I am not from this time."

"It would take a lot more than that to surprise me."

He turned away from the window. This could make things a bit easier. "Can you help me return to Leisos?"

The happiness in Vanessa's eyes faded. "No, I can't."

He zeroed in on her. "Are there things you are not telling me?"

"Perhaps. But none that will help your situation." She crossed over to him. "I can't help you, at least not in the way you want me to. But I think Kelly can. I don't know why or how, but it's not a coincidence you were brought to her."

"She does not believe me."

"She will, Jarek. Give her time. She's had a lot to come to grips with in the last few days. She'll come around. Until then, what do you plan to do?"

"Wait until I hear from Narena."

"You could stay here. In this time."

"No. I must return and find out who tried to murder me."

Vanessa's eyes flew wide. "Murder! Are you sure?"

"It is the only explanation. I believe my family is also in danger. Or more precisely, the throne of Leisos. If that is the case, it is imperative I return to protect the crown. Besides my family, other lives may be at stake — servants and trusted staff loyal to my father. In all good conscience, I cannot turn away from my people and remain here if there is any way of getting back to warn them."

"Didn't anyone in your family realize the situation?"

"I do not think so. My brother, Rayja, came by once to see how I fared. A few of the maids wished me a speedy recovery, but toward the end, I had no visitors. Perhaps they were afraid of getting sick themselves. The day before Narena sent me here, I came to the conclusion I had been poisoned. The royal healer could not explain my lack of recovery."

"I'm sure if there is a way for you to return to your time, Narena will make it happen," she said, keeping a reassuring hand on his arm. "Come sit down and tell me all about Leisos."

The vestiges of the late-afternoon sun warmed her back as Kelly walked up the stairs to her aunt's house, knocked once on the door, and stepped inside. After driving around for a few hours, trying to come to grips with all she'd learned in the past few days, it was time to accept the recent turn of events. No matter how outrageous the idea, there was no denying people with powers had existed—maybe still did — and she was a direct descendent of a sorceress.

And that meant Jarek had been telling her the truth from the very beginning. She'd been such a heel.

Standing in the foyer, she felt ashamed. She needed to ask Jarek's forgiveness for all her doubt and for scoffing at his claim of time travel. Talk about unfeeling and cruel. Hopefully he'd understand.

In the sunroom, Vanessa sat on a chair, reading a book. She had family, someone to depend on, who wouldn't leave. Kelly's heart swelled. She wasn't alone anymore.

The tall, sexy time-traveler who'd dramatically appeared in her life wasn't in the room. Her stomach fell at the idea of Jarek taking off because she'd been off wallowing in self-pity.

"He's outside in the garden."

Kelly sighed with relief. "Sorry about leaving you two here."

"No apologies needed. It was a lot to grasp in one sitting. Are you okay?" Vanessa came over and laid a hand on the side of her face.

She nodded, stepped into a warm embrace and sighed contentedly. This was home. After a moment, she pulled away. "I need to speak with him. Can you give us a few moments alone?"

"Of course, dear. Take all the time you need."

Her hand touched the door latch when Vanessa spoke again. "Kelly, everything that's happened to you has happened to Jarek as well."

She gave a silent assent, stepped through the portal and down the steps to a flagstone path leading to a magnificent garden. Jarek stood with hands in his pockets near a massive oak tree. Lines of apology rambled through her head. She stopped a hair's breath behind him.

"Forgive me," she whispered.

The man remained silent for so long, she thought he hadn't heard her apology. He turned, bracketed her face, and captured her mouth in a soul-searching kiss that went on and on.

Fear, relief, and joy rocked through Kelly's system as she finally accepted who and what he was.

Her arms slid up, around his neck. She threaded hands through his thick, brown hair, luxuriating in the feel of it running through her fingers. He deepened the kiss, his tongue delving into her mouth. Her breath hitched. Her body became soft, pliant, needing to get closer to him. Strong arms wound around her shoulders, lifted her up until toes barely touched the ground, and brought her intimately closer. His hand traveled down her back, pulled her hips against him. Hot desire crashed through her. She wanted this man. Now.

The reality of where and what they were doing came crashing in. Kelly broke off the scorching kiss and stepped back. She softly caressed Jarek's face, searching his eyes for absolution.

"I'm sorry for doubting you, Jarek."

He flashed a wolfish grin that stole her breath. Those amazing hands cradled her face once more. "I was not sure you would return."

A half-hearted smile tilted the corners of her mouth. "For a while, neither was I. I guess we're in this together."

"Is everything all right? Do you wish to talk?"

"Yes, but not here. Not now. I found out what I needed to know for the time being. I want to spend the remainder of our time chatting with Aunt Vanessa."

"Would you like me to leave the two of you alone?"

"No." Kelly took his hand, walked back to the house. "As I said, we're in this together."

Chapter Sixteen

Jarek rubbed a hand over his brow, turned to look out the window. They were on their way back to North Carolina, and Kelly attempted to pull him into conversation, but he was in no mood to talk. He was trapped. Not by the metal of the vehicle he sat in, but by his growing feelings for the woman beside him.

Since this afternoon, when Kelly had left so abruptly, his desire to see her again overpowered his need to bed her. Even his goal to return home.

The silence in the car lengthened.

"Jarek, what's wrong?"

When he remained quiet, she pressed further. "I don't understand. I thought you wanted me to believe you, and now that I do, you won't talk to me. What gives?"

"Things have become more complicated."

"Are you kidding me? How could they become more complicated than they already are? You're from another time with no knowledge of how to get back."

"Trust me. They have."

The woman beside him threatened his focus. He was always aware of her — the way she moved, her voice, her scent, her body. His hands clenched in an effort to control the desire igniting his blood. He wanted to reach out and capture her mouth again and again. Biting back a groan as she parked the car and turned off the ignition, he wondered how much longer he would be able to stay away from her.

"Do you wish to spend the night in the vehicle?"

Kelly blinked. Her mouth opened and closed before finally replying. "Well, of course not." Her apartment building loomed above in the night. The parking lot was quiet this late hour. "I...listen Jarek...I'm not sure I under—"

With a stony expression, he unlatched his seatbelt. "Then might I suggest we make our way to the apartment? It has been a long day." The car door closed behind him with a resounding thud.

"What the...grrr...I'm gonna smack him upside the head in a minute if he doesn't smarten up," she muttered, reaching into the back seat for her purse. She slammed her door shut with more force than necessary and stomped to the entrance of the building where he waited. She went inside, strode purposefully to the elevator, knowing full well he didn't like it. Too bad. She jabbed the "up" button. When he walked past, toward the stairs, she felt like sticking her tongue out at him. This guy was getting under her skin.

A ping signaled the car's arrival, and she stepped inside. The quick ride wasn't long enough to calm her ire. Of course Jarek was already waiting at the apartment when she exited onto on her floor. He crossed his arms over his chest, as if she'd kept him waiting for hours. She took her time walking down the hall. Childish, but if he didn't want to tell her what was bugging him, fine. Let him stew.

She practically muscled him aside to unlock the door. Her purse landed on the hall table, followed by her keys, which slid off the other side. The full head of steam working in her brain didn't allow her to stop and pick them up. Instead, she motored into the living room.

"If you do not mind, I wish to clean up," he said.

"Fine, go ahead." The reply choked her throat. Once he was out of sight, her composure fell, and she sank onto the couch. What the bloody hell was going on? This afternoon he'd kissed her like he couldn't get enough, and now he treated her like she had the plague.

Maybe a glass of wine would help her relax. She uncorked a bottle of red on the counter and poured the burgundy liquid into a glass.

"To hell with letting it breathe."

Back in the living room, a red flashing light on her answering machine caught her attention. It was probably work, although they knew she'd be gone for a couple of days. With a shrug, she hit the play button.

"Hi, Kelly. It's David. Umm...how are you? Guess this is a bit of a shock, huh? Well, I...eh...I was hoping to talk to you, but I guess you're not home. Maybe I'll try again tomorrow. I, uh...I've been thinking a lot about you. And anyway, you can call me on my cell at 555-3939. Bye."

Slivers of panic inched up her spine, pushing her heartbeat to thunder in her ears. Vision narrowed to a cloudy, unfocused gray. With shaking hands, she deleted the message. Her sickening stomach warned this was only the beginning.

Oh my God, it's David. What am I going to do?

A grip clamped her shoulder, eliciting a scream from her throat, and she whirled to face the attacker.

"Kelly! What is it? What is wrong?" Jarek's wide eyes searched her face. He spun around, looking for unseen peril, his arm going protectively around her shoulders.

The last of Kelly's restraint evaporated, and she threw herself into the safety of Jarek's embrace. His shirtless torso, still slightly damp from his shower was warm. Muscles bunched and tensed as if sensing danger. She flung her arms around him and hung on for all she was worth. He must have realized they were alone because his stance relaxed and he held her close. He softly kissed the top of her head.

"Shhh. It is fine. You are all right. I am here."

She shut her eyes in a vain attempt to stop the tears from forming. A lump formed in her throat at the care and concern reflected in his words. Eventually, her quiet sobbing ended, and her tear-streaked face tilted upward. Deep brown eyes connected with hers. An anchor against the storm. His thumb brushed away tears, and he curled a strand of hair behind her ear.

"Better?"

"Yes."

On the couch, she nestled under his arm with her head on his shoulder.

"Do you wish to talk about it?"

"It..." She cleared her throat and tried again. "It was David," she whispered through trembling lips. "He wants to talk to me."

Jarek ran his fingers through her hair, kissing it every now and then. The simple gesture comforted her. She sighed. There was no getting away from her demons now. David was here.

"You said before you had no wish to resume a relationship with this man."

She nodded.

"Then you must tell him so. If you do not, he will continue."

"I know you're right. I was hoping it wouldn't come to this. I can't believe he found me. It's kind of freaky, actually."

"Explain freaky."

That brought a tiny smile to her lips. "Not very nice in an odd, unpleasant way."

"Ah."

She plucked at her jeans. How could this man cause her feelings to ricochet in so many different directions in such a short time? It was exasperating, not to mention unnerving.

"Thank you for being here," she whispered. Physical and emotional fatigue pulled at her. She wanted to go to bed, but didn't think she had the strength to sleep alone with David so close. She picked at her jeans again, trying to find the right words.

"Jarek." Her voice croaked. "Jarek. May I ask a favor? You don't need to say yes, because, well...It might be unconventional in your time...but..."

"By the time you finish, it will be morning."

She cast a nervous glance sideways. "Would you mind sleeping beside me tonight?"

He leaned back, his mouth slightly open. His gaze probed deep into her eyes. "You wish me to lay with you?"

Yikes. "No. Not in the way you mean." *Liar.* "We would keep clothes on. I only ask because I know I won't be able to sleep. But don't feel obligated to..."

His eyes sparked with amusement. "It is fine, Kelly. I understand."

"Oh. Good." The scent of his skin filtered through her foggy brain. "Speaking of clothes, you don't have a shirt on."

"I am in need of more clothing, I am sorry to say."

"Hmm. When we went shopping, I hadn't expected you would still be here. I only bought enough for a day or so."

"Is that a problem? I have already said I will repay you."

Now it was her turn to chuckle. "Don't worry about it, and no, it's not a problem. Since I have tomorrow off anyway, we can get some more clothes." Sleepiness struck her, and she yawned.

"Sorry, guess I'm really tired. It's been a pretty wild day. I...uh...I'm going to get ready for bed. You can, um...stay up for a while if you like, or get some rest now. I'll only be a moment." Eeks, she'd never make it

119

as a sex kitten. She leapt off the couch and zipped to the bathroom.

"Sleep, not likely. A gorgeous guy is sleeping in my bed, and all I want to do is rip his clothes off." She gazed at her reflection in the mirror. Oh God, she was falling for him. But when it was time for him to leave, would she be able to let him go?

Chapter Seventeen

Jarek lay in darkness. Across the bed, Kelly was on her side, back to him, rigid, tense. She should be relaxing and getting some much-needed rest.

He was one to talk. For the past hour, he'd stared at the ceiling, searching for anything to take his mind off the warm female body next to him. His right arm pillowed his head, giving Kelly room to cuddle closer if she desired. She hugged the opposite side instead. One wrong move, she would end up on the floor.

Covers obscured her soft curves. He ached to touch her hair, kiss the nape of her neck, caress her skin. He yearned to bring her body to life. His teeth bit into his lip to stifle a groan. He couldn't hold out much longer without touching the creamy skin beneath her silky garment. Did the woman not own something more modest?

The need for her was so strong, his body shook. But he would not break. He would not instigate lovemaking, even though his body, mind, and soul cried out for it. The choice had to be hers. She had to desire him. Her needs came first.

But oh, the temptation was excruciating.

A heavy sigh broke into his thoughts. The bed shifted as Kelly turned over. Light filtering through the window reflected off the side of her face. She snuck a glance at him, turned again, cushioning her head in her hands.

"Can't sleep either, huh?"

"No."

"Want to talk about it?"

Jarek bit back a naughty grin. He could imagine what she'd say if he spoke aloud the things he wanted to do to her. With her. For her. She'd probably demand he leave the room and slam the door in his face.

Or she might surprise him and acknowledge the desire he sensed she felt for him. Over the past few days, he caught her looking his way when she thought he wouldn't notice. And today, in the garden, her response to his kiss was warm, inviting him to give more. Her heart had hammered in sync with his. He'd almost lost control when she'd flicked her tongue over his. It had been heaven and hell at the same time.

He smothered a groan, his control hanging by a thread.

"Okay, if you don't want to talk about why you can't sleep, then tell me all about Leisos. I want to know. What was it like growing up there?"

A smile spread across his face. At last, he could share his world with her. "My uncle, Lord Tavarian, took me fishing when I was a child. There was a lake a few hours' ride from the palace, where *surduatas* chirped in the citron trees that lined the banks along the water. One spot along the shore sloped gently toward the lake, so you could lie and look at the clouds in the sky. No one ever bothered us there. It was the only place where I always caught something, and he never did. Each time, he was determined to hook more fish than me. Secretly, I think he made sure I caught more than he did. He also taught me how to skin and fillet the fish, which was when I first began to admire knives."

Kelly scrunched the pillow under her head. The corners of her mouth swept up in a relaxed smile. "What about your brother? Did he like to fish as well?"

"Not as much. Rayja preferred to hunt, which made him a better tracker than me. But I am more proficient with the knife."

"And your father? What is he like?" she asked.

Jarek hesitated. "Lord Daylen is a good man and has ruled Leisos for many years."

"Why do you call him by his title?"

"His title is King. When we speak of royalty, we use the more familiar term of Lord."

"But you don't call him 'Father.'"

"When I am in his company, I do." But that hadn't been for some time, which still bothered him. Why had his father not visited as he lay sick in his bed?

"Are you going to tell me about the women there, or shall I guess?

Kelly's question brought him back to the present. "The women?"

"Oh, don't play cute, Jarek. You're a man. You must have bedded lots of women."

"It is not something to speak about, especially to another female."

Kelly giggled, poked his ribs. "You're embarrassed."

"I am not embarrassed." He didn't want to discuss other women with Kelly. It felt wrong. Her laughter and teasing stirred his blood, and he returned the playful banter. "What of you and your other conquests?"

"Conquests? You make it sound like I run around, trying to rule men."

He propped himself up on his elbow to look down at her. "You are a woman. Is that not what you set out to do?" He enjoyed evoking a fiery spark in her eyes.

She reached out to smack his arm, but he caught her wrist, pinning it close to her chest. He was about to make another teasing barb when her eyes widened slightly, and the mischievous spark changed to desire.

Her breathing faltered. The brush of her breasts against him kicked his craving up a notch. Her scent drifted over him. Heat radiated from her skin. His gaze narrowed on the accelerating pulse beating in her neck. But it was the tip of her tongue, inching out to moisten her luscious mouth that was his undoing.

"Kelly." He ached for her. "I do not know how much longer I can resist you. You cannot look at me that way and expect me to do nothing. I think it is best if I sleep in the other room." He desperately wanted to kiss her lips, devour them, but after one touch of their petal softness, there would be no turning back. His body burned, and his control slipped.

The breath left Kelly's lungs. Jarek's skin was hot, and judging from the smoldering glint in his eyes, he wanted her as much as she wanted him. Delicious flashes of want leapt through her, settled in her belly. Hunger to have him inside her grew. She shifted position and brushed against the strain in his jeans. She gasped. Flames in her belly turn to liquid fire.

His comment barely registered in her foggy brain but when it penetrated, she realized she wouldn't let him go. Not with this raw desire clawing through her. He bent his head to kiss her brow, and she funneled her fingers through his hair, rising to claim his mouth. Her world teetered, thundered, crashed. She wanted more.

Jarek groaned and Kelly pulled his body closer, melting into him. He took command of the kiss, delving into her mouth with his tongue, eliciting a whimper as her hands roamed the hard planes of his back and shoulders. Her hips inched off the bed, nudged against him. Jarek broke off the kiss, breathing ragged, eyes glazed.

"Kelly," he rasped, cradling her face. His body quivered next to hers. "Is this what you want?"

"I've never wanted anything more." Her hands splayed on his rock-hard chest, flitted lower to trace the well-defined abs. She kissed his bronzed skin directly above his heart. "I've never wanted any man more."

Jarek pushed her back onto the bed, sending his hands beneath her silk teddy, pulling it over her head in one move. He trailed his fingers down the column of her throat, past her collarbone, onto her breasts, teasing the nipples to stiff peaks. She groaned as his hot mouth suckled the rosy buds, and with each flick of his tongue, the pull deep down in her belly increased. Her body was on fire. Everywhere Jarek touched with his hands, his mouth, burst her skin into flames. Her breasts settled into his palms. Kisses rained over her torso. He rolled her nipples between his thumbs and forefingers, and with each gentle play, her hips rose off the bed.

Kelly no longer knew where she was. Hunger for him drove her crazy. He trailed his tongue from her breast down her stomach. His hands danced across the juncture of her thighs, then dipped into the band of her teddy bottoms. Jarek inched them down her legs until she was naked beneath his smoking gaze. She felt sexy. Alive. Wicked.

Her hands shook as she unbuckled his belt. The button of his jeans popped free after the second try. She lowered the zipper slowly. The rasp of metal echoed in the room. Jarek snagged her hand in a tight grip.

"There is no turning back, Kelly," he said with ragged breath.

She traced his hard length before delving into his jeans and cupping him. Jarek's face contorted as he groaned and closed his eyes. Her fingers danced along him, tickling, teasing, each movement eliciting a gasp.

Sexual power surged within her, heady and potent. She wanted him to feel the same longing as she did.

He growled deep and primal. Jarek snaked an arm around her waist and flipped her underneath him. His pants came off with harsh urgency. Raw lust glowed from his eyes. He sat up, lifting her effortlessly and settling her directly on top of him. Her bent knees caged his hips. She lowered herself onto his shaft as he drove himself upward. The instant penetration into her hot moistness rocked her system. Each thrust from him fueled her blood. She careened closer and closer to the edge.

Their gazes connected. The inferno in his eyes flamed hotter with each rock of her hips. His arms bunched with increased tension. Hands splayed on her waist, locking her to him. Her fingers slid down his arms and tripped across his abs, making muscles quiver and dance beneath his skin. He increased the tempo, commanding her body to do the same.

She whimpered as exquisite torture consumed her. His head tilted back. She grasped his arms to anchor her as the pulling, coiling, tightening built, pushing her higher and higher, up, up into the clouds. Jarek muffled a grunt and pulsed inside her. Then Kelly called his name and finally let go.

Her body trembled with delicious aftershocks. She lay on top of Jarek, her face hidden in the curve of his neck and tumbled back to earth. Good God Almighty, what had she done? She had literally thrown herself at a man she barely knew for mind-blowing, molten hot sex. So much for the analytical thinker who explored all avenues of a situation before deciding the best course of action. She sure as hell wasn't here.

Strong arms encompassed her, holding tight. The hammering of Jarek's heart echoed hers. His ragged breathing resounded in the room while they both settled down from their lovemaking. She shifted to roll off him, but he held her fast, a low moan of pleasure rumbling in his chest.

"Where do you think you are going?"

Sexual intent still glimmered in his eyes. She placed her palm against him and sat up. Surely he wasn't ready for more? Still inside her, he stirred and filled her again. He clamped his hands on her waist. A tide of heat swirled through her as her body came alive of its own volition, clutching him inside, causing him to moan.

"You cannot tell me you wish to leave now." He thrust upward.

A gasp of pleasure escaped her lips. "Stop. We can't do this."

"Why not?"

A wolf grinned back at her, and her hips rocked to match his rhythm. She shook her head. This needed to stop, right now. She had never been able to climax more than once during a lovemaking session. She inwardly cringed. They'd both end up feeling frustrated, and he would be disappointed at her lack of sexual ability. She'd had sex to get him out of her system, that should have been enough.

Her body wasn't listening to her mind. It craved more.

"Jarek, I can't." She couldn't meet his eyes.

"Again, I ask you. Why not?" He tilted his head to one side but continued to move.

"I...I've never..." This wasn't going well. Maybe she should say she had a headache.

"Do not fret, my sweet." He framed her face, making her look at him. The brown orbs staring back at her were filled with sincerity. "Let me show you how you make me feel. This time, it will all be for you."

He sat up, captured her mouth in a slow, sensuous kiss. He knelt, bent her back over his arm, exposing her throat. His lips burned a path down her skin — lower to her aching breasts — and worked in tandem with his other hand. He journeyed over each white globe, leaving no inch of them undiscovered.

Kelly arched her back, giving herself up to Jarek's exquisite torture. He continued rocking. Her hips ground against him, harder, more demanding with each pass. When his teeth grazed her nipple, she gasped, shuddered, as a wave of heat gradually rose through her.

"Jarek, I'm not able to..." But she couldn't finish the words as a slow burning coiled in her belly, working its way through her bloodstream. He murmured words in a language she couldn't understand and thrust harder, deeper. She stared into his eyes, entranced by his intensity. She caught a glimpse of something else, but the heat consuming her drove all thoughts from her brain. A cry of ecstasy escaped her when his hand slid intimately between them to her sensitive nub. The burning turned into an inferno.

She couldn't breathe. She couldn't think. She could only feel. Urgency spread until it begged for release. She clamped her legs together like a vise and rode the wave to a shuddering release with him. This time when she called his name, he stole her breath with his kiss.

A single tear made of joy and sorrow trailed down her cheek. Jarek was the only man who had given her the gift of being able to experience multiple orgasms. And when he left, he would take the gift back.

That and something more—her heart.

Chapter Eighteen

As she dragged herself from the depths of a deep sleep, the first coherent thought in Kelly's mind was a warm, hard, muscular body nestled against her back, and a protective, heavy arm draped across her waist.

The next thought was that she was in serious doo-doo.

What on earth had she done? A flush of embarrassment heated her face at the memory of what had transpired last night and how she had reacted. She'd no intention of sleeping with Jarek when she asked him to stay with her. She needed comfort after the disturbing phone call from David and didn't want to be alone.

But instead of taking Jarek's offer of solace, she practically threw herself at him. Yeah, this was the twenty-first century, and it was perfectly acceptable for a woman to go after what she wanted. But she didn't want *him*.

Okay, he was hot, sexy, and she wanted his body. She thought having sex with him once would scratch the itch. Then she could keep their relationship, for lack of a better word, on a purely platonic level. Hah. The sensation of his hard planes against her back sent shivers of delight coursing though her. Her heart tripped while the embers she had banked last night started to smolder again.

She had let herself go with Jarek, focusing on what her body wanted. The first time had been wild and heavy, but having two amazing orgasms took her breath away.

Jarek had only thought of her pleasure. Maybe that was the difference between him and her previous partners. He put her first, set her world on fire.

She couldn't help reaching back and touching him, giving in to the compulsion of connection. The sexual itch returned. A quiet moan escaped her lips. She needed to get out of bed. Now.

"If that was a plea to continue where we left off, I could not agree with you more," Jarek whispered. His hand inched up from her waist to capture her breast and gently kneaded it.

Kelly bit her bottom lip to keep from groaning again. She refused to turn around. One look at his eyes would capture and sweep her away again. She needed distance from him, both physically and emotionally. It was the only way to protect her heart. He would leave soon, and each time they made love, he would own another piece of her. Until there'd be nothing left.

His fingers swept the inside of her thigh. Oh, he made it very difficult to say no. His tongue glided down the back of her neck, slipping lower. If she didn't get out of bed now, they would end up spending the entire day beneath the covers.

Gritting her teeth, she pulled away from his embrace and swung her feet over the side of the mattress.

His hand trailed a heated path down her spine to her waist. "Do not leave. Can you not think of a better way to greet the day than by giving each other pleasure?"

The deep rumble of his voice made her tremble. *Courage, Kelly.*

"It's late. We should get going." Her short robe had fallen to the floor. She stooped to pick it up, self-conscious of her nakedness. She fumbled with the sleeves.

"Why do you cover yourself up so quickly? You are not embarrassed, are you?"

She didn't look at him.

"Kelly, you have no reason to feel shameful." His voice softened. "We shared something wonderful last night, and you have a beautiful body. One I wish to explore some more." He moved across the bed, the covers slipping dangerously low.

She gulped at his muscled chest, the long dark brown hair tousled from sleep. He looked at her like a cat would a bowl of cream.

"I'm going to get cleaned up," she squeaked, darting into the bathroom and locking the door.

She needed time to think. Her reflection in the mirror gave no answer to the questions nagging her brain. What was she going to do now? Since he had nowhere else to go, she couldn't very well toss him into the street. But would she be able to stay away from him?

Her feelings for him couldn't deepen. He wouldn't stay. He was from another time and place that didn't include her. The best solution was to take a huge step back, keep her distance, and wait to hear from the sorceress. She only hoped it wouldn't take too much longer. Because the more time spent in Jarek's company, the more pieces she would break into when he finally left.

Hands folded beneath his head, Jarek lay on the bed, staring at the ceiling, reliving what he and Kelly shared the previous night. Their lovemaking had been a wonderful, sensual experience. The more she enjoyed it, the more he gave of himself. Satisfaction blossomed when he helped her achieve pleasure so quickly after the first time.

The corners of his mouth curved in a grin. He would like to share more with her. Delicious fantasies began to form in his mind. In this day and age, there must be new things she could show him. Given time, it would be fun to pull Kelly out of her analytical shell and help her explore her erotic side.

That thought stopped him cold. He didn't have time. There was no future with Kelly because as soon as Narena contacted him, he'd go back to Leisos and seek retribution.

He tossed aside the low-lying covers, rose from the bed and reached for his clothing lay on the floor. *Focus.* He yanked the shirt over his head, pulled it snugly over his chest. Sunlight from the window glinted off the metal armband encircling his bicep.

With a soft oath, he stepped into his jeans. If he stayed here too much longer, he might not have the strength to leave Kelly and return to Leisos.

Would he even want to?

Kelly spent the rest of the day buying more clothes for Jarek and replenishing groceries. The air between them was not strained or tense, just a bit uncomfortable. Whenever he stood beside her, she took a tiny step back. Distance, she reminded herself.

The last stop was the morgue. Being close to Jarek, but refusing to listen to his body calling hers, drained her emotional strength. The beginnings of a headache manifested.

In the parking lot, she turned in her seat to give him a pointed stare. "I need to check into work for a minute and let them know I'll be in tomorrow evening. Just wait here. I don't want to have to go looking if you wander off." Her words were harsh, cruel even. It wasn't her intention; she just needed to collect her thoughts. What better place than the perfect, predictable, uneventful world of work.

"Where else would I go?" His softly spoken question made Kelly regret what she'd said.

She attempted a reassuring smile. "I won't be long."

She exited the car and walked to the employees' entrance. She had no intention of staying more than a few minutes. Then it would be straight home for a nice long hot bath. Maybe that would ease the tension building in her shoulders.

Her steps echoed along the passageway. She was just about to enter the morgue when a head poked out of an office farther down.

"Ah, I thought I recognized the footsteps," Cal McDonald said. He came out into the hall. "Ms. Richards. My office. Now."

Chapter Nineteen

Every instinct begged her to run. But she couldn't. This was her boss, and he looked thoroughly pissed. She braced herself and followed him into his office.

"Yes, Mr. McDonald." She hadn't done anything. Hell, she'd been away.

"Have a seat, Kelly."

At least he was calling her by her first name. It couldn't be that bad.

He rounded the desk and sat across from her. He picked up a file, moved it to one side and laid his hands flat on the bare surface. Hmm, not a good sign.

"I'm still trying to get to the bottom of our little lost-body fiasco."

Uh-oh. "Okay."

"I spoke with Marcus yesterday while you were away. He swears there were five corpses to be autopsied when he signed off his shift Sunday afternoon." He stared at her, expressionless.

She prayed her face was as placid as his. "Well, I didn't actually count the cadavers. I wasn't aware we needed to." Even if she had, it wouldn't change the fact Jarek was there instead of the overdose victim.

"Let's put that aside for now. When you came to my office on Wednesday, I showed you a video tape of you and your cousin leaving the building."

"Yes." Her stomach tightened.

Mr. McDonald reached for the remote sitting on the corner of his desk. "After speaking with Marcus, I decided to do a bit more digging."

Shit. Okay. It's okay. Just breathe. There was no way her boss could know Jarek wasn't her cousin.

"And imagine my surprise when I checked the incoming hallway video for that day and didn't see your cousin enter the building." He clicked the remote to start the videotape, staring at her with a look that was anything but curious. "Do you have any explanation for that?"

Kelly swiveled in her chair to view the television screen, but she knew what she would find. Jarek's image wouldn't come up on the screen because he arrived by magic. And she had no clue how to explain it to the man sitting across from her. She silently watched the video play in fast forward, all the while desperately trying to think of something to say. After a moment, the tape stopped, and the screen returned to darkness. Mr. McDonald leaned forward expectantly.

"No, sir. I don't have an explanation. Maybe there was a glitch in the video." Her stomach went from clenching to shaking.

"Not that I'm aware of. And I also see that two police officers came in as well."

"Yes."

"Any problems?"

Should she lie and say it had to do with a case? Each fabrication got harder to keep track of. She opted for the truth instead — sort of.

"Not really. I placed an outside call and inadvertently dialed 911 by mistake."

"Oh? Were you distracted?"

Crap. She should have stuck with lying. "You're telling me," she muttered without thinking.

"Pardon?"

"Uh, I said, yes, that's me. Sorry, I had a lot on my mind."

Panic flared up and exploded in her chest. She had to get out of there. Now. The longer she stayed, the more likely she would trip up, and the results would be...scary. The blood drained from her cheeks.

"Uh, I don't know what to say, Mr. McDonald. Frankly, I'm not feeling well to begin with. The visit with my aunt was traumatic." It was, she told herself. "I returned only a few hours ago." When had lying become a daily routine? "Can we talk more about this tomorrow?"

"Tomorrow is Saturday, Ms. Richards. I don't work weekends." He sighed, shook his head. "That will be fine." The hard tone of his voice softened slightly.

She almost jumped up to escape from the room. Jarek was in the car. What if her boss went outside and cornered him?

"Go home and get some rest, Kelly. You do look a bit pale."

I can imagine. She nodded and opened the door.

He shot her a parting comment. "I will get to the bottom of this."

She smiled tentatively. "I've no doubt about that, sir." She walked out of the office, down the hall, careful to keep her pace steady.

"Hey, Kelly." Her co-worker, Simon, emerged as she passed the morgue.

"Not now, Simon. I'm not feeling well, and I need to get home."

"But I have a message for you—"

She shoved open the door. Air. She needed air.

"Kelly."

She spun in the direction of the voice. A tall, slim man dressed in dark blue slacks and a light grey shirt stepped away from the side of the building.

David.

Her insides quaked. She shifted her focus to the door behind her. Going back in wasn't an option because she already said she wasn't feeling well. Car trouble, maybe? But someone would come out, check her car and find it working just fine.

Which was the lesser of two evils? Kelly relaxed her death grip on the car keys. It was broad daylight, and they were in a public place. He wouldn't try anything here. She just needed to let him know how she felt in a calm, cool manner. After that, they would part ways. And she could stop acting like a scaredy cat.

"David. What a surprise," she said, her voice strained.

"Kelly, it's good to see you." He stopped in front of her, smiling warmly. "How have you been?" A slight breeze rustled his short blond hair.

"Fine, fine. How about you?"

"Good. Did you get my message?"

"Yes, I did. I've been away."

"Well, I was wondering if we could get together, to talk."

She hesitated. Should she flat out tell him she didn't want to see him, or let him down easy and say she'd moved on?

"Um, David, there's really nothing to talk about."

"Sure there is." He reached for her hand. She stepped back.

Unease prickled goose bumps onto her flesh. The slightest sense of foreboding whispered over her, but vanished before she could be sure.

She'd never felt threatened by him before. He was just a bit overbearing.

Hello, her conscious bellowed. If you didn't feel threatened, then why did you leave? Why did you disappear?

"You left without saying goodbye," he said as if reading her mind. He grabbed her hand before she could snatch it away.

"It was better that way, David. I needed to sort things out."

"And did you?"

"Yes."

"Well then, we can try again. Pick up where we left off."

His thumb rubbed over the top of her hand. When Jarek did it, the gesture was warm and exciting. But with David, the contact felt foreign, wrong, almost cold.

David's blue eyes reflected concern and caring for her. Maybe it was best to end this now.

"We can't try again. Things have changed. I've moved on."

He narrowed his gaze, increasing the pressure on her hand. "What's changed?"

"I don't feel for you the way you obviously feel for me." She tried to tug her hand free, but David held fast.

"Why not?" he demanded. A spark of anger flashed from his eyes. The threatening feeling from a moment ago intensified.

"David, let go of my hand."

"Not until you tell me what's changed. Why don't you feel the same way?"

"Because she has me," Jarek said evenly from behind Kelly.

Chapter Twenty

David's head snapped up. "Who the hell are you?"

"I am her lover," Jarek replied calmly, pulling Kelly under his protective arm.

Well, shit. Nothing like saying it out loud. And what did he mean by lover anyway? They had sex once and she didn't have any plans on a repeat performance.

Her gaze leapt between David and Jarek. God, please, don't let there be a butting of heads or other body parts. What was it with men and staking their claim on someone? It would have been nice if she and Jarek could have at least talked about their relationship before announcing it to the world.

Kelly pushed out from under Jarek's arm and placed herself between the two men.

"You," she said firmly, pointing to Jarek. "We have things to talk about." She pivoted to David. "You, we have nothing to talk about." She turned and strode to her car.

The two men stared each other down before Jarek walked back to her vehicle and climbed in. He started to speak, but Kelly raised her finger to halt him.

"Not a word. Not now. We'll discuss this when we get back to the apartment."

She sped away, leaving David glaring after them. She ground her teeth the whole ride home. It had been a one-night stand for goodness' sake.

Or maybe not.

When they arrived at her building, she got out of the car and stormed through the door, into the elevator, working up a good head of steam for her argument. They could not continue being lovers. There would be no more scorching kisses, no more nights of passion, no more lovemaking. From now on, it would be strictly platonic. Period.

After taking the stairs, Jarek caught up with her as she entered the apartment. He closed the door behind him and followed her to the living room where she stood, hands on hips, looking outside from the patio doors.

"I have made you angry. Again." She thought she heard confusion and a hint of frustration in his voice.

She whirled on him. "You had no right to say we were lovers."

Jarek leaned back, as if struck and gaped at her. "But it is the truth," he said softly.

Kelly closed her eyes and sighed. He was not going to make this easy. "It was one night, Jarek."

A frown furrowed his brow. "You do not wish to make love with me again."

She caught a glimpse of pain before he cloaked his gaze. When he said, "make love" like that, it felt warm, inviting. She wanted to do again but couldn't.

"It's not that simple."

"Why not?"

"Because it just isn't." She turned to the beckoning darkness. Running away would be so much easier than facing her feelings.

Hands rested on her shoulders from behind. "I want this to continue. Why do you not?"

Kelly bit down on her lip to stop it from trembling. When he said what he felt, it made her question her own feelings. She didn't want the relationship to continue because in the end it would be more painful. He had to see that.

He slid his arms around her waist and nuzzled her hair. "Talk to me."

She stepped away and turned to him. "Do you still want to return to Leisos?"

Jarek blinked. "Of course."

Gaping, she stalked past him to put some much-needed distance between them. If she were being honest with herself, she did want them to be lovers. But she wanted more than the sex. Her feelings for him were already growing into something deeper. And by his nonchalant comment, his weren't.

"It's only a matter of time before Narena contacts you." She huffed when he only raised his eyebrows. Fine. She would spell it out for him. "When she contacts you, you'll go back to Leisos."

"Yes. You knew that from the beginning."

Of all the nerve! "So, until then, you think you can get your rocks off, have sex with me, and then adios, see ya later?" The protective shell around her heart thickened.

Jarek closed the distance between them in two quick strides and clamped his hands around her arms, his eyes flashing with anger. "I do not understand what 'getting your rocks off' means, but if it implies what your tone has said, that is not the case."

"Oh, give me a break."

He shook her when she tried to wriggle free of his grasp. "What we shared was more than sex, and I wish to continue for the remainder of my time here. There is nothing wrong with that." He searched her face, gazing deep into her eyes, her soul.

"I can't." The words came out in a whisper.

"Why? Do you not feel the same way about me?"

"Yes, I do." He'd pushed her into a corner, making her acknowledge what she was too afraid to.

"Then tell me."

"Because you'll leave me like Stephanie did—in a million pieces. I don't have the strength to put myself back together. I will not make a choice that will turn out badly. Not again."

He held her close. "Showing someone you care will not bring remorse."

The door to Kelly's past flew wide open, and all the pain and heartache that came with it flooded through her. Deep brown eyes looking down gave her courage to continue.

"Have you ever lived with a decision you regretted from the moment you made it?" she whispered, vision wavering with unshed tears.

He brushed a stray lock of hair from her forehead. "Tell me." He led her to the couch and pulled her onto his lap. In the warm cocoon of his arms, she laid her head on his shoulders and bared her soul.

"My parents died in a car accident when I was eighteen. I had just finished high school and was planning to go to college when it happened. Everything changed for me that day. I became the parent to my sister, Stephanie, who was four years younger than me.

"There was no other family to take care of us, so I gave up the college dream and found work. Things were pretty shaky for a while. Stephanie was resentful, rebellious—as any teenager who had lost her parents would be. But we got through it.

"After a couple of years, I used some of the money Mom and Dad had stashed away for my college and enrolled in some night courses. Stephanie rebelled again, thinking I was deserting her. The only reason

I took the courses was to get a better paying job, for a better life for the both of us. I wanted to send her to college. My life revolved around work, school, and raising my sister."

"I am sure you did the best you could," he consoled.

She continued as if he hadn't spoken. "One night, I got selfish. I had a date with a guy I'd been seeing, and we went to a concert of one of the best bands around. Stephanie wanted to go with us so bad, but it was a school night, and I didn't want her staying out late. Truth is I wanted to spend some time with David, just him and me out for some fun. No sister, no house, no school.

"Stephanie knew the rules. On school nights, she had to be in bed by ten. There were some evenings when I wouldn't get home from class until eleven, but she'd never disobeyed. I guess the lure of the band was louder than the threat of being grounded, so she snuck out and went to the concert herself. How she got there, I have no idea.

"David and I left the concert as soon as it was over. We didn't stay for the first encore. I wanted to get home. From the news reports, a riot broke out just after we left. Fans went nuts and stormed the stage. Fights erupted, fans were hurt, somehow a fire started. It was pandemonium. Some people were trampled to death...Stephanie was one of them."

Kelly didn't realize tears were streaming down her face until Jarek gently brushed them away. Two years of heartache erupted in wracking sobs. Tremors shook her body while her soul begged for redemption. She cried for the empty hole in her heart and for the world that wouldn't know Stephanie's spirit.

He laid down, spooned her on the couch, kissed the top of her head, and wrapped an arm around her while she grieved.

Jarek slid his arm from under Kelly's head and eased off the couch. She had finally fallen asleep, her face streaked with dried tears.

He stepped to the patio doors and searched the night sky. His heart grieved for her loss, guilt and hardship. To bear the responsibility of caring for her sister at such a young age, and then having the person she cared most about snatched away from her by an accident must have been a horrible experience. He glanced over his shoulder. She slept the sleep of exhaustion, both physical and mental. Maybe in dreams she would find her atonement.

His gaze returned to the darkness, his thoughts turning onto a different path. David. Kelly had spoken his name when she recounted the events leading to her sister's tragedy. It was no wonder his arrival opened up old wounds. Did David wish her harm, or was he truly interested in rekindling what he had lost?

When David had snatched Kelly's hand in the parking lot, protectiveness roared in him, pushing adrenaline through his blood. Although the man produced no weapon, he could have been concealing one. Jarek would have beaten him senseless for grabbing Kelly if she'd not stepped between them. David sent an explicit challenge by way of a heavy glare. Jarek was sure they hadn't seen the last of him.

A murmur broke into his thoughts. Kelly would be more comfortable in her bed, but he didn't want to wake her. Sleeping on the floor would have to do, but he didn't mind. A grin split his face as he made his way down the hall. She didn't want to be lovers, but she would get used to it—he'd make sure of that.

In the bathroom, he turned on the water for a shower and stripped off his clothes, leaving them in a pile on the floor. The dark shadow reflected on his jaw in the mirror reminded him he needed to shave. He grabbed the razor to take into the shower with him. When he glanced up, a blurry visage stared back at him from the mirror. He whirled around, but no one was there. He spun back to the mirror. The image sharpened, and a familiar woman smiled at him.

"Narena!"

He touched the face in the mirror but felt only glass.

"Jarek. Forgive me for taking so long to contact you. It has been difficult."

Relief surged. Narena was alive. He smiled widely. "Narena, I have been very worried about you. When I did not hear from you, I feared the worst."

"As you can see, I am fine, although the task of sending you forward was more difficult than I anticipated. Are you well?" Minute lines etched the corners of her lovely violet eyes.

"Yes, I am fine. You succeeded in your task. I was healed by a very talented woman, who I believe is your descendant."

"I know. She was the one I chose. I thought she would be best to aid you in your condition."

"Narena, tell me of Leisos. Is Rayja all right?"

"My prince, I do not have much time. Even now my strength is leaving. In two days, at midnight, I will call for you. When I do, you must be ready and unclasp the armlet. Only then can I bring you back to Leisos. If we fail, our next opportunity will come at the following cycle of the moon."

"Why not take me now?"

"It would not be wise. I am not strong enough. We must wait and use the power of the full moon to aid us. Do not worry, Jarek, I will succeed again."

The vision of Narena began to fade.

"What about Kelly?"

The image blurred, but Narena's soft voice echoed from the distance. "Only one can pass."

Chapter Twenty-one

The screaming of a buzzer snapped Kelly out of a deep sleep. She bolted upright and sprang off the couch before her brain was fully awake. She didn't register the form of a man lying on the floor beside her and stumbled when she connected with his body. Jarek grunted at the contact. He covered his ears with a groan as the buzzer wailed again. She staggered to the door.

"Who is it?" She rubbed her eyes.

"Flower delivery," came a muffled reply from the other side.

Kelly stifled a yawn, unlocked the door, and inched it open.

A young man held a bouquet of beautiful red roses out to her. "Kelly Richards?"

"Yes." She swallowed over a scratchy throat.

"Sign here please." The deliveryman thrust the flowers and a thin clipboard into her hands.

Kelly laid the cellophane bouquet across one arm as she scribbled her name on the paper. "Who are they from?"

"I don't know ma'am. I only deliver them."

"You're a bit early, don't you think?"

The stranger quirked an eyebrow and looked at his watch. He took the clipboard with a polite nod. "Have a nice day." He turned on his heel and headed down the hallway.

Kelly shut the door and inhaled the glorious fragrance from the roses before searching for a card. On the way to the kitchen, her fingers plucked a small white envelope from the wrapping. The big glass vase on the top shelf in the cupboard would be perfect to display the arrangement.

She couldn't remember the last time someone sent her flowers. They were probably from Aunt Vanessa. Warmth filled her heart.

Her smile fell away as she read the inscription written in neat, bold strokes on the card: "They didn't have blue ones. We need to talk. David"

Oh no. He must not have believed her when she said she didn't want to see him again. And he obviously didn't care about Jarek's claim they were lovers. He wasn't going to give up.

Great. Just great.

"They are beautiful flowers," a deep voice rumbled. She turned to Jarek, who leaned against the counter behind her.

"Yes, they are," she said, laying the card down. She reached up to the cupboard above the sink, grabbed the vase, filled it with cool water, and unwrapped the roses.

"Are they from your aunt?"

She could lie, but what would be the point? She stepped around him to place the flowers on the table. "No, they're from David."

"Why did you accept them?"

Good question. Why did she? "I don't know. I guess I wasn't thinking clearly. It's still too early. The guy woke me up."

He glanced at the clock on the wall and then back to her. She copied his movement. Past ten a.m. No wonder the deliveryman looked at her strangely. The morning was almost over. She'd overslept, probably because of the emotional upheaval of the night before.

"You can always return them."

Yes, she could. And she should. But a part of her wanted to keep them to show Jarek another man desired her. It was childish and petty, but his lackadaisical comment about continuing to share the same bed, knowing he would return to Leisos ticked her off. Yes, she was keeping the roses out of spite, as awful as it sounded.

"It's too late now," she mumbled with a wave of her hand. Her gaze drifted to his well-developed chest underneath the unbuttoned shirt. She followed the lines of muscles down to his six-pack stomach. And lower. Heat flared through her as remnants of last night's steamy, sexy dream of her and Jarek floated through her brain.

No, no, no.

She smiled innocently in an effort to hide her thoughts. "Is there something you wanted to do today before I go to work?"

Desire igniting Jarek's eyes could have started a forest fire. If she didn't get out of there now, she would either self-combust or do something she'd regret later, like rip his clothes off and go from there.

"Think about what you want to do, or a place you wish to go." The words rushed out as she circumvented the table and hustled her way to the bathroom.

Her attempt at keeping a safe distance from Jarek was not working. She stripped away her clothes and turned the shower on. How was she supposed to keep things platonic when a gorgeous hunk who curled her toes slept in her apartment? It was enough to make a woman weak in the knees.

Maybe she should take him up on his offer of sex for the remainder of his stay. Then when the time came, she'd say, "Thanks for the memories," and send him on his way.

As Kelly stepped into the shower, her conscious knocked loud and clear. She couldn't take the sex and be done with it because it was already past that. Her connection to Jarek was deeper, stronger than the sex, almost as if they were *supposed* to have met. Maybe he was meant to come to this time — to her — and she was meant to know him.

She sighed at the complexity of her wonderings, closed her eyes, tipped back her head, and let the hot water flow through her hair and over her body. The images from her dream rose to her consciousness again. The soft click of the shower door closing indicated she had company. She stayed motionless, waiting, anticipating, until she couldn't bear it any longer.

Just when she was about to open her eyes, there they were. His hands. Strong, and slick with soap, they caressed her body, starting on her shoulders, moving in slow, sensuous circles, down her arms, across her collarbone to her breasts. He encircled each one, covering every inch of them with soapy fingers. She sucked in a lungful of air when he rolled and gently squeezed her nipple between his thumb and forefinger. The pull reached deep in her belly. Her body arched backward in silent offering. Her hands rested on opposite sides of the stall. Ragged breathing ensued as Jarek continued his relentless exploration of her skin, bringing her body to life.

Soft moans escaped her parted lips. His hands traveled to her abdomen and lower still to the hot, aching part of her that begged to be loved. His caressing became more sensual, more intimate. She leaned against the back of the stall for support. His fingers slipped inside her, withdrawing, sliding in, again and again. Her hips matched his rhythm. She bucked against his hand, wanting more. She whimpered as a spiral of need curled inside, coiling sensuously with heat. When she couldn't it take anymore, his hot, wet mouth tantalized the most sensitive part of her body until she exploded into a million pieces. She trembled and sagged from the power of her release.

"Wrap your legs around me, Kelly," he said, lifting her, his husky voice filled with hunger and need.

He widened his stance for support. Her legs clasped around his hips, and he slid in. He was thick, heavy and so wonderful she wanted to die with pleasure. With her shoulders pressed against the wall, his hands gripped her waist, holding her tight as he thrust deeper and deeper.

Kelly locked her ankles behind Jarek's back, matched his rhythm, and rode him while hanging on for dear life, digging her fingers into his shoulders.

"This is what we share—this and so much more. The meeting of our bodies, hearts, even our souls." He crushed his lips over hers, sealing off any response.

She felt the hunger in his tongue delving deep into her mouth, and in the way he filled her with each stroke. His breathing hitched. She tensed. With one final thrust from him, they both cried out and went over the edge together.

They were united in a world of steam, panting, and trembling.

"We had best leave before this becomes painful." Laughter rumbled in his chest. "Can you stand?"

With a nod, she slipped from his grasp onto shaky legs, reached over and shut off the tap. She wiped the wet hair from her eyes. Jarek framed her face with his hands.

"You cannot tell me this was merely sex to you," he whispered.

Unable to bear the intenseness of his gaze, she turned her head away and nodded.

"Come, my precious one." He led her out of the shower, scooped her into his arms and carried her to bed. "Let us find out whatever we can about each other, both in body and in mind."

"Who do you think might be behind your poisoning?" Kelly didn't look at him when she spoke. Absent caresses from her gentle fingers skimmed across his chest, and little lines furrowed between her brows. She was beginning to care for him. Her troubled eyes and tone of voice told him so, even if she couldn't. He hung onto that hope.

"I honestly do not know who it could be. I hope Narena will be able to supply some insight."

"Narena." Kelly's eyes widened, locking onto his. "Have you heard from her?"

The open honesty on her face captured him. He couldn't lie to her, even if it would be easier to evade the question or pretend he hadn't heard from the sorceress and simply disappear in two days time. He stilled her hand and brought it to his lips, placing kisses at the tips of her fingers. Her soft smile warmed him. He kissed her once more, let her hand fall, and slid from the bed.

"Jarek?"

He couldn't look at her. He gazed around the bedroom at the simple, clean décor. Not many items lined the shelves. There was a sharp, life-like image of a young couple standing beneath a tree. He glanced at Kelly and back at the man and woman. Probably her parents. He stepped away from the bed, picked up the silver square holding the image of her family, and turned it around.

"How is it possible to capture a likeness of another?"

"Uh...it's called a picture, or a photograph. Basically, an image is reflected by mirrors onto what we call film. By exposing the film to light and an object — in this case, my parents — the subject becomes permanently etched onto it. Color, like you see there, has only been around for the last forty-odd years. Before that, all pictures were made in black and white. And you never answered my question."

"Yes. I heard from Narena."

"When?"

He didn't share her excitement. "Last night."

Silence.

"She plans to bring me home tomorrow night."

"I see. And when did you plan on telling me?"

He cringed. Not because of her tone, but because of what it implied. If she hadn't asked the question, they probably wouldn't be talking about it now.

Coward. His fingers touched the glass protecting the faces of her family. When he left, would she give him a picture of herself so he could gaze upon her likeness every day?

He turned to her. "I just did."

Her icy stare could have frozen the biggest lake in Leisos. "Holding out for all the jollies you can get, were you?"

Air hissed through clenched teeth. "Are you speaking for yourself?" he glowered.

She gasped, her face crumbled with hurt.

He rushed on. "This morning was a meeting of more than just bodies, Kelly. The first time we kissed, our souls connected. I know this. I was hoping you would see it as well."

"Yeah, okay. Whatever." Kelly launched herself off the other side of the bed, hastily gathering up clothes.

He stepped into his own jeans, slid them up, and fastened the button. An object on the shelf caught his eye. He reached up and took down an old dagger, turning it around, inspecting the weapon for markings. The whole thing was made of metal with the handle forged to the blade. It balanced perfectly on his finger. The dagger came alive in his hands, flipping through the air so quickly, it blurred.

He caressed the handle and tested the blade. Very sharp. He intended to ask her about it, but she was gone. He was very proficient with the blade, something he would need to instruct Kelly on in the next few days. After he left, there would be no one to protect her. Teaching her how to defend against an attacker was the one thing he could do for her before he walked out of her life.

With a heavy sigh, he replaced the dagger on the shelf.

His thoughts turned to how he would plunge one just like it into the heart of his would-be assassin in two days.

Chapter Twenty-two

Kelly was grateful there was so much work waiting for her when she clocked into the morgue. As morbid as it sounded, she preferred answering the questions the dead left behind than thinking about Jarek.

Bastard. He lied to her.

She flung the bloody set of latex gloves into a biohazard container. She couldn't believe he didn't tell her Narena had contacted him. Typical man. Thinking with the little head.

She stomped around the morgue, slamming drawers and generally pouting until tears in her eyes made it impossible to see.

He was leaving. Tomorrow night. And he would take her heart with him. She sat at the desk, pulled a tissue from the box, and blotted her eyes. It wasn't like they hadn't talked about him going back, but that still didn't make it any easier.

"Face it, girl," she muttered to no one, "it was more than sex to you, too. How could you be so stupid as to fall for a guy from another time?" Damn.

She blew her nose and tossed the tissue into the trash. And since she was coming clean, she reluctantly admitted Jarek really didn't lie. There'd been no time. After she bared her soul about Stephanie last night, she'd fallen asleep. Then this morning with the flowers, and the shower...She blushed at the hot and heavy memory.

Jeez, she'd acted like an ass. No wonder Jarek had been hurt. When he stiffened and stared after her oh-so-lady-like comment about him getting his jollies, pain radiated from his eyes. She needed to make amends. Again.

And if she didn't have enough to worry about, the missing body was also on her mind. Thank goodness it was Saturday, and her boss didn't work today. He wasn't going to let the matter drop. Her own bit of investigating revealed no family member had claimed the overdose victim. The body was catalogued as John Doe number thirty-eight. She thought about taking both videotapes Mr. McDonald had shown her, but that would really make her look guilty. Stealing another cadaver for a replacement was out of the question.

Oh God, what was she thinking? Breaking the law. That was just crazy.

She groaned and finished her last report. Her life was a mess.

John, her shift relief, came into the room, and they exchanged pleasantries. Kelly brought him up to speed on what cases were still pending.

Jarek was supposed to be waiting for her outside. Though it had been a bit tense when she left for work, he asked her to drop him off at a park a few blocks away from the apartment. Later he was supposed to see a local theatrical production of Hamlet and meet her here after work.

Outside, Kelly waved to Jarek across the parking lot, but when she drew closer to her vehicle, she realized with dismay the man was shorter and thinner than Jarek.

David. Again. Why couldn't he leave her alone?

A shiver rolled down her spine and she scanned the shadows. No Jarek. She didn't want to be alone with David, especially at night. Her hand fumbled inside her purse and closed around car keys. She slid them between her fingers. Not the most effective way to defend herself, but it was better than nothing.

Pasting on a tight smile, she approached David. He leaned against the car, relaxed. She stopped a few feet away.

"David. What are you doing here?"

He straightened, his legs slightly apart. She surveyed the parking lot.

"Did you get the roses?"

"Yes, they were lovely, but you shouldn't have done that." Jarek's earlier comment rang in her head. "I should have returned them."

"Why?" he demanded.

Too late, Kelly realized the foolishness of her words. The last thing she needed was to aggravate him. She tried to ease the tightness of her smile. "Because, as I said last night, we really have nothing to talk about."

Her former lover jabbed a hand through his hair. "I think we do. I want us to get back together, Kelly. I'd like another shot."

"No, David."

"Why? Because of him? Is that it?"

"Partly."

"What else?"

There was no getting around it. She had to tell him the truth, as difficult as it would be for both of them.

"David," she began, stopped, tried again while fiddling with the purse on her shoulder. "I enjoyed being with you, but no matter how hard I try, seeing you brings back a lot of painful memories of the night at the concert. And Stephanie."

"But it wasn't my fault."

"I know that." She lowered the pitch of her voice. "It was nobody's fault. It was an accident. I know it isn't right to label you 'guilty by association,' but I can't help the way I feel. If I had never gone to the concert with you, my younger sister would probably still be alive. Stephanie was the last remaining member of my immediate family. I'm still dealing with her death. Please try to understand. I need to get on with my life, and as painful as this sounds, I just don't see you as a part of it."

His eyes narrowed. The mouth she once enjoyed kissing thinned into a hard line. "That's not fair."

"You're right, it's not. But neither is the loss of a young, vital, beautiful sixteen-year-old."

He remained unmoved.

"Didn't anyone ever tell you life isn't fair?" she said wearily as she stepped to the driver's door.

David's hand whipped out and gripped her arm. "Please. Let me help you get through this."

"No one can help me," she whispered, trying to tug out of his grasp.

"I see this is beginning to become a habit with you." Jarek's voice rang from across the lot.

Relief surged through Kelly. Jarek's black clothes blended into the shadows from where he emerged.

"It's amazing how you seem to arrive just in the nick of time." A sneer distorted David's face. She'd thought him so handsome once. He released her arm.

"If you would leave Kelly alone, there would be no need for me to come to her rescue."

"No one is rescuing anyone," she said, wanting to diffuse the situation. "David, are we clear?"

"For now." He glanced at Jarek and strode away.

Jarek made to follow, but she held him back.

"Leave him be."

"He has manhandled you again."

Kelly smiled at his wording. "No harm, no foul." She faced her savior. Despite the harsh words spoken between them, he had been there, protecting her. A personal knight in shining armor.

Her eyes gazed up at him. "I'm so sorry for what I said earlier." She touched the collar of his shirt, her hands nervously flitting, never resting in one spot. "You were right. What we shared was more than sex. A lot more. And that's what scares me. Deep down inside, I knew it, but I didn't want to admit it."

He gathered her hands into his own, bent his head, and kissed her softly on the mouth.

In the silence, the strength of their embrace spoke volumes.

Kelly stepped back, palmed a tear from her cheek, and smiled tentatively. "I was wondering what we should do after work. First I thought of going to a bar or grabbing a coffee, but I think I have a better idea. Did you like the play?"

"I would have enjoyed it more in your company. As for now, I am sure you know what I would prefer doing." His hands trailed from her neck, down her back, and over her hips.

"Later," she promised. Being with him felt really good. "What do you know about banana splits?" Kelly grinned and signaled for him to get into the car.

Pigging out on gooey desserts would be a great distraction from her encounter with David and would lighten the mood between them. As Kelly pulled out of the parking lot, headlight's beams flashed on a man-sized shadow. When she checked the rearview mirror, nothing was there. She must have imagined it.

Although she didn't like how David reacted to what she said, he'd never do anything to hurt her.

Would he?

Chapter Twenty-three

"I have no more bones in my body. You do realize that," Kelly mumbled sleepily.

She stretched, nestled her butt intimately against Jarek's groin, pulled the light bed covers up a bit higher and with a contended sigh, she closed her eyes.

"You did not complain last night." He chuckled. His deep, throaty morning voice sent shivers up and down her spine.

It was unnerving how her body reacted to the sound of his voice. If she were a cat, she'd be purring right now. She stretched, rolled over, and faced him.

"Now, why on earth would I complain?" A grin split her face. He was so deliciously manly, it took her breath away.

"If you are not protesting, then we should continue." His devilish smile almost stopped her heart.

"No way. I can't. I don't have enough strength."

"You do not need any. I will do all the work."

"Work," she mocked. "I didn't realize making love was work to you."

Jarek blinked. His mouth opened, but no words came out.

"I'm only teasing."

The laughter died on her lips. This was their last day together. She wondered if he was thinking the same thing and if he was struggling with the same mixed feelings as she was. To stop the onslaught of tears, she bit the inside of her cheek, welcoming the resulting sting. It would be nothing compared to letting Jarek go.

"You are troubled."

"Just thinking." She would miss this, the talking. Her heart constricted. She smothered a cry of despair and changed the subject. "Tell me about Narena."

The corner of his mouth lifted, but a touch of sadness settled in his eyes.

"Narena is remarkable. She sees things—sometimes events yet to be, sometimes things that have come to pass. My father values her opinion and relies on her suggestions. She has never failed him."

"How long have you known her?"

"Since we were children. She can be very stubborn. When we were growing up, she and I got into such mischief. One time, Narena had to create a smoke spell so we could get away without being caught."

"What were you doing?"

"We were in the larder, trying to sneak out with a pie that was supposed to be for after supper."

"Did you succeed?" she chuckled.

The lopsided smile widened into a full grin. "Yes. But as it turned out, the confection was not for us, as I had thought. Once we escaped, Narena took the dessert and gave it to a family with six children. They were very poor, and she wanted them to have a treat. She is like that, giving to others, caring for others...like you."

Even though her heart swelled at the compliment, her gaze fell to the covers on the bed. This was so hard.

"Tell me of your parents. What were they like?"

She rolled onto her back, stared at the ceiling before beginning. "Mom and dad were great. My childhood was nothing exciting. Dad worked as a shift supervisor in a manufacturing plant, and Mom was a substitute teacher. Every year, we would all pack up and go on a road trip to somewhere different. Some vacations were long, but all of them were good. We got to spend quality time together. I didn't think it was so hot then, but now I value what we shared."

"You must miss them very much." He threaded a strand of hair behind her ear.

"Yes." She always would.

He was silent for a moment, hesitant, and nodded toward the far wall. "I noticed a dagger on the shelf."

"Yeah. Dad found it at an old antique shop on one of our yearly trips. I thought it was pretty cool, so he bought it for me." She brought the memory forward fondly. "I couldn't wait to try it out, but Mom wouldn't allow me to play with it. She said if she ever caught me, I'd never see it again. I kept my promise for the longest time, handling it very carefully when she wasn't around. I didn't want to see if she would follow through with the threat or not. So I left it on the shelf, forgotten until after they died."

"Have you ever used it?"

"Never had a call for it and hope I never do. Besides, I wouldn't know how."

Jarek smiled at her. "I can teach you."

"Yeah, right. We'll just go out into the parking lot, and you can practice on passersby."

The smile left his face. "I am serious." He grasped her shoulder.

She nudged him away, but his fingers tightened on her skin.

"I will not be able to aid you should David come around. It is important you learn how to protect yourself." Gone was the man who softened her heart, made love to her in the gentlest ways. He eyed her with steely determination.

"I've taken self defense courses before, Jarek."

"In hand-to-hand combat, you will lose. David is a man. He is stronger. I will teach you how to use a dagger."

"I don't know..."

"Please, Kelly." He rose from the bed and paced the room like an angry panther. "It is difficult enough for me to leave. It will be less painful if I know you have the basic understanding of how to handle a knife."

"You had to bring that up, didn't you?" She hugged her knees, resting her head on her folded arms.

He grabbed the dagger, returned to her side, and took her hand. "I have never hidden my intention of leaving. What I had not intended was to care for you so deeply." He placed the dagger on the bed between them. "Do this one thing for me. Please."

His anguish softened her resolve. It wasn't the best way to spend his last day here, but at least they'd be together. She nodded, took the knife, and put it on the bedside table.

"We'd better get going." She crawled off the bed, picked up her discarded clothes, and tossed them into the hall. "I, ah...I have to throw in a load of laundry before we go. Clothes for...work." Her words cracked as the tenuous hold on her emotions began to slip. Jarek didn't need to see her cry. There would be plenty of time for that later, after he left. When she picked up the pieces of her shattered heart.

Half an hour later, Kelly stepped into the hall, closed the stairwell door behind her, and almost dropped the jug of laundry detergent. Two uniformed police officers were walking down the hallway ahead toward her apartment. They slowed to a stop just outside her door. Blood rushed to her head. Her hands began to shake. One officer raised his hand to knock.

"Can I help you, officers?" she called out, quelling the desire to rush over and block their path into her place. Jarek was behind that door. She hoped her raised voice carried into the apartment and stopped him from opening the portal. Both men turned in unison, and Kelly wanted to crawl into a hole. Heckle and Jeckle. The two police officers from the morgue the night Jarek arrived. Great. What on earth could they want?

The men came closer. She stopped half way down the hall, making them come to her. *Must get them away from the door.*

"Ms. Kelly Richards?"

"Yes." The jug of detergent started to slip from her sweaty palm. She switched hands.

Both men stopped in front of her. One quirked an eyebrow, and the other barely suppressed a grin.

"Hello again. We were wondering if we could speak with you for a moment."

"I'm kind of in a hurry, fellas. I was just heading out."

"It'll only take a moment."

"Sure, okay."

"Maybe it would be better to take this inside your apartment," the other officer said.

"Sorry, the place looks like a bomb went off inside. What's this all about?" Her insides quaked. If she let the police in, they might look around. She couldn't let them find Jarek.

"You were working last Sunday night?"

"Yes. You know that, you both were there."

"Apparently there's been a bit of a mix-up regarding one of the bodies."

"I thought that was being taken care of internally. I've already spoken to my boss. What do the police have to do with this?" This was getting worse by the second.

"The missing man's next of kin have come forward to claim his body. Naturally, they were a bit upset when he wasn't there. They've filed a missing persons case."

"For a dead body?" She couldn't hold back the bark of laughter.

The younger officer shrugged. "I'm sure some papers got lost or something. Anyway, we still need to ask you a few questions. Strictly routine."

She nodded. *Don't lose your grip now.*

"When you started your shift, there were five bodies in the morgue?"

"Yes."

"Did you ever leave the premises?"

"Yes, once. To do a pick-up."

"And did you lock up?" The older officer pulled her attention to him.

"Definitely."

"When you came back, there were five bodies?"

"No."

"I beg your pardon?" the young officer interjected.

"I brought a body back with me. That would make six." But one was still alive. Wouldn't be prudent to point that out, though.

"Oh. Right. Did you see any strange people hanging around?"

"No." Not hanging around, just lying there, pretending to be dead.

"You're sure?"

"Very. Look guys, I'm running late. Can we finish this up some other time?"

"Just a few more—"

"Car twelve, what's your status?" a shoulder mike squawked.

The younger of the two men reached up and dislodged the mike. "Twelve here."

"Roger, twelve. Caller asks you to return to the morgue."

"Roger. On our way. Twelve out."

"Can we stop by again and ask you a few more questions?" The older officer stared at her, his eyes penetrating.

"Sure. You know where to find me."

The two men stepped past her, went down the hall, and took the stairs at the end.

"I'll just have to make sure Jarek is gone before you come back," she muttered, hurrying toward her apartment.

Chapter Twenty-four

The knife hit its mark with a muted *thunk*.

"You're quite proficient at that."

Jarek gave Kelly a lopsided smile and retrieved the dagger from a stump. The late afternoon sun warmed his shoulders. They were alone in the meadow, a perfect place for Kelly to hone her knife throwing skills. Or more precisely, her survival skills.

Against David or any other man. A lead ball formed in his stomach.

"Hey, are you thinking of calling it quits too?"

Her call took him out of his musings. The sunshine surrounded Kelly's golden hair in a halo. She smiled at him and air rushed out of his lungs. These were the memories he would take with him when he left. Her beautiful face, haunting blue eyes. Her generous spirit.

"I'm done," she said. "My arm feels like it's about to fall off." She massaged her forearm. "How long did it take you to get so good?"

He winked. "I am a man. Therefore, not long at all."

She gave him a shove and took his hand. "Let's go relax by the stream."

They sat and dangled their feet in the gently flowing water. It was peaceful and serene. He couldn't remember the last time he felt so happy. Or so sad. He'd chosen family over the love of a woman.

Love. He did love Kelly. Earlier this morning, when they had pleasured one another in bed after their shower, he had called her *akitra* — soul mate — an endearment not given lightly, for it was a proclamation of commitment. He hadn't explained that to her. It would only make things worse.

The thought of leaving her constricted his heart. He squeezed his eyes shut to stem the onslaught of tears.

"You're awfully quiet," Kelly said. She pulled her feet out of the stream and wrapped her arms around her knees, wiggling her toes on the warm rock.

Jarek gazed over the water. "Hmm. I am enjoying this day, being with you in the sunshine, listening to the wind in the trees, and feeling the water on my feet."

"What will you do when you get back?" Her whispered words tugged at his heart.

"Seek my vengeance."

"Don't you need a suspect first?"

"With Narena's and Rayja's help, I will find out who tried to kill me." And when he did, he would take great pleasure in slicing the person's heart out.

"What time does the transfer take place?"

He gazed down at her. The bluest ocean couldn't compare to Kelly's azure eyes. "At midnight I will unclasp the armlet. That is how Narena will locate me. She will recite a spell and take me back."

"Can I come with you?" Kelly spoke so softly he almost didn't hear her.

He'd hoped she wouldn't ask about the one thing he had trouble facing. He would rather endure the pain of a thousand dagger wounds than hear the wistfulness in her voice.

"Only one can pass," he repeated Narena's earlier words. But his voice was thick, and his throat ached so much, he couldn't swallow.

"That's okay," she whispered.

He couldn't speak. Instead he gazed out over the water, and the two of them sat in silence for a while.

The growl of his stomach broke the quiet. And the sadness.

Kelly giggled. "Let's get something to eat. Then I have a surprise for you."

"Will you be the dessert?" He tried to make light of the situation, but he wanted so desperately to make love to her once more.

"No." The laughter didn't reach her eyes. "A co-worker lent me a telescope. I noticed how much you missed the stars, and I thought we could go stargazing tonight."

"I would enjoy that very much."

They slipped their socks and shoes back on. Jarek rose, offered his hand, and pulled Kelly to her feet. She looked up at him, hesitating.

"Instead of dessert, how about an appetizer?" she said, leading him back to a blanket they had spread out near the car.

Cal McDonald sat at his desk, bouncing a pencil against a file. A frown tightened his brow. He glanced up to the two policemen sitting across from him in his office and back to the folder. He shook his head, leaned back in his creaky wooden chair.

"You're sure about this?" He rubbed a hand across his chin. The knot in his stomach tightened.

The younger officer spoke up. "That is the information we found on Martin and Lucille Richards. There is an aunt in North Carolina. But no mention of any cousin named Jarek."

The knot in Cal's stomach grew into a boulder. "There's something not right here, gentlemen. You can't find any information on her supposed 'cousin.' He wasn't seen entering the building, but his image was captured on tape when he left with Kelly on Sunday after her shift.

So, who is this guy, Jarek, and what's his connection to our missing body?"

Chapter Twenty-five

After a delicious seafood dinner at a restaurant on the outskirts of town, Kelly and Jarek left the lights of the city and drove a few miles to the quiet hillside she visited when she wanted to be alone. She parked the car and climbed out. Jarek retrieved the telescope from the trunk, she grabbed the blanket from the back seat, and they headed to a flat area. She assembled the telescope and showed him how to operate it.

Kelly sat on the blanket over a patch of mossy ground. Jarek's gasp of surprise at finding certain constellations made her smile. It was like learning about the cosmos again through a child's eyes.

He turned to her, a huge grin on his face. "This is wonderful. What an invention. We are lucky it is so dark, and we can see so many stars. Come, have a look at the moon."

She joined him beside the scope and focused the instrument on the lunar landscape.

"What time is it?"

Her watch read ten thirty. "Still early. We've got lots of time."

"You have done this before?"

"Yes, although not for many years. Dad had a cheap telescope. Stephanie and I would set it up in our back yard and look at the stars when we were kids." Her voice drifted off.

He gazed heavenward, tilting his head. His fingers clasped hers.

"Maybe she is up there, looking down and smiling, knowing you are taking pleasure in it again."

She gave permission to let the pain drift away. Funny, even a month ago, she wouldn't have been able to revisit the precious memory of stargazing with her sister and not be torn apart by it. She had Jarek to thank for that. Her head lay against his shoulder.

"Thank you," she whispered.

His chin rested on the top of her head. "For what?"

She shrugged, leaned forward to look through the eyepiece again.

They spent the next half hour or so checking out countless constellations. Before long, it was time to leave.

Jarek had to return to Leisos.

During the ride home, Kelly gnawed on her lip, debating whether to ask the question weighting heavily on her heart. She finally gave in. "Will you ever come back?"

Tires hummed on the pavement. Minutes ticked by. Jarek remained silent for so long, she didn't think he was going to answer. Interior dash lights reflected in his brown eyes when he turned to her. "I do not know."

She waited for a more substantial explanation, but none came, and she didn't press him. She couldn't get her hopes up. The only good thing about all this was once Jarek left, she wouldn't have to hide him from her boss or the police.

It seemed like the trip back to her apartment took half the time that the drive out did. She steered down her street, almost deserted at this late hour, and pulled into her parking lot.

"The telescope can stay in the trunk since I have to take it back tomorrow."

Jarek took the blanket. She grabbed her purse, and to anyone watching they looked like a couple returning from a nice outing, instead of a final one.

Once inside, Kelly dumped everything onto the couch. "I'm going to get my laundry from the dryer."

He glanced at the clock on the wall and stopped her. "Don't worry about the clothes right now." His anguish almost killed her.

As much as she wanted to spend every last second with him, she was going to lose it any minute. "Hey, that's easy for you to say. You're not the one who will have to iron the wrinkles out. I've left them in there too long already. I just hope no one has stolen anything." She made to move past him, but he tightened his grip on her arms.

"Kelly." He stared intently into her eyes. "Kelly, I want to tell you I...I..."

The door to her apartment flew open with a thunderous crash. Kelly shrieked. Jarek spun, pushed her behind him. A man entered the living room pointing a gun.

"Aww, how sweet." David sneered, aiming the weapon at Jarek's chest. "It's about time you got back. Did you go out on a little date? A picnic under a full moon? I saw the blanket curled beneath your arm when you passed my car."

"David! What are you doing? You can't possibly think this will solve anything." She tried to step out from behind Jarek, but he held her back.

"Think? I'm done thinking. That's all I've been doing for the past two days. Trying to get you to come back to me. But when you made it clear you had no plans of ever returning, I decided if I can't have you, he can't either."

The gun never wavered as it was aimed at Jarek's chest. Jarek didn't move. He remained expressionless — no fear, no quivering.

"No!" Kelly swallowed hard.

"David." Jarek's flat voice was laced with steel. "You do not want to do this. You are frightening Kelly. She has no desire to go back with you. Harming me will not change that."

"Jarek, he's got a gun. He'll kill you. Please, let me talk to him."

"No. I will not put you in danger."

David tilted his head to one side. "You don't have much choice."

Kelly's world began to crumble all over again. Just when she let down her barriers, finally inviting someone into her life, her heart, he was going to die. This could not be happening.

Jarek focused on the clock, spun around, blocking her view of David. He reached up and unclasped the metal armlet from around his bicep, thrust it into her hands, and pushed her away from him.

Her eyes flew open wide. Realization dawned. She held the magical homing beacon out to him. "No, Jarek!"

"Forgive me. I cannot leave you here to face him alone." He grabbed her, kissed her roughly, and let her go. "I love you, *akitra*."

He dove to the side, hit the carpet, and rolled.

The image of the room began to distort.

A far away, soft voice chanted. Walls shimmered. Jarek and David faded. Dizziness forced Kelly to her knees, the armlet grasped tight in her hands. As her vision darkened, something tugged at the center of her body, an unseen force pulling her. Blackness closed in. Her head felt like it was trapped in a vise. She tried to raise her arms, but it was as if layers of lead weighed them down.

Vertigo set in. Her stomach rolled. Ears rang. Each beat of her heart exploded in her brain. With every ounce of strength she had left, she screamed, "Jarek!"

And her world evaporated.

Chapter Twenty-six

"What the bloody hell is going on?" David swung the gun between Jarek and the spot where Kelly had been standing only moments earlier.

Jarek gasped. It worked. Narena had come to his aid like she promised. David's wide eyes darted around the room as if he might find Kelly hiding somewhere else in her apartment.

David turned toward the kitchen.

Now.

Jarek dropped to a crouch and tackled him, pounding the man's body to the living room floor. His hands clawed at the weapon in David's grasp. Bunching muscles in his forearms, he poured all his strength into his hands and bent his rival's wrists back. The gun inched to the left by degrees. Jarek applied more pressure. David screeched through clenched teeth.

Sweat popped along Jarek's brow, dripping closer and closer to his eyes. David's other hand clamped his lower arm. His fingers pressed hard into Jarek's wrist. Jarek gritted his teeth against the pain. He was stronger, but David's rage fueled him. Judging by the maniacal look in David's eyes, there was little chance of a peaceful outcome.

A blow connected with his kidneys, and he rolled away. He lashed out with his fist at the last second, connected it with David's jaw and scrambled to his feet. There wasn't enough time to make it through the front door, and even if he did, David would kill him before he made it out of the building.

He darted down the hallway and to Kelly's bedroom. Her dagger lay on the shelf. Footsteps pounded in chase. He lunged across the room. In one fluid motion, he grabbed the dagger, swung his arm up, pivoted on his foot, and threw it as hard as he could.

A second of silence followed by a whimper. The figure standing in the doorway gurgled a phrase he couldn't understand. The dagger had found its mark, embedded to the hilt in David's chest. The gun thumped onto the carpet.

David sank to his knees, astonishment written on his face as he stared at the blade protruding from him. He raised his head, looked at Jarek, and toppled into a heap on the carpet. Blood pooled around him as a final breath escaped his lips.

Panting from exertion and adrenaline bombarding his system, Jarek went over to the dead body. He closed his eyes in regret. Although David had threatened his life, as well as Kelly's, he had not relished killing the man.

He sunk to the edge of the bed, bent over inhaling a gulp of air to calm his erratic heartbeat and dropped his head. He took a moment to clear his thoughts, ran a hand over his face and walked out of the room. He noticed the front door had slammed shut on the rebound from the wall.

Someone must have heard the commotion.

Jarek went back to the spot in the living room where Kelly had disappeared. Pain and anguish gripped his heart. His breath hitched in a soft sob. She was gone. He'd lost his soul mate after knowing her only a short time.

Sending her back to Leisos instead of him had been a split-second decision and his only choice. He couldn't leave her here with David. He would deal with the repercussions later.

What now? He didn't know anyone in this time who could help him.

Wait. He did know someone.

Kelly's Aunt Vanessa.

Jarek stepped to the telephone and opened the worn green address book lying beside it to the page with Vanessa's number. He tried to remember how to use the phone. The memory of Kelly using the instrument rose in his mind, making it difficult to concentrate. He pushed it aside. *Focus.*

He picked up the phone, punched some buttons, and held it to his ear. Nothing. After numerous failed attempts at placing the call, he finally heard a voice on the line.

"What number were you dialing?"

Jarek stared at the device before answering. "I am trying to contact a person but am unsure how to do so. Are you able to help me?"

"What is the phone number you wish to dial?" The voice sounded impatient.

He recited the numbers written beside Aunt Vanessa's name.

"One moment please, and I will connect you."

"Thank..." A soft tone rang in his ear. He waited, unsure what to do next. The ringing stopped.

"Hello." It was Kelly's aunt's voice.

"Vanessa."

"Jarek? Is that you?"

"Yes."

"My goodness, it's very late. Is everything all right? Where's Kelly?"

"I find it difficult to explain."

Vanessa's tone changed, holding an undercurrent of urgency. "Jarek, tell me what's wrong. Is Kelly all right?"

"I believe her to be, but she is not with me."

"Why not? Where is she?"

He hesitated a moment. "I believe she is in Leisos." He prayed she'd arrived there safely.

"What? How?"

"It is a long story and one I will tell you, however, I have a more urgent matter. I do not know your laws, but I doubt things have changed much in two thousand years. Kelly's former lover attacked us. There was a struggle, and David is now dead. I do not know what to do."

Vanessa gasped. "Oh, Lord. Okay. Where are you now?"

"Kelly's apartment."

"And where is the body?"

"Here, in another room."

"Jarek, you must listen to me and follow my instructions carefully. I'll come and get you, but you must leave the apartment. Now."

"Why? How will you find me?"

"You need to go before someone calls the police. I gather it was self-defense?"

"Yes."

"Be that as it may, if you remain, you will be taken into custody. You're from another time and have no identification. You cannot let them find you. Can you drive?"

"No, I do not know how to operate the car."

"Okay. Leave as soon as you hang up the phone. Take nothing. Whatever you do, don't go near the body, and try not to touch anything else. Is there a park or a store near her place where I can meet you?"

"There is a park close by. Do you know how to get to Kelly's apartment?"

"I'll find it on the Internet using her phone number. Don't worry. It will take me a few hours."

"I appreciate your help."

"Just be careful."

"I will do my best. Thank you."

"And Jarek?"

"Yes?"

"We'll figure something out, okay?"

"I hope so."

He hung onto the instrument until the tone replaced Vanessa's voice. He pushed the end button and put the phone back into its holder. He turned to inspect his surroundings.

Just then, three loud knocks on the front door stopped him dead in his tracks.

Chapter Twenty-seven

Jarek froze.

His eyes flashed to the front door, heart galloping in his chest. On silent feet, he crept to the portal. Barely breathing, he listened to the conversation on the other side.

"Doesn't seem to be anyone home. You're sure you heard something?"

"Yes, officers. I live right next door."

Jarek's head snapped back. Officers. It was the same term Kelly used to describe the men who came to the morgue when he first arrived.

"What did you hear?"

"There was some banging around and raised voices."

Jarek pressed his back against the wall. Would these men try to come into the apartment? Dread clawed its way up his spine.

Three more knocks. Each rap reverberated through his body.

"This is the Lackton Police. Please open the door."

The raised voice startled him. Should he try and get out through the glass doors in the front room? Kelly's apartment was quite a ways up. He'd surely be injured if he jumped.

"Does she have a boyfriend?"

"Not that I'm aware of, but I have seen a man come and go recently, like only in the past couple of days."

"Have you heard any arguing before?"

"No. She's always been fairly quiet."

"Then for all we know, you may have heard the television."

"Did you see anyone leave?"

"No, but after I phoned you, my sister called from Atlanta, and I wasn't near a window. Don't have one of those portable phones. They're bad for you. Edna is always saying, 'You ever on one of those phones, standing by the window when there's a thunder storm, you'll get struck by lightning.' Acts like some kind of conductor. And those new fangled cell phones nowadays. I'm never gonna get me one of those. No way. Causes brain cancer, my sister is always saying."

"Riiight."

Jarek held his breath through the ensuing silence.

"Hey, isn't this the apartment of the woman from the morgue? We were here earlier today. Ms. Richards probably left for work."

"Well, she could have gone down the back stairs," the neighbor conceded.

"Tell you what. We'll swing by her work to make sure."

"I would feel much better, officers. Thanks."

Footsteps retreated down the hall. The muffled sound of a door closing seeped through the barrier. Jarek sagged against the portal. He had to leave. Now.

He strode quickly to the living room, turned off the lights, and opened the door a crack to peek into the hallway. All clear.

Instead of leaving via the usual exit, Jarek turned and went to another set of stairs. He eased the door shut so as not to make a sound, zipped down the steps, and exited the building.

At the road he turned left. His eyes scoured the streets, keeping watch for the return of the officers. Unfortunately, he didn't know what they looked like or how they would present themselves. His best bet was to avoid anyone who tried to approach him.

It would be few hours before Vanessa arrived. His footsteps echoed in the night. He was grateful there were no other pedestrians or traffic on the street. He wanted to be alone with his thoughts.

Shoulders hunched, he shoved his hands into his pockets, pressed his lips together and concentrated on putting one foot in front of the other. Kelly. Losing her had ripped his heart and soul apart. He'd assumed once he got back to Leisos, and the killer was found, he would resume his princely duties and learn to live without Kelly. He never expected a twist like this. Now, he had lost not only his home, but also half his heart. Kelly was gone. Maybe forever.

He reached the park within fifteen minutes. As he turned in, a black and white car drove by at a normal rate of speed. The bar of lights across the roof remained unlit.

Glow from a lamppost illuminated a pathway leading into murky shadows. Cool night air danced across his bare arms. He wished he'd taken the blanket from Kelly's apartment.

A darker object loomed ahead on the left. A bench. He sat down, his gaze resting on the white ball of the moon, a faceless orb looking down on him. Narena had said she needed the power of the full moon to bring him back. Would he have to wait another cycle for her to try again? By now she must have realized what happened.

All hopes of returning home were dashed when he remembered he didn't have the armlet anymore. The blue crystal around his neck was all he had left. A second chance maybe?

Narena had given Jarek the armlet with no explanation, yet it was a tool required for his passage back to Leisos. Could the same be true for the crystal? A faint glimmer of anticipation blossomed as Jarek sat back and waited for Vanessa to arrive.

Hours later, footsteps rustled in the grass. Jarek sat up, his eyes squinting at the form coming his way through the darkness. He breathed a sigh of relief. The silhouette belonged to a woman.

"Jarek?"

"Yes, I am here." He rose and walked toward the figure.

Vanessa's face was grave. She placed a hand on his arm. Worry lines creased her face. "Let's get you out of here. My car is parked right out front."

"Where will we go?"

"Back to my home. You look exhausted. You can sleep in the car on the way."

"I apologize for the inconvenience."

She stopped him with a touch. "It's no inconvenience. Although we were only recently reacquainted, Kelly means the world to me. I will help you get her back."

They walked to the car and slipped inside. Vanessa drove away from the curb.

"Do you know how Kelly can return?"

Vanessa's gaze flicked between him and the road ahead. "No. I don't. But that doesn't mean we can't figure it out. I cannot believe a sorceress as great as Narena would not have thought of something like this."

"I was supposed to come here, find an antidote to the poison I was given, and return to Leisos. I never planned to come back."

"So, Kelly would have been left here, alone again, once you were gone."

The words stung. "You must believe me. I had no plans of becoming involved with anyone. Nor would I ever hurt Kelly."

"What's done is done, and we can't change it. Obviously Narena contacted you at some point or you would both still be here. Tell me everything she said."

"She came to me in a vision two nights ago. It was only for a few moments, but she said she needed to wait until midnight of the full moon to bring me back, that she was not powerful enough to do so sooner. At midnight I was to unclasp the armlet, but not before."

"She must have placed some type of tracing spell on it. Unclasping the armlet unlocked the spell. But she would have had to do something on her end. Did you hear anything when Kelly disappeared?"

"No. I cannot say if Kelly heard anything. She only called my name. Then she was gone."

Vanessa's lips pursed. "Did Narena tell you anything before she sent you here?"

"No. I recall nothing of significance."

"Did she give you anything else, another armlet, a charm, anything?"

His heart beat wings of anticipation inside his chest. "Yes. When I arrived in this time, I found this crystal," he yanked it from under his shirt and held it out, "around my neck."

"Hmm." Vanessa nibbled on her lip. He averted his gaze. Kelly did the same thing. "Narena said she needed the power of the full moon to aid her. Granted, it is at full strength at midnight, but there are also three days prior and three days after when one can call on the moon's power for help."

"Narena contacted me two nights ago. We have another three nights. What do you plan to do?"

"I don't think it's a coincidence Narena gave you the crystal. Gems like that can have tremendous power when paired with something else. Once she realizes Kelly returned to Leisos instead of you, Narena will contact us, and you can switch places."

"But Narena said only one can pass. If I must remain until the next full moon, it will be up to Kelly and Narena to find out who is behind my attempted murder. They both know how important the throne of Leisos is to me."

"Why can't they just go to the king and tell him?"

"Because I do not know whom to trust. I think someone close to me might be involved in the plot to kill me. For all I know it may be the king himself."

Chapter Twenty-eight

Kelly was going to throw up.

This might be one of the worst hangovers she ever had. Problem was, she didn't recall drinking anything. She clenched her teeth and took a deep breath to push back another wave of nausea.

A groan escaped her lips. Jeez, even her eyes hurt. She eased them open and struggled to sit up, but a gentle hand on her shoulder pushed her back down.

An unfamiliar female voice spoke unintelligible words. A blurry form loomed above her. She slammed her eyes shut again, took another deep breath, and waited for the nausea to pass. What the hell happened?

A hand slipped beneath her head, and the lip of a cup touched her lips. Water. Thank goodness. Maybe that would help quell her stomach. She took a sip, and a bitter taste rolled across her tongue. What the hell was this? She spit the liquid back out, clamped her mouth shut, and turned her head aside.

The person treating her spoke again, but Kelly couldn't understand. The cup pressed against her lips with more urgency. She fought back. Someone was trying to drug her. Or worse, poison her. She struggled weakly. Her eyes opened to a blurry face leaning forward. Fingers pinched her nose and others pried open her mouth.

"No. Don't." She moaned. "Jarek..." The rest of her words were silenced as the bitter brew trickled down her throat, making her cough.

A few of the woman's words broke through. "Must...drink...understand."

Kelly shook her head to clear her mind. Wait a minute. The strange words she didn't comprehend a minute ago now made sense. A little. She eyed the stranger cautiously. The woman nodded her head and motioned with her hands for Kelly to drink more from the cup. She took another sip. The nasty brew brought a grimace to her face.

"Rest and gather strength."

The last of the liquid slid down her throat.

"Illness from the travel will pass. Be patient." The woman rose, her feet barely making a sound as she walked about the room.

"Am I alive?"

The stranger chuckled. "What do you think?"

"I can't think. That's the problem."

"Yes, you are very much alive."

"Where am I?"

No answer. Kelly's vision cleared. She was lying on a bed. Her hand stretched over rough fabric. A blanket. But not the soft quilt on her bed at home.

A small stand stood beside the bed. A rug in the center of the large room held a square table with a crockery pitcher and two chairs. Soft glow from stubby candles didn't quite reach the corners. The snap of a burning log pulled her gaze to the hearth where a black pot sat off to one side, steam wafting toward the ceiling. The odor of wood smoke drifted through the air.

Where was she?

"You didn't answer my question."

"Maybe it is better for you to rest before I reply."

Oh God. There must have been an accident. She was in a hospital. But she didn't remember being in a car. And a hospital wouldn't have a fireplace. Kelly strained to remember what happened before she blacked out.

Oh no, David! He'd come into her apartment with a gun. Jarek thrust something in her hands. Then her body felt like it was being pulled through a knothole backwards. She couldn't see Jarek. Had David done something to him?

"Jarek!" She pitched forward to a sitting position.

"Hush. You are fine. Everything is all right." The stranger spoke from across the room.

"Please, he's in great danger. Someone was trying to kill him. You must find out if he's okay."

The female standing by the fire turned. "Kelly, I believe Jarek is fine. I would know if something had happened to him."

"How do you know my name?" she whispered.

The woman moved forward and sat on the edge of her bed. The candles highlighted her long, raven-black hair. Flames reflected in amazing violet eyes. She pushed a lock of hair behind one ear, and Kelly glimpsed something on her neck. A picture burned into her brain and recognition dawned.

She gasped. "Narena?"

"Yes, Kelly." Narena smiled back at her. She rose smoothly from the bed, crossed the room to retrieve a goblet, and returned to her side. "Here, take a sip of water."

Narena. This woman was the sorceress Narena.

Holy shit. She was in Leisos.

"How can I understand you?"

"The potion I gave you to drink is a variation of one I gave to Jarek when I sent him to you so that he would be able to communicate."

"What now?"

Narena narrowed her eyes on Kelly. "I do not know."

"What do you mean, you don't know? Send me back. Now."

"It is not that simple."

"Like hell. You're a sorceress aren't you? Wave your magic wand or whatever the hell you do, and get me back to my time." Panic vaulting up her spine projected through her bitter words.

Narena's eyes glowed with an inner fire. "My dear girl, when I tell you it is not that simple, I do not lie. I cannot 'wave a wand' as you say and send you away. Traveling through time is not accomplished with a snap of my fingers. I must have an anchor, something I can call to. Plus, to do this task, it takes a tremendous amount of energy, most of which I spent bringing *you* here."

"But, I don't *want* to be here."

"You have made that clear. However, here is where you are. Jarek would not have sacrificed his chance to return and ensure the safety of his twin without good reason."

Kelly wanted to scream, wail, hurl something and throw a temper tantrum. She wanted to smack Jarek, throttle the life out of him, and then kiss him.

Tears slipped from beneath her lids and trickled down her cheek. He sent her here to save her life. If he had come back instead of her, she would probably be dead. David wouldn't have taken no for an answer.

She swiped away her tears and grabbed Narena's hand, squeezing it, desperate for anything to ground her rising anxiety. "You said you would know if Jarek was okay. Please, tell me the truth."

"I do not know if he has been harmed, however, I have not sensed his death. Tell me what happened."

She curled her hands tightly around the top of the blanket, pulled it up to her chin, and relayed the events with a quavering voice. She ended her story with, "He said he loved me and called me something like *akitra*."

Narena's eyes widened. "That would explain it," she said softly, staring at the wall above Kelly's head.

"Explain what?"

She pinned Kelly with a serious gaze. "*Akitra* is a name granted a special person. It means soul mate. In our culture there is a reverence associated with it, showing the binding commitment between two people. I have never heard Jarek speak of love for a woman. He would never call you *akitra* unless he truly believes he has found his soul mate. He regards your life above his own and his family's."

"What do you mean, above his family?" This was more confusing than ever.

"Jarek must return to secure his family's reign in Leisos. If he does not, Rayja will be the next king."

"But at least Leisos will have a ruler."

"True. I have been unable to find out who poisoned him. I have my suspicions. If Jarek does not return, the same fate may come to Rayja."

Dread filled Kelly. Jarek had said the most important thing was ensuring Rayja's safety. "You think someone will try to kill his twin brother? Can't you go to the police or whatever authorities you have around here?"

"Other than Jarek, I do not know whom I can trust. At one point, I even suspected Rayja, but Jarek would not hear of it. I do not have access to the palace unless the king summons me. Therefore, I cannot ensure Rayja's safety."

"Well, can't you contact Rayja and tell him?"

"I am friends with Jarek, and he trusts me. I do not have the same type of relationship with Rayja. He would want to know why I suspect his life is in danger."

"So? Tell him Jarek thinks it is."

"If I went to Rayja explaining this, it would mean I had something to do with Jarek's disappearance from the palace, and although that is true, admitting it could cost me my life. Although Jarek has been missing from Leisos for a number of days, this information has not been made public in the village, which leads me to believe the person who wishes harm on the family is within the walls of the palace. Everyone in the palace still believes Jarek is unwell and not allowed visitors. If the prince really had gone missing, word would have spread to the village almost immediately."

Kelly sat back in stunned silence. Whoa. This was too much. Two weeks ago, she lived an ordinary, predictable life in the black and white world of science, and now she was in the past while her soul mate was still in the future.

Soul mate. Sure, she was falling in love with Jarek, but she didn't think her feelings went that far.

Narena gripped Kelly's hand, returning her attention to the present. "I have to bring Jarek back within the next few days. If I wait any longer, the power of the moon will wane, and I am not strong enough to attempt this without it. Should I be unsuccessful, he will have to wait until the next full moon. Would he understand this and go to someone else for help?"

Well, no. Jarek didn't know anyone but her. He never met her co-workers. He only met...Aunt Vanessa.

"Jarek was with me when I went to visit my Aunt Vanessa. In fact, after Jarek told me about you, she was the one who verified our connection." Kelly touched Narena's birthmark and pointed to her own.

"Does your aunt also have one?" Excitement tinged Narena's voice.
"Yes."

"Good. Hopefully, he will contact her for help."

Narena rose and left the room. She returned a moment later with a bowl, which she placed on the table beside the pitcher of water.

"What are you doing?"

"I will attempt to contact your aunt. If she is a believer as you claim, I should be able to send her a message, which she will give to Jarek."

Kelly began to get out of the bed, but the sorceress stopped her. "No. You must rest. You will need all your strength."

"Why? For what?"

"Because I am going to need your power, as well as your aunt's, to bring Jarek back."

Chapter Twenty-nine

"Nothing is ever one hundred percent certain when it comes to magic," Narena said.

Not a comforting thought, especially when it could cost a man his life.

They were sitting in the sun on top of a hillside. Stiff grasses sprouted nearby in the soil. A copse of trees marked the border of rugged hills off into the distance. Leaves gently rustled from the occasional breeze. The sun warmed Kelly's back, easing her tension.

"The look of doubt in your eyes tells me you do not believe me."

"I wasn't thinking about what is and isn't certain regarding magic," Kelly intoned. "I was more worried about your claim I have powers. And that you need them to help you bring Jarek back to Leisos."

"Without your powers it will be almost impossible to return the prince to this time." Narena tilted her head to one side. "When you healed the sick, were you always this unsure of yourself?"

"No."

"Why question your abilities now?"

"Because I've never seen or felt them."

"Just because you cannot sense something within you, does not mean it is not there. Your power only needs to find a way to make it known."

Unable to come up with a reply, Kelly studied the woman sitting beside her. Narena sifted through a shallow basket filled with herbs and flowers lying between them. She'd collected the plants in preparation for the spell tomorrow night, the third and last night to use the moon's power. The woman's calm and self-assured movements directly contrasted Kelly's fear and trepidation about bringing Jarek back. The sorceress hummed softly, seeming totally at peace. What Kelly wouldn't give to feel like that.

"How long have you been a sorceress?" she asked.

"Quite a while."

"Have you always known this was what you were meant to do?"

Narena stopped her inspection of the cuttings. "Kelly, I may have always known I would be a sorceress, but I too had choices to make. They were not easy, and I struggled, just like you. However, once I made my decision, it was easier to walk on that path than to stumble in the dark."

"You and Yoda must be related," Kelly mumbled. She waited for Narena to elaborate on what choices she'd made, but the woman remained silent. Must have been personal. "How did you know you picked the right option?"

"Because it felt right. There are many times we select resolutions that do not feel right, yet we make them because it is less difficult. Instead of listening to our inner voice, we choose to ignore it and usually pay the price. When you carry out the correct choice, you will feel it in your heart and in your soul. You will be at peace."

"Any misgivings?" An image of Stephanie floated in Kelly's mind. She would always regret not taking her younger sister with her to the concert.

Narena watched over the landscape. "Certain outcomes have been more difficult to bear, but I know I made the right choices. Therefore, to answer your question, no, I have no qualms about my decisions."

The sorceress went back to inspecting the plants in her basket.

Kelly was disappointed at the woman's vague answers. Perhaps she'd been hoping for a simple option.

Narena rose, grasped the basket, and offered Kelly hand. "Come, there is something I wish to show you."

She stood and brushed away dirt clinging to the free-flowing dress Narena had given her.

With the basket of herbs draped over her arm, the sorceress led the way to the rising countryside.

Kelly scanned the area but couldn't tell where they were heading. "Where are you taking me?"

"Not far, but there is something important I think you should see."

They continued a short while longer, until Narena stopped near three large rocks standing against one another in the form of a pyramid. The ground at their feet still held grass and soil but melded into less fertile terrain twenty yards ahead. The harsher topography continued all the way to the rugged hills.

Kelly peered down to the ground. "What's this?"

"The grave of a man I buried."

Her head whipped up, eyes wide. She stared at the sorceress, waiting for clarification. A quick glance of the immediate surrounding area provided no indication of a graveyard. Her eyes returned to Narena's face.

"Was he a friend?"

"I did not know him."

Unease pricked at her insides. Did the sorceress kill someone?

Narena met her gaze, the violet orbs softening at Kelly's wary stare.

"You look at me as if I have committed a heinous act. Do not worry. This man relinquished his place in your world so Jarek could meet you."

The missing body from the morgue. Kelly practically sagged with relief. So this was where he ended up.

"Did you dig this grave yourself?"

"Yes. After I helped Jarek escape from the palace, I took him to a shallow cave nearby. I couldn't take the chance of him being seen. The night I sent Jarek forward, there was no room for him where you work. Since I did not have the time or an anchor to transport the man's body to another place, I brought him back here. It was the easiest way. I apologize if it made things difficult for you.

"That extra burden, coupled with performing the ritual alone, put tremendous strain on me. When I woke almost two days later, the man's body had to be dealt with. I returned to my home, retrieved a shovel and buried him."

"Well, at least I'm off the hook for one thing. He was an addict."

Narena glared at her. "Despite how the man lived, Kelly, he deserves respect for the role he played."

"You're right. Where I come from, drug abuse is a global problem and I've seen how much it can harm the patient and those around them. As a physician, I know how people can get started down that road, but have never understood the reasoning. Maybe that's why my tolerance isn't as strong as it should be. Regardless, I shouldn't judge. I'm sorry." She paused, thinking back to her conversation with her boss. "The man's family came forward to claim the body for burial. Please don't tell me we have to switch them again."

"To do that Jarek would need to be in the morgue. Unfortunately, this man's final resting place will be here. I sympathize the family will be unable to bury their loved one."

Kelly bent her head and said a silent prayer of thanks to John Doe number thirty-eight and hoped his soul finally found peace.

Narena took her hand. "It is time to go. I thought you might like to see the village."

She stared, open-mouthed to the woman beside her. "You're going to let me be with other people?"

"As long as we keep to ourselves, it should be fine. You are dressed properly now and will blend in."

A short while later, Kelly and Narena walked amongst the citizens at a market set in the village square. Clothing, wares, and an array of food crowded the tables. The rich aroma of spices drifted on the breeze.

Narena had instructed Kelly not to speak unless necessary, as her dialect might draw unwanted attention. It didn't matter to her. She was so enraptured with the sights and sounds surrounding her, it was enough just to be an observer.

A group of children played in the square, darting between tables, much to the annoyance of some of the adults. Their laughter made her forget her present situation, even if only for a little while. She moved off to the side and took a moment to enjoy the simple pleasure of watching mankind's innocence.

Narena stepped to a table displaying candles, momentarily blocking Kelly's view of the children. She jumped when a scream of pain ripped through the air. All conversation ceased in the market. Everyone's attention shifted to a young girl lying in the dirt, bleeding from a gash on her leg.

The child's blood mixed with the earth, turning it to blackish mud. Kelly gasped in horror. Her first instinct was to run and help, but a strong hand clasped her arm, holding her back.

"No. You must not intervene." Narena's stern warning made Kelly struggle against her grasp.

"But the girl is hurt. She's bleeding." Her heart hammered, sending fear coursing through her veins. Where were the parents? What happened? She scanned the area near where the child had fallen. A rusted metal hoe blade lay beside her, a hint of blood the evidence Kelly needed.

"That girl gouged herself on a piece of rusted metal. Where is your doctor?"

"If you mean a healer, there is one who takes care of many villages, including ours. However, I believe he left for *Saltera*. Someone will ride out and bring him back."

"How far is that?" Adrenalin spiked through her system. Her mind was already mentally flipping through pages of medical books she had studied, working out how the injury would be treated.

"A two day ride."

"Two days! The child could be sick from an infection by the time he gets back. Surely someone else can help her. What about you, can't you do something?"

"I am a sorceress, not a healer. I do not have the skills to help the child."

"But I do." Determination tangled with her panic.

A man cradled the sobbing child in his arms and carried her down the street. Kelly watched his retreating back. She whirled around and glared at Narena. "Why wouldn't you let me help her?"

"You are two thousand years in the past with no medicine. How would you treat the child? And do you think her parents would let you? These people do not know you."

As much as she hated to admit it, Narena was right. She couldn't do much for the poor girl other than bathing the wound with clean cloths and hoping for the best. Penicillin hadn't been discovered yet. Her jaw clamped tight to fight tears of frustration.

She stared at her useless hands. "I want to leave here. Take me back to your home. Now." Shoulders slumped, she turned away from the market and walked back in the direction they had come.

Hours later Kelly stared into the low flames of the fire, reliving the accident with the little girl. Her heart ached for what was to come. The child would die. And Kelly was at a total loss as to how to prevent it.

A tear slid down her cheek, and she angrily brushed it away. There must be something she could do.

Okay, first she had to get a grip. Overreacting wouldn't help matters. She needed to think. Modern medicine hadn't been invented yet. How did ancient people treat their ill? *Think, Kelly, think.*

Her head snapped up. Of course. How could she have been so stupid? Most modern medicine was derived from plants. She just had to remember which plants would help combat infection. She wished she had her medical textbooks. Wait. She vaguely remembered reading something in a book about alternative medicine.

She concentrated until the answer sprang into her mind. Frankincense. Besides being used for muscle soreness and sunburns, the sticky resin of the plant also had great anti-inflammatory and antibacterial properties. She could make a topical treatment with some oil. Shouldn't be too hard to find the plant, she was somewhere in ancient Arabia. And instead of three wise men, all she had to do was ask a wise woman to help her locate some.

As if the idea called to her, Narena appeared in the doorway, corners of her mouth twitching. "Do you wish to get some rest? It is getting late."

"No. I need your help. I think I know how to treat the little girl from the market."

Narena smiled. "Do you?"

"Yes. I'm not sure the Leisos name for it, but what I need is named Frankincense." Kelly described the plant and the aromatic smell. "With your help, I can make a compress which should combat any infection. But we'll need to get to the child as soon as possible. Any delay will only make it worse."

"And how will you explain your presence?"

"I was kind of hoping you could help me with that. Everyone here knows you. Maybe you could tell the people I'm a distant relation or something." A second later the irony hit her, and she grinned. "Well, at least you wouldn't be lying."

"Dried valerian root would help the child with the pain. I have some over on the shelf." Narena motioned with her head. She stepped to the door. "I will gather what you require. Please do not leave the house. I will return soon."

She went out, leaving Kelly to pace the room with impatience. She had no way of knowing how long it would take for Narena to get back. Hopefully, she wouldn't be too late.

Chapter Thirty

Vanessa opened the door to two uniformed policemen.

Oh dear.

"Good day, officers. May I help you?"

"Good afternoon ma'am. I'm Officer Campbell, this is Officer Lawson from the Petersburg Police." The middle-aged man in blue nodded. He was tall, easily six feet, with jet-black hair peppered with grey at the sides. A courteous smile stretched across his angular face. He removed his reflective sunglasses and dropped them into the pocket of his shirt.

"Are you Vanessa Summers?"

Vanessa glanced to the other officer who spoke. He was older, shorter and heavyset but not obese. The deep lines on his face and thinly pressed lips indicated he had weathered some hard years. Probably seen a lot of things on the job he wished he could forget. She did a mental assessment. He must be the bad cop of the good cop/bad cop tag-team.

She masked her rising nervousness with a pleasant smile. Jarek was safely hidden away in the corner of the basement behind several boxes of old clothes. When she'd spotted the police car from the front window as it had swung into the driveway, she hustled Jarek downstairs with instructions to be absolutely quiet.

"Yes, I am. What is this about?" she responded to their question.

"We're looking for your niece, Kelly Richards. Is she here?"

Vanessa held her hand against her side to keep it still. "No, she's not. Is something wrong?" She injected just enough concern in her voice to sound worried but not panicked.

"May we come in?" Officer Campbell said.

"Yes, of course." She stepped aside and motioned for the two men to enter, closing the door behind them. As long as they stayed in the hall, she and Jarek would be fine.

"When was the last time you spoke with your niece?"

"A few days ago on the phone before she left."

"Left? For where?" Lawson took a step forward.

Vanessa refused to be intimidated and didn't retreat. "She's on her way to Florida for a few days."

"Without her car?"

Apparently, they'd already been to her place and spotted her vehicle in the parking lot. Her insides trembled. "She's having problems with it. I gave her some money to rent one. Now will one of you please tell me what's going on?"

"Kelly didn't arrive for her shift," Campbell said.

"And the Lackton, North Carolina Police Department called across the line to the Petersburg, Virginia Police Department because she didn't show up for work? Really gentlemen, isn't that a bit extreme."

"You don't sound too worried about her," Lawson said with a grunt.

"Of course I'm a bit anxious about this news. However, I'm sure if something bad happened, I would have been contacted by now. What does concern me is she either didn't tell her boss she was leaving — which is very unlike her — or there was a miscommunication. What's the real reason you want to talk to her?" Vanessa said. Officer Lawson's thin, unkempt hair, ruddy complexion, and rumpled clothes reminded her of Columbo sans the trench coat. The only things missing were the glass eye and cigar.

"We want to ask her some questions about a missing persons case in North Carolina." Campbell interrupted her thoughts.

Her eyes widened. "What missing persons case?"

"Sorry. We're not at liberty to say. Do you know where she's staying in Florida?"

"She didn't have any definite plans."

Lawson narrowed his eyes. "Was she alone?"

Vanessa bit her tongue. She really didn't like him. In her present state of nervousness, she inanely wished she had some of Narena's powers, so she could turn him into a toad. And immediately tamped down the notion before the image of the surly policeman hopping around in a trench coat made her start laughing. "She wasn't here, so I don't know." If they went asking around, they might discover someone who had seen Kelly when she and Jarek were there. She prayed they wouldn't do that. At least not yet.

Officer Campbell brushed past his partner and offered her a card. "If you hear from her, would you please let us know? We only want to ask her some questions."

Vanessa took the card. "Yes. Of course. She said she would only be gone for a few days, so I'm sure you or the Lackton police can ask her yourselves when she returns. And I will speak to her about her irresponsible behavior. "

Officer Campbell nodded. "Thank you for your time, ma'am. Sorry to disturb you." He opened the door and stepped out. Lawson followed.

"No problem, officers," Vanessa said, resting one hand on the knob. She was about to close the door when Officer Lawson turned.

"Do you have a son named Jarek?" he said, piercing her with a predatory gaze.

"No. My son is named Tyson. Why?"

"Nothing." The man turned and walked to the police cruiser.

"Damn little toad," Vanessa muttered as she shut the door. She leaned against the portal and collected her thoughts. They came here because of a missing body and not because of David. That meant they hadn't gone into Kelly's apartment yet.

But when they did, Vanessa was sure they would be back. Possibly with a search warrant.

And that meant Jarek had no place to hide.

Chapter Thirty-one

The little girl whimpered, the soft sound tearing at Kelly's heart.

The odor of cooked meat and soiled clothes mingled with sweat slammed into Kelly with such force, she had to breathe through her mouth so she wouldn't gag. The room was windowless, lit only by a single candle. Unwilling to step into the injured little girl's house without being invited, Kelly hung back behind Narena and waited. Her eyes darted to the form lying on the bed. The child's face was ashen, and a thin film of sweat dotted her brow.

"I have brought a wise woman, one who can heal the child. Do you give permission for her to do so?" Narena said in a low voice.

"I have not seen this woman before. She is well known to you?" The mother clutched a rag in her hands.

"She is my distant kin, but not from this land. I trust her with my life."

Kelly's mouth opened slightly, and her throat constricted. Narena's words caught her off guard. The acceptance touched her.

At the mother's nod, she stepped toward the listless child. She murmured comforting words as she sat on the edge of the bed.

"Hey, there, how are you feeling, sweetie? Let me have a look at your leg, okay?" She pushed the scratchy blanket to one side, exposing a leg with a bloodied rag wrapped around the wound. She stopped herself from shaking her head. These people didn't know about infections. They were doing what they could. It was up to her to help

205

them now.

"I need a pan of boiling water, some clean rags, a needle, some thread, and a couple of clean towels. Also a cup with hot water to make a tea for her to drink."

Narena drew out a few pieces of cloth from a pocket in her robe, handed them to her and retreated to help the child's mother gather what she needed.

Kelly put the items in her lap. One held dried valerian tied into a pouch. The other was a small square of linen with Frankincense and oil mixture folded inside. She sat beside the child on the bed, caressing the girl's forehead.

A cursory examination showed the little girl to be in relatively good health, although there were contusions on her upper arms. Bending closer, Kelly placed tentative fingers on the bruises, and the child gave a soft groan. The markings had the vague shape of a hand. The young one had been abused, not necessarily beaten, but gripped hard enough to create black and blue marks.

Kelly shifted her attention to the mother and Narena, who brought the pan of hot water and other items. She took the cloth containing the valerian and dunked it into the steaming liquid. Once the tea turned light brown, she added some cold water to the mix so the patient could drink it.

"Do you have another pan and some soap?"

When the mother returned with the second pan, Kelly gave her the sedative mixture to administer to her child.

Kelly poured half of the heated contents from the first pan into the second. She immersed her hands and hissed at the near-scalding temperature. She quickly lathered them with soap, rinsed away the suds, and wiped them on a towel. A quick dip of the needle and thread into the other pan of clean, hot fluid sterilized her tools.

Kelly unwrapped the bloodied cloth from the girl's leg. It fell to the floor with a plop. She wet a rag with sanitary water and gently rinsed off the dried blood from the edges of the wound. The mother stepped away from the bed, empty cup in her hands.

Kelly caught both women's attention. "I have to sew the gash on her leg. The valerian should work quickly to provide some relief, but it will still be very painful for her. The child must be kept immobile." She motioned the mother to the top of the bed. "Hold her shoulders down. Talk to her while I work. The sound of your voice will help calm her." Kelly turned to Narena. "Place your hands on her knees and press down firmly. She mustn't move her legs."

She looked once more at the mother and Narena. "Are you ready?" They nodded.

Kelly tied a knot at the base of the thread. Using one hand to hold the skin together, she sutured the little girl's wound. The child's whimpers turned to screams, jagged and shrill and it took all of Kelly's resolve to concentrate on getting the job done as quickly and neatly as possible.

After ten agonizing minutes, Kelly slipped the last stitch through skin and knotted it tightly. She sat back and closed her eyes over tears threatening to fall. She took a deep breath and swallowed the lump in her throat.

Her gaze fell to the mother who was crying silently.

"You can let go now, but continue speaking to her. Let her know the worst is over. I will put a dressing on the wound, and then she can rest."

She addressed Narena. "Keep hold of her legs, but just enough to prevent her from moving too much. Once I put the compress on, I'll need you to lift the leg so I can wind a clean bandage around it."

She retrieved the compress, unfolded it to expose the wet side where she'd dribbled the Frankincense resin mixture. Taking it by the edges, she placed the medicated side on the wound, wrapped another clean rag around the girl's leg, and anchored the compress with a knot.

She sat back. Now that the ordeal was over, her once-steady hands began to tremble. The nervousness and anxiety of the last half hour weighed heavy on her. Hopefully, the extract would do its work and keep infection at bay. Only time would tell.

Kelly rose from the bed. The mother covered her child with a blanket, placed a soft kiss on her brow. She watched the display of affection with wistful remembrance.

Narena came to her side and withdrew a miniature vial of opaque liquid from the pocket of her dress. Kelly took it and handed to the mother.

"After one full day, undo the dressing on her leg and check it. If there is any dark redness or pus seeping from the wound, you must come get me at once. If the wound looks clean, make a new compress with a clean cloth, and sprinkle the remainder of this liquid on it. Put the medicine side down on the wound, and secure it like I did here."

The woman clasped her hands over Kelly's, face filled with appreciation.

"She looks like a strong little girl. She should be fine." Kelly comforted.

"I cannot thank you enough. You truly are kin to the sorceress. I sense greatness about you."

Hardly. She bit back the comment and withdrew her hands from the woman's grasp.

"I will be by in a few days to check on the child." Narena placed a hand on Kelly's shoulder, signaling their departure.

Approaching footsteps drew everyone's attention to a male figure silhouetted in the doorway.

The mother's eyes shone with hope. "The sorceress has brought a great healer to save our child."

The man assessed Narena and Kelly. He walked forward, reached out, and lightly grasped Kelly's upper arm. Her heart slammed into her chest. Thin wisps of malevolent darkness slithered across her skin. Oppressive. Violent. He dropped his hand and advanced toward the child's bed. "I give you thanks for tending my daughter." The voice was gravelly, hard with no affection.

Kelly nodded, not trusting herself to speak. Tendrils of hatred seized her throat. She couldn't breathe. Her stomach revolted, and she recoiled from the couple.

"Kelly, what is it?" Narena whispered.

"I...I'm tired, that's all. If you don't mind, I would like to get back and rest. It has been an emotional time." She didn't wait for an answer, but forced herself to walk out the door when what she really wanted to do was run.

Once she stepped into the night, she ran to the edge of the clay building, bent over, and heaved. She dropped to her knees. Her whole body shook while sweat poured down the sides of her face. Another wave roiled and she vomited again. Her hands slapped to the ground to keep herself from falling into the dirt. She inhaled blessed fresh air into her lungs.

A cool hand touched her sweaty forehead. "Kelly. What is wrong?" Narena asked.

She could only shake her head. She didn't understand. In training, she'd gotten sick watching her first autopsy, but since then her body never reacted like this. She sat back, took the edge of her dress in a shaky hand, and wiped her mouth.

"Are you all right?"

Kelly nodded, stood, facing Narena. Deep lines of concern

furrowed the woman's brow.

"I'll be okay."

"Can you tell me what transpired? Is your power trying to come through?"

"I'm not sure. Nothing like this has ever happened to me. It felt as though I touched...evil."

Chapter Thirty-two

Kelly sat at the table with a cup of Leisos' version of coffee in her hands. The brew was strong enough to raise the dead, and she couldn't have been more grateful. It had been another hellish night plagued with weird dreams and she felt like she could sleep for a week.

"You look troubled," Narena said, raising her own cup of coffee.

"Nothing a week at a spa couldn't fix. You wouldn't happen to have one close by, would you?" The words sounded flippant, but she was overwhelmed. First by coming here, then by tending to the injured girl. The weirdness of what happened to her after the little girl's father touched her still didn't make sense.

And oh yes, there was tonight.

At midnight, she and Narena would attempt to bring Jarek back to Leisos. Only she hadn't found her so-called power, and time was running out.

"I'm sorry, just don't pay any attention to me. I'm cranky, tired, confused, and really scared."

"About tonight," Narena correctly surmised. She put down her cup and reached across the table for Kelly's hand. "Do you still doubt your ability?"

"Of course, I do. I don't have any ability."

"What do you call what you did last night? You saved the child's life."

"Medical training, although the voice in my dream didn't seem to think so."

Narena went still, tightening her grip on Kelly's hand. "Tell me."

"There's nothing to tell. A female voice spoke to me, but I couldn't see a face."

"You must tell me exactly what she said."

She concentrated, trying to remember the words the woman used, a few of which she'd never heard before. "She said, 'Seek the light in the shadows, for it will guide you, give you strength and purpose. Once you embrace the sense, so too will you be able to see it in others. It is done. Your path of discovery has begun. Welcome to your destiny, *Tabibu*.'

"I may have gotten some of the wording wrong..."

"You are sure about the word she used — *Tabibu*?" Excitement threaded through Narena's voice.

"Pretty sure. Do you know what it means? Is it important?"

The sorceress's eyes blazed. "Yes, Kelly, it is very important. The woman you heard was Rehema, the Goddess of Empathy. *Tabibu* means healer. The message she sent has proclaimed your gift. Your power has been granted."

"Here we go again with the power. I don't feel any different."

"You will not know until you try."

"How can I when I don't know what to try for?" she said with a mix of exasperation and frustration. Why couldn't Narena face the fact she was not special? She didn't have any secret powers, and she couldn't do hoodoo voodoo. It was hopeless. Staring down at the table, she wished the whole world would just go away and leave her alone.

She sensed Narena looking at her but refused to meet her gaze.

The sorceress's soft voice broke the silence. "How can you explain what happened last night after the man touched you?"

Kelly's head tilted back. "I can't. Nerves maybe. Overreacting to stitching up the little girl. I dunno." She shrugged.

"That is not what you said last night. Stop doubting yourself. You said you sensed evil. There is no need to be afraid or ashamed. Did you see anything?"

"No. It was more like I felt a dark heaviness." She hesitated. "I think he abuses his daughter."

"Why do you think so?" There was no derision or skepticism in the woman's eyes. Only interest.

"When I treated the girl, I noticed bruises on her upper arms, like someone had gripped her too hard. It takes a lot of force to create those types of marks."

"It could be the mother."

"I didn't get the sense from the mother, just from him."

A knowing smile crossed Narena's face, as if the answer had just been spoken. "The 'sense.' It is the second time you have used that word. You relied on an inner feeling to give you direction, and that feeling has spoken."

"What do you mean?" She was more confused than ever.

"When the mother touched your hands, what did you feel?"

"Nothing."

"Close your eyes, relive the moment. Breathe in and clear your thoughts. Now, bring to your mind when your two hands touched, and experience everything again. Think about what you were exposed to."

Kelly did as instructed, focusing only on the few seconds of contact with the mother. She pictured the woman in her ragged dress. The calloused hand. Her dry skin.

"What did you feel?"

Her eyes widened. "I sensed gratefulness and hope."

"Anything else?"

"Maybe a touch of awe?" She wasn't sure that was the right word,

213

but there was no other way to describe it.

Narena gave her a wide smile. "That is your power, Kelly. Feeling. Sensing. You are an empath."

"What's an empath?"

"Someone who can sense what another is feeling. With practice you will be able to tell *exactly* what people feel. When you touched the father, you became aware of darkness in his soul. If he had done nothing wrong, or if he had done it only once and was repentant, his soul would have been cleansed of the transgression. But because he abused the child, and perhaps the mother too, his soul bore the stain, the blackness you sensed in your mind. This is the gift of an empath."

"So you're telling me I can read people's minds?"

Narena chuckled. "No. Only their emotions."

"How do I know this wasn't a one time deal?"

"Rehema would not have come to you if you did not already possess empathy. She has given you the power to tap into it, broaden it, and use it with your gift of healing."

"I don't know how that will help me. Don't forget, I don't actually heal people. I see them once they've died. And something tells me I don't have the ability to bring them back from the dead."

"No one has the ability to do that. But you can use your power in whatever way you choose. You have the training to heal. You already proved it with Jarek and now with the young child. Why do you question yourself? There is no reason you cannot use your training on the living instead of the dead. And as an empath, you may be able to do more. It is all up to you."

Kelly gnawed on her lower lip. Narena was mistaken. She didn't have the power to be an empath.

Did she?

"If I had this ability, this empathy before now, wouldn't I have noticed it?" Or maybe she had and didn't recognize what the ability was. She gave up her practice as an MD because the onslaught of emotions from her patients and their families had been too overwhelming to bear. But she'd never felt anything this strong.

"Has there ever been a time when you felt something was wrong but were unable to identify what? Or sensed a person wished to unload their burden but was reluctant to do so?"

"I guess so. When I was younger, I could tell when something was bothering one of my friends, but I didn't think there was any sort of magic involved."

"Do you not have the ability now?" Narena frowned.

"I haven't paid any attention."

"Then something has changed."

"Nothing's changed other than being thrown back in time."

"A power is not buried unless one chooses to suppress it. If you had this ability before, something in your past caused you to turn away from your gift."

There was only one thing that could have affected her on such a deep level. "I don't want to talk about it."

"But you must. Time is of the essence. Tonight is the only chance to bring back Jarek, and you have not fully tapped into your power. You must bring to the surface whatever binds you to your past and release it, or we will fail."

"No! Just leave me alone." She stalked to the fireplace, searched the flames for peace. Bringing up the past wasn't going to help. It would only rip open old wounds.

"Kelly, our task is dangerous. If you do not believe in your power, if you have any doubts, your connection with me will falter, and Jarek will pay the price."

She whirled around and glared at the sorceress. "Look, I get it. Jarek needs to come back now to save his twin. I understand his brother may be in danger, but really, we can try this again next month. By then I'll have more practice, and I'll be less likely to fail."

"If I knew Rayja was safe, I would concede and give you another moon's passing before attempting to bring Jarek back. However, I cannot and will not risk Rayja's life. There is also something else you must know. Tonight, when we begin, I will contact your aunt. She will lend me her power. Together, the three of us will transport the prince through time. However, once he has left your time, our concentration cannot falter. During the spell, if you waiver or the spell is broken before he arrives here, he will be lost between both worlds. Forever."

Chapter Thirty-three

Jarek paced like a restless animal. Inactivity drove him crazy. He shoved a hand through his hair, a low groan of impatience rumbling deep in this throat.

"You keep growling like that, and I'll have to put you in a cage," Vanessa teased, peering over the edge of her book.

Late morning daylight heated the sunroom, but he didn't feel it. He would not be warm until he held Kelly in his arms again.

"I am unaccustomed to waiting," he retorted.

Vanessa arched her eyebrow in response.

He returned to his chair. "Tell me about Kelly's family." Maybe this topic would help pass the time.

Vanessa studied him, closed the book and placed it on the table beside her. "What did she tell you?"

"Very little. She spoke in brief of her parents and their accident. The subject of Stephanie is very sensitive to her."

"I'm sure. Unfortunately, I don't know much. You see Kelly's mother — my sister, Lucille — and I had a falling out after Kelly was born. We spoke only once after that."

"Why did you not contact Kelly after their accident? She was left to bring up Stephanie by herself." That had been bothering him for a while, especially when Kelly told him how difficult it was raising Stephanie.

Regret flashed across the woman's face. "I made a promise to

Lucille I wouldn't have any contact with either Kelly or Stephanie."

"But why?"

"Lucy refused to believe we were descendants of Narena, even though she carried the birthmark. That was what we spoke about the last time. I wanted her to tell Kelly about her lineage, but she wouldn't hear it. And when I told her about my powers, she cut off all ties to me. I never heard from her again." A far-away expression clouded Vanessa's features.

"It must have been very difficult for you," he said. His brother Rayja came to mind. He couldn't contemplate severing ties to his twin. His stomach tightened as if a fist had punched him.

"It was. I didn't expect her to be so closed-minded. After that, I never spoke of my power to another soul again. Not even to Kelly. I said some women in our line possessed powers, but I didn't tell her I actually had them."

"What is yours?"

Vanessa turned away, gazed outside.

"I will not pass judgment. You do not need to convince me. My being here proves magical powers exist. Besides, Narena is my friend."

"I can speak with people of the past," she admitted. "But only if they contact me. I have visions or they come to me in dreams, like Narena did."

"You have not communicated with Lucille?"

"Like I said, they must contact me. She never accepted our lineage, let alone the prospect of her sister having abilities. No, I will never hear from her again."

"It is unfortunate you were not able to be a part of Kelly's life."

"Yes, but I kept tabs on her through other people. I read about Stephanie's death in the paper. When Kelly left, I didn't know where she had gone, which was why I was so pleased she contacted me. By the way, how did she find me?"

"The same way I did you. Your name was written in an old, green leather book. The pages were quite worn and yellow."

"Lucy's telephone book," Vanessa said with a hush. "I gave it to her when she went to college so she could fill it with the names of new friends she'd make there." She put trembling fingers to her lips. "I can't believe she kept it all these years."

"Apparently, part of her was unwilling to let you go."

Jarek rose from the chair and went back to the window. His gaze lingered on the spot where Kelly and he had kissed. He pictured her golden hair and blazing blue eyes. He ached to hold her again, to make love to her until their hearts and souls merged. He couldn't wait to see her. His pacing resumed.

Vanessa cleared her throat.

"Forgive me. As I mentioned, I am unaccustomed to waiting, and I do not know what is happening in Leisos," he sheepishly said, returning to his seat. "And I have been wondering if Narena has persuaded Kelly to use her powers. Something, I think, will not be easily done."

"What will you do once you get there?"

"Ensure the safety of my brother and uncover who was trying to kill me. I will also find a way to send Kelly back," he said hesitantly.

As much as his heart wanted to have Kelly near, as much as his soul cried out for its mate, he doubted she would want to stay in his world. Her life was here, with her job and now her aunt. Leisos was different, no modern amenities, like her car or money. His world wouldn't have these things for over a thousand years.

"Kelly can't come back. Ever."

He snapped his eyes to Vanessa. Her fingers were gripped tightly in her lap.

"Why not? I am only thinking of Kelly. Her world has more to offer."

"She will have you."

"That may not be enough. If Kelly wishes to return to this time, I cannot deny her the right."

"As her aunt, I can. She can't come back because of David."

"But David is dead."

"Exactly." She sighed. "There is a dead body in Kelly's apartment. If the police haven't found it by now, they will soon. When Kelly doesn't show up for work from her supposed trip to Florida, they will search her place. Once they find the body, a murder investigation will ensue. She'll be the prime suspect, even though she didn't do it."

"I am the one who killed David."

"Yes, but you won't be here. She can't very well say some man from two thousand years ago came through time and killed David in self-defense. From what you said, her fingerprints are on the dagger."

"She could stay here with you."

Vanessa shook her head. "This is the first place they will look. I wouldn't be able to hide her. And though she didn't do it, she had means, motive, and opportunity. No jury in the world would let her go free. Don't you see? To keep her safe, she must stay in Leisos with you."

Jarek rubbed his hands over his face, wishing he could rub out the last few days as well. "I am sorry."

"You did what you needed to do to keep her safe, and so must I. She can never come back to this time. Ever."

Chapter Thirty-four

"Forever, as in indefinitely? Can't you track him or something?"

Kelly gaped at Narena as if the sorceress had told her the world was coming to an end. And in a way it was. There was a possibility Jarek might not make it back home.

This couldn't be happening. Not again. She wouldn't be responsible for another person's death.

"I must have an anchor to locate him," Narena explained. "Once the spell has begun, Jarek will shatter the crystal he is wearing, releasing the anchor inside for me to locate. If we fail or the spell is interrupted, I will not be able to find him. Now do you understand why you must be ready?"

Kelly's senses reeled at what was required of her. "Did you have an anchor when you sent Jarek?"

"No, and the energy required drained me. I almost died. There is only so much power I possess," Narena said. "Although I had thought myself prepared, it was harder than expected. If I attempt to do this without you and am unsuccessful, I will not survive to try again later, and Jarek will stay in the future for the rest of his life." Narena palmed Kelly's cheek, compassion shining in her eyes. "I am sorry to put such a burden on you."

Kelly's heart felt like it was being sliced open. Everything rode on her. Jarek's life. Rayja's safety. Even Narena's life. She was pretty sure the sorceress would attempt to bring Jarek back even without her help.

"Help me, Narena. How do I tap into my power?" Her voice cracked.

"Let go of what haunts you. When you set your burden free, you will be free."

A sob broke from her lips. "I had a sister."

The story of Stephanie's death spilled forth in a rush. It all came out. The guilt. David. Her self-imposed exile into the world of the dead. As the wave of words ebbed, she rested her head on her folded arms, exhausted, yet strangely lighter. Narena held her until the sobs eased to whimpers.

When Kelly's tremors ceased, Narena lifted her chin and gazed into her eyes. "If you had taken Stephanie with you that night, would you have stayed until the end of the show?" she asked.

Kelly wiped away tears. "Yes, I guess so."

"And if you had, would you have remained to hear what you call the encore?"

"Of course. Sometimes it's the best part."

"Then you might have perished with your beloved little sister, too. Had you died, Jarek would not be alive right now, and the future of Leisos would be in peril."

"I suppose it's possible," she conceded.

"Kelly, all things happen for a reason. If Stephanie had lived, you would not have taken the path you are on now. It would not have led you to Jarek. Sometimes one must die for another to live."

The tightness gripping her heart made it hard to breathe. Her soul tore into pieces, and she wasn't sure if she had the strength to put it back together.

"I need to be alone." She rose from the table and walked to the door.

"When do you plan to return? There is much preparation to be done for tonight."

Kelly glanced back at the woman and held her gaze for a long moment. She turned around and stepped out the door without replying.

"Are you all right?"

Kelly snapped out of her dream. She raised a hand to block out the blinding afternoon sun and looked at the young couple bent over her. She struggled to a sitting position and inched away from the outstretched hand.

Great. The last thing she remembered was being alone. She'd needed a place to think and came to the same spot Narena had shown her yesterday. The warmth of the sun, accompanied by the past few nights of fitful sleep, had taken its toll. She must have dozed off. Her fingers rubbed the grit from her eyes. Narena's words of caution echoed in her mind. No unwanted attention.

"I'm fine, thank you."

"You are not from here." The man's eyes narrowed warily.

"No. I'm from far away." Keep to the facts, she reminded herself. "I am kin to the sorceress Narena." Would these people recognize the name?

"Oh, yes the sorceress," the young woman gushed, sitting down beside Kelly on the hill slope. "I have not met her, but all know of her greatness and wisdom."

Kelly nodded. She had been dreaming of Stephanie. The dream was bittersweet, not like the usual nightmares, which had plagued her since her sister's death. In this one, Stephanie was smiling and happy. They stood together, enveloped in mist. No sound. No breeze. No feeling.

An aura of peace surrounded Stephanie as she opened her mouth to speak, but the couple woke Kelly before her sister could speak. All she wanted was go back to the dream. God, she missed Stephanie. She would always miss her.

"Laisa, show me the flowers you like. I will collect them while you speak with the newcomer." The young man extended his hand to the girl and helped her to her feet.

"I will return shortly." They walked, fingers clasped, down the slope.

Kelly watched the couple wistfully, their devotion making her miss Jarek even more. She felt so alone without him. Her hand massaged her chest over her heart, as if rubbing it would ease the pain. Knowing she would see him again tonight made her hang on.

Arms around her knees, she rested her head and struggled with the oppressive weight of responsibility.

"Kelly."

She snapped up, eyes wide, heart hammering in her throat.

Stephanie?

Her head whipped around. No one behind her. Oh God, she was losing her mind. Now she was hearing voices.

"Kelly."

Kelly whirled back. An ethereal figure in a flowing dress was floating in mid air. Her eyes widened and then they slammed shut. A strangled cry caught in her throat. It was Stephanie. She was hallucinating. Her heart rate skyrocketed as she heaved for air. First the voices, and now she was seeing things. She wasn't losing her mind—it was already gone. Her head swayed back and forth in denial. Was this what having a nervous breakdown felt like?

The voice spoke softly as if coming from a great distance. "Kelly, it's me."

"No. You're not real. Go away. I'm not seeing you."

"Kelly, it is me. I don't have much time. Please look at me. You aren't hallucinating."

She refused to acknowledge her.

"Rehema sent me."

She opened her eyes. Stephanie's semi-transparent body hovered above the ground within a soft white aura. She smiled, her beautiful face softening under the peaceful glow.

"Hey sis," Stephanie said.

"Is it really you?" Kelly's voice broke as tears streaked down her cheeks.

"Yes, it's me."

"How..."

"The young couple will be back any minute, and I need to talk to you."

Overwhelmed by the deluge of emotions, Kelly said nothing.

"Everything is okay, really. I don't blame you for what happened, and you shouldn't blame yourself."

"Oh God, Stephanie. I was responsible for you."

"I know you're the older sister, but for once in your life, listen to me. You have to let me go."

"I don't know if I can."

"You have to. Only then will you be able to follow your destiny, to tap into your power. Don't let my death be in vain. You were always there for me, Kelly. Let me help you. Embrace your power, and let me go."

"Will you forgive me?"

"It's not me who has to forgive. Time for me to go."

"Will I ever see you again?" she sobbed. Saying goodbye was like losing her all over again.

Stephanie smiled. "What do you think?" As her image faded, she whispered, "I love you." And she was gone.

A soft breeze drifted across Kelly's face, and she could have sworn she heard the word "Believe." A light heat permeated her, like a hug from an old friend, a loved one, a sister. She closed her eyes and filled her lungs with air, holding the warmth within her. It flowed through to her soul. The shell surrounding her heart cracked, let in light and warmth, split wider, welcoming Stephanie's love, until she was filled by it. With a mixed cry of joy and sadness, Kelly let go of her inner demon.

She faced the sun, and peace enfolded her. She was enveloped by the scents of the earth she sat on, the grasses and flowers around her, the clean air. A smile stretched across her face. The weight lifting from her soul was immeasurable. For the first time in over two years, she felt whole, and it was because of Stephanie. Her little sister had given Kelly permission to forgive herself. It was a gift she would treasure always.

It was time to move on and embrace her destiny. She had to learn how to tap into her power before Narena cast her spell, or Stephanie's forgiveness would be in vain. No way was Kelly going to let that happen. Jarek had to come back tonight, and Narena needed her help. Like the sorceress had said, maybe Stephanie died so Jarek and his family could live.

Kelly spotted the young woman approaching and wiped away the last of her sadness.

Laisa sat down beside Kelly, slipping her arms around her bent knees.

"Ravell and I will have our *nafstahd* tonight. He is collecting flowers for my floral crown." Laisa stared, dreamy-eyed, at her companion walking farther down the hill. She tilted her head. "If you are kin to the sorceress, do you profess to know magic?"

226

God, she truly hoped so. Kelly managed a half-hearted grin. "I am a healer." Admitting it out loud was strange, yet enlightening.

She believed she was a healer and not just someone who worked on dead bodies. Now she needed to believe she was also an empath.

And here was a patient sitting beside her.

But how was she supposed to read people's emotions?

Laisa enthusiastically rattled on about the upcoming ceremony, completely oblivious to Kelly's silence.

Kelly breathed to relax and clear her mind of all thoughts. Remembering what Narena had instructed, she searched for the calming center of her body where everything was still. Her heartbeat became her focus. Its rhythm slowed to match her breathing. She concentrated on the beat, opening her mind, inviting smells in the air, the rustle of grasses, even welcoming the excitement in Laisa's voice.

At first she felt a glimmer in her chest. She couldn't put her finger on the sensation. Kelly tried to grab hold of the impression, investigate it to define what it was, but it floated away. Gritting her teeth in frustration, she cleared her mind again. The awareness returned, only this time, she let the feeling come on its own.

She reached out with her mind to grasp the slippery tendrils of mist. Vapor-like awareness built until it was tangible, fluttering like butterfly wings against her heart and lungs, swimming through her veins. It built, took form, filled her until it was recognizable.

There. The thrill of tapping into another person's emotions increased her heart rate. She concentrated on lowering it to a steady, slow beat. Laisa's feelings became her own. The young woman was excited.

It was no surprise Laisa would be delighted about getting married. Maybe there was something else. Something deeper. A feeling Laisa wouldn't readily share.

A flicker of hesitancy pushed into her thoughts. What she was about to do constituted as invasion of privacy but she was running out of time. Besides, she rationalized, she was a physician and this could be classified as doctor/patient confidentiality. She continued. Maybe physical contact would enhance her connection to Laisa's emotions, just as it had with the injured girl's father. It was worth a try.

"Laisa, Tell me more about this *nafstahd*. Would you show me how it is done?"

"Ravell and I will clasp hands, like this," she said, grabbing hold of Kelly's lower arm just above the wrist.

Ancient handfasting. Kelly ignored the words and focused on finding her center of peace. Her mind opened and let Laisa in. Excitement again. Kelly acknowledged the emotion and let it go, concentrating on uncovering what lay beneath the surface.

"The overseer in our village will bind our hands together with a cloth I stitched," Laisa continued.

Somewhere deep down, a kernel of trepidation budded.

Laisa was scared.

Kelly wanted to jump up and down and yell her head off. She had done it. But she couldn't tell Laisa she sensed her fear. To do so would only scare the young woman, and then Kelly would have to explain she was more than just a healer.

But she wanted verification.

"You must be very happy," Kelly said.

Laisa let go of her hand. "Oh yes, I cannot wait to start a new life with Ravell." The young woman's face lit up with anticipation.

"Are you nervous?"

"No. Ravell is the one for me. We have known each other since we were children."

Hmm, this was going to be harder than expected. And it wouldn't be long before the groom was due back. "If it was me, I would be nervous. Maybe even a little scared."

"What is there to be scared of? We love each other."

"What if he found out something about me I didn't want him to?"

"One should not have secrets from another," Laisa said, looking away.

Aha. She was right. Laisa was hiding something.

"Yes. But sometimes things happen we are ashamed of, and we don't want others to know."

Laisa's eyes flew open wide and snapped to meet Kelly's gaze. "What do you mean?"

"There are things I have done in the past I'm not proud of and would find difficult to tell anyone, especially my husband."

"Why would you, then?" The young woman searched Kelly's face.

"Because, like you said, husbands and wives shouldn't have secrets. In the end, the secret comes out anyway. The other person might resent you didn't tell him or think you didn't trust enough to let him know right from the start. Or think you didn't love him enough."

"But, I do love Ravell with all my heart," Laisa cried.

Kelly regretted pushing the girl, and needed to make amends and help her. "If Ravell truly loves you, he will love everything about you, no matter what secrets you hide."

"How did you know?"

She smiled ruefully. "Well, Narena is my kin."

"I am so scared Ravell will not want to have me after I tell him."

"I'm sure he will. And if he doesn't, what does that say about him? If he had a secret like yours and he told you, would you still want to marry him?"

"Yes."

"Then give him a chance."

Laisa looked down at her hands clasped tight in her lap. "I am no longer a maiden," she whispered. Tears flowed down her cheeks. "At night, after the ceremony, Ravell will find out, and he will revoke his pledge."

"Laisa. It's something he would have found out eventually. You can't hide it."

"I had hoped it would grow back." Laisa looked up with pleading eyes. "You are a healer. Can you not make it grow back?"

Kelly's heart broke at the bride's naiveté. In this age, women didn't talk about sex. They were lucky to know what was expected of them. No wonder Laisa was hoping her body might return to the way it was before.

"That's something I cannot do. Was it an accident?"

"One of my brother's friends forced me. I have not spoken of it to anyone."

Kelly had a few choice words for men who violated women, but voicing her opinion wasn't going to help matters. Laisa needed emotional support. Would Ravell give her that?

"You must tell him. Don't wait until after the ceremony. Ravell will think you tried to trick him. Explain what happened. He will understand. If he loves you, it won't make any difference."

"But what if he does not want me any more?"

"Then you are too good for him, and another will come along who will want you. Believe in yourself, Laisa. It is your greatest power."

Kelly smiled when she realized she quoted the words her sister had spoken. Brought out in this light, she realized how true they were. And she did believe them. With her whole soul.

Laisa wiped the tears from her face and gazed down the hill at the approaching man. She turned to Kelly. "I would like to thank you, but you have not spoken your name."

"It's Kelly."

"Thank you, Kelly."

She brushed back a strand of hair from the young woman's face. "You'll be fine Laisa. I wish you and Ravell all the happiness in the world."

Laisa rose to her feet. "Our ceremony is tonight. Can you come and join us in the celebration?"

A different ritual demanded her attention this evening. "I'm sorry, but I can't. Thank you for asking."

Her companion nodded with a sad smile. When Ravell met up with them, she took his hand. He carried a basket of beautiful wild flowers in the other.

"You'll make a beautiful bride, Laisa," Kelly said.

"Be well, Kelly." Laisa turned to Ravell. "Come, there is still much to do and something I wish to talk to you about."

The young couple walked away, and all Kelly's dreams and well wishes went with them. Hopefully, Ravell would look past custom and see how special Laisa was.

It would have been nice to see a traditional handfasting, but she had her own ceremony to prepare for. No matter what, she was going to make sure her soul mate came back to her. And that meant she needed to get her act together.

Chapter Thirty-five

The waiting was killing Jarek. Time was his enemy, ticking slower with every minute. Almost midnight. The moment would be here soon, when he would leave this wondrous new place and go back to his home and his love.

With an impish grin, Vanessa touched a finger to his brow. "You look so menacing when you frown, Jarek."

He took her hand in his and held it. This was the one regret. Over the past two days, he'd started to care for the strong, vibrant woman sitting beside him. Though she didn't know him, Vanessa had invited him into her home without hesitation. She'd become a true friend.

"Don't worry Jarek," Vanessa said. "Everything will be all right. Narena came to me in a dream last night and revealed the words of the spell I must recite once you shatter the crystal. You will be back in your own time soon."

"Did she say anything about Kelly?"

"No. The message was very brief. But I'm sure everything is in place. She wouldn't try this unless she could bring you back with Kelly's help."

"Do not be too sure. I have known Narena all my life. She would sacrifice herself in an attempt to bring me back if it would guarantee the safety of our people."

"It's almost time." Vanessa rose and walked to the windows, peered through the glass, and closed the curtains. A frown puckered her brow.

"What is it?"

"There is a police cruiser parked outside. They've driven by before."

"Do you think they will want to come in the house?"

"Possibly," she said. "My guess is they found David's body and might be waiting for a search warrant. Let's hope Narena is on time."

She pushed the coffee table off to the side. For the next step, she retrieved five white crystals from a box on the couch and placed them in a circle on the floor. She took a hammer from the toolbox, set it inside the circle, and stood back.

Vanessa glanced at the mantel clock above the fireplace. "It's coming up on midnight. You need to be inside the circle when the ritual begins."

His hands settled on her shoulders. He swallowed the tightness in his throat. "I cannot thank you enough for all you have done. You have risked your life for me, a debt which I cannot repay."

"Your payment will be to ensure my niece's happiness."

"On my word, I will love and care for her the rest of my days."

"I only ask one thing. When you see her, tell her that I love her and that she can find me in her dreams." Vanessa stepped into Jarek's embrace and held him tight. "Safe travels."

Closing his eyes, he hugged her. He regretted Kelly would never get to know this wonderful woman.

Vanessa disengaged herself and wiped a tear from the corner of her eye. She led him to the center of the crystal circle, moved the hammer to within his reach, and stepped back. Taking a piece of paper from her pocket, she breathed deeply. The first stroke of midnight chimed out just as the doorbell pealed.

Kelly's knees shook. She had never been so nervous and scared in her life. This was it. Almost midnight. In a few moments, Narena would begin the ritual to bring Jarek back to Leisos.

Fear and doubt clouded her mind. An irrational thought pulsed through her brain. Maybe this was all just a bad dream.

But of course it wasn't. She was in Leisos, and she had a job to do.

She and Narena were alone in a clearing a short distance from the sorceress's home. There was no more time for practice. A horse stood beneath a nearby tree, munching grass with idle abandon. They were blessed with a calm night. Kelly gazed up at the moon. It was three days past full but still beautiful. The orb's rays caressed her skin. She looked at it differently now. It wasn't a scientific symbol anymore, but a representation of power.

Narena placed five white crystals in a circle on the ground and set one lighted candle between each, for a total of five. The sorceress lifted her face, raised her arms to the inky heavens, then lowered them to her sides. She took a deep breath and focused on Kelly.

"It is almost time. Come, you must stand beside me. At the precise moment, I will take your hand so I can receive your power."

The weight of the world rested on Kelly's shoulders. "We didn't get a chance to try transferring my power to you."

"You know what needs to be done and how to do it," Narena said. "Do you love Jarek?"

Kelly's step faltered. She had asked herself that very question many times since she arrived in Leisos. It was always the same answer. Jarek's charm, laughter, caring, and love for her taught her to live again. He was her soul mate, and she would do anything to get him back.

"Yes, I love him," she admitted.

"Then you can do no other than succeed. If you wish to see him again, you must help me. Once we start, we cannot stop. My power alone is not sufficient. If you do not give me yours, Jarek will either be left in your time or between worlds. You will remain here. And I will not survive the casting."

Narena caressed Kelly's face. "You have given me a wonderful gift, Kelly. You have shown me how strong the women of my line will become. I am proud you are my kin."

Kelly grasped Narena's hand and squeezed tightly.

"Let's get on with it, shall we?" She took a step back, let go of Narena's hand, and filled her lungs with the night air, pushing all negative thoughts from her mind. Her eyes closed, and she focused on the image of Jarek, as Narena had instructed her earlier. Her racing heart slowed down. Her breathing became shallower. She reached for a place in her mind where all thoughts, all emotions were gone. Only calmness remained.

The mental image of Jarek remained sharp. Narena recited the spell, and Kelly joined in the chant.

> *Over land and sea and sun*
> *To the time that is to come*
> *We call the one we hold dear*
> *We call for Jarek to be here*

Kelly repeated the spell again. The air began to quiver. She desperately wanted to open her eyes, but it would break her concentration. Narena grasped her hand. Tuning out Narena's voice, she focused on the light within her. It grew, filling her up, consuming her. Her body no longer felt corporeal. It became a huge ball of energy. Heat flowed through her, down, and out her clasped hand. As she chanted the spell for the third time, it felt like her soul left her body.

Narena's grasp on her hand tightened. Power exploded out of Kelly like a million rays of light.

One minute, she was a ball of pure energy, and the next, she staggered back on wobbly legs. She shook her head to focus on the scene in front of her.

Narena lay in a heap on the ground, cradled in Jarek's arms.

Chapter Thirty-six

Kelly wasn't sure whether to laugh or cry. Jarek knelt in moonlight, the orb's radiance dancing off his dark hair. Her heart sang with joy, and the flooding relief made her legs weak. She staggered forward, eager to touch him, to prove he was really there.

Jarek lowered his head and cradled Narena's motionless body closer.

Pain squeezed like a vise around her heart, and a lump rose in her throat as she fell to her knees.

"Oh no, Jarek. Is she okay? Please tell me she's alive." Losing Narena now would be unbearable. In their brief time together, they formed a special bond. The sorceress taught Kelly she could achieve anything if she believed in herself.

"She breathes, but just barely. I do not know what to do." His voice cracked.

"We need to get her back to the house," she said, moving to get the horse.

She would not let Narena die.

The bell rang again, followed by four sharp knocks on the door.

A tear pricked at the corner of Vanessa's eye but she forced it back. Jarek was gone. She prayed Narena and Kelly were successful and that he arrived safely back in Leisos.

She had her own problems.

She gathered up the crystals, put them back in the box, and placed the hammer on the coffee table.

"Coming," she called. She dashed to the kitchen, retrieved a broom and dustpan and hurried to the door.

"Who is it?"

"Petersburg Police Department. Please open the door."

Vanessa summoned the appropriate shock and concern in her voice as she opened the portal. "What's this all about?"

Officer Lawson held up a paper. "We have a search warrant for your house. Please step aside."

Vanessa moved back and let Lawson and another officer into the front hall. Mr. Good Cop, Officer Campbell, was not with them.

"It's a bit late, don't you think?"

Lawson shrugged and continued to move through the structure.

"What are you looking for?"

He stopped and shoved the paper into her hand. "Not what. Who. Your niece." He nodded for the other officer to go upstairs. Rich deep red carpet muffled the sound of the man's progress.

"I told you before, Officer..." Vanessa peered at his nametag, but she didn't need to. She stopped herself from calling him Officer Toad. "...Lawson. Kelly is away in Florida."

"Funny. We can't verify that. No record of any car rented to Kelly Richards in Lackton or Petersburg. We even checked to see if you rented one for her."

Oh, if only she had stronger magic. "I gave her the money. I didn't rent the car for her."

Lawson walked toward the hall leading to the kitchen, stopped and turned to her. "You always clean your house this late at night?" He pointed to the broom and dustpan in her hands.

"Not any more than you search houses. I dropped a glass in the living room when you rang the bell."

She moved past him into the living room. He followed, his footsteps loud on the hardwood floor. She ignored him, crouched down to the throw rug, and swept the shattered crystal fragments into the pan.

"Why are you searching for Kelly? Does it have to do with that missing persons case?" Vanessa left the room and headed toward the kitchen. Lawson trailed behind her like a puppy. Or a bloodhound.

"It's more than a missing person's case now," he said watching her every move.

She dumped the fragments into the garbage, stowed the broom and pan in a nearby closet, and rounded on him. "What's changed?"

The other officer stepped into the kitchen. "Nothing upstairs. No trace of anyone other than the occupant."

"Check downstairs," Lawson ordered. "Murder, Ms. Summers," he said with a probing, accusatory gleam in his eye. "We found a dead guy in Kelly's apartment, stabbed with a dagger. Your niece's fingerprints are all over it."

"That's impossible. Kelly would never kill anyone!" Thank God Jarek had told her what happened beforehand, or she would have died from the shock.

"Won't know until we find her and ask her." Lawson left the kitchen and met up with the officer coming from the basement.

"Place is clean," he said.

Lawson turned. "Where is she, Ms. Summers?"

"I have no idea."

"Aiding and abetting a murder suspect is a federal offense."

"I'm not helping Kelly in any way. I haven't heard from her in days."

"Come on, Lawson. There's nothing here." The second man headed toward the front door.

Lawson moved into her personal space. "There is no statute of limitations on murder, Ms. Summers. Somehow you're associated with this. No matter how long it takes, I will find the connection," he warned and stepped out of the house.

Chapter Thirty-seven

The sorceress was still unconscious.

"I will help you onto the horse first, and then lift up Narena. You will have to hold her between your arms," Jarek said.

Kelly bit her lip. Now was not the time to mention she *really* didn't like horses. They had to get back to Narena's home, and this method was the quickest way. Jarek didn't wait for a reply, simply boosted Kelly up and settled her on the horse. The animal shifted, tensing beneath her. Jarek hoisted Narena to the front and she adjusted the woman's body against her own. She held her friend close as he led them back to Narena's home.

The stillness of the night was both comforting and eerie. Stars glittered in the sky. The heavenly lights were the trio's only spectators as they made their way through the shadows.

"We need to keep her warm. Put her on the bed and cover her. I'll stoke the fire," Kelly instructed as Jarek carried the unconscious Narena through the door. She dumped the sack with the crystals and candles on the table.

She crossed to the hearth, poked at the embers of the fire, and blew until it came to life. She lit one end of a thin piece of kindling and brought the flame to the wick of a lavender scented candle. Its calming properties would help Narena heal.

Kelly commanded herself to think. There was no physical evidence Narena had suffered any type of trauma, so she must be unconscious from the strain of conducting the ritual. She crossed to the bed, eased back the covers, and listened to the patient's breathing. It was shallow but steady. The pulse on her wrist felt slow and regular. Good. Unless Narena woke and told her of any internal pain, the best remedy was rest.

Except Kelly could use her powers. She might be able to sense what Narena was feeling. Kelly breathed deeply to clear her mind, laid a hand on Narena's forehead, and closed her eyes. She sought an inner place of peace and opened herself to Narena's emotions. Even though the sorceress was unconscious, her subconscious was aware and active.

Concern drifted into her. The sorceress was aware of her success in the ritual but distressed for the well being of her prince. And something else hid deep, locked away. She concentrated harder. There. The emotion was dark, heavy, laced with regret and fear.

What could Narena possibly be scared of?

"Kelly, is she all right?" Jarek said.

"Yes, I believe so, but I think she's troubled." She had an idea. If she could sense emotions coming from others, then perhaps she could reflect emotions back. Anything was worth a try.

She centered herself and projected thoughts of accomplishment, calm, and joy. Rest, Narena. You have succeeded. All is well. Don't worry, she whispered into the sorceress's consciousness.

Her open mind caught a glimmer of happiness coming from the other and the woman sighed softly.

Kelly disengaged herself mentally and physically from Narena and rose from the bed. When she turned around, Jarek's wide-eyed look of wonder drove home the realization they had succeeded in bringing a human through time. Her heart filled with joy.

"You're here," she whispered, touching his face with a shaking hand. He captured it and crushed her to him.

"I did not think coming back would be possible," he said in a low, ragged voice. "Thank the gods you are all right." He pulled back, cupped her face.

"Thank Narena."

"Is there cause for alarm?" His gaze drifted to the sleeping woman on the bed.

"I don't think so. She just needs rest—"

The words were silenced with an explosive kiss. Jarek's lips devoured hers. Kelly invited him in, and he deepened the contact, delving into the crevices of her mouth, exploring her.

Her world spun in an upswing of joy and need. The kiss became scorching and demanding, igniting a banked fire. Blood pounded in her ears.

"I didn't think I would ever see you again," she said. The ragged breathing and passion in his eyes mirrored her own.

"I am sorry."

"Shhh, it's okay," she murmured, kissing his eyelids and cheeks. "We can talk later. For now I need to know you are truly here and not just a dream."

Jarek swept her up and gazed around the room. "Where can we go?" he asked, his intention clear.

Kelly pointed to a curtained doorway. "In there." She was pretty sure Narena wouldn't mind if they used her sleeping chamber.

Jarek carried her into the room and placed her on her feet. He grabbed the quilted covers from the bed and tossed them on the floor over a braided rug in front of the hearth. The cooling embers of a spent fire emitted a hint of warmth, enough to heat their bodies before the internal fire burned from within.

His smoldering gaze ignited her blood as he stared deeply into her eyes. "I have yearned for you every second since we parted. Through every waking hour and in my dreams, I have waited for this moment. You are the most beautiful woman in the world. In this time and in yours."

She tapped into her power and opened up to Jarek's emotions. His love, his hunger, his fear of never seeing her again came in wave after wave. She framed his face with her hands, letting her own feelings flow into him, and watched with fascination as awareness dawned in his eyes.

"We will never be apart again. You are my love until the end of time," he vowed.

They held nothing back. In every touch and every sigh, their love flourished. And when they sailed away into oblivion, they called to each other – *akitra* — soul mate.

Chapter Thirty-eight

Snuggled up against Jarek's rugged body, Kelly woke the next morning to the slow, steady beat of a heart beneath her ear. There was no place on earth she would rather be. After their double round of lovemaking last night, they'd grabbed the covers and crawled into the narrow bed. Her body was languid and sated.

She couldn't believe she and Narena had done it. They had transported a human back through time. It was inconceivable. Her scientific mind begged to know how such a feat was possible. She wished she could unravel the mechanics of the magic they'd used, but for now she'd have to be content that she'd had a hand in it.

She slipped out from under the blankets, grabbed one of Narena's robes and tiptoed into the main room to check on her patient. The steady rise and fall of the sorceress's chest indicated she rested peacefully. Kelly placed a gentle hand on Narena's face and found no trace of fever. Good, since she had no medical supplies, and the closest healer was two days away. It was a wonder people survived in this day and age. She checked Narena's pulse, and finding it normal, folded the covers around her. Sleep was the best thing.

Soft footfalls came from behind.

"Good morning. How is she?" Jarek whispered, peering over her shoulder.

"Morning. She's resting," she replied, moving away from the bed.

Jarek poked embers in the fire. After a bit of coaxing, he added some kindling to the small flame.

This time and place was beautiful but harsh, she mused. What she wouldn't give to be able to go out for breakfast, or plug in the coffee pot. But here, the preparation of food relied on having a fire. Cooking was an endless chore, and she looked at the women in this time with renewed respect.

She filled a pot with water for tea and placed it on the hearth to heat. As she turned away, Jarek captured her again in his arms and kissed her passionately. His fingers cradled her face, and intently studied her eyes.

She arched an eyebrow. "What?"

"When we were apart, I knew the color of your eyes, yet it was difficult to recall the exact shade. I knew the feel of your skin but could not remember how soft it really was. I made a promise to myself that when I returned to you, I would find the answers to these questions. Now, even if we are apart for only a short time, I will be able to conjure you in my mind so clearly, it would be as if you were standing in front of me."

Kelly's breath hitched in her throat. His proclamation stole her breath. She drowned in his heavenly brown eyes, swept away by the love residing there.

He crushed her to him. "I will never be apart from you again. I swear it."

Emotions coming from Jarek careened through her system, overwhelming her. She had to learn to mentally distance herself. Touching him was not helping. She knew how to tap into her empathic powers to sense what another was feeling, but not how to stop the feelings from overtaking her. It was something to ask Narena about.

She checked on the water; not boiling yet, but soon. Stepping to a shelf close by, she measured loose tea leaves from a wooden box and threw them into two cups. A bowl of grapes sat on the table. It wasn't much for breakfast, but she didn't have the heart or the knack for cooking something more substantial. Thank goodness she had no plans for remaining in this time.

Jarek took the cups to the hearth, poured some simmering water into each and moved the pot farther away from the low flames. He returned to the table, sat across from her, plucked a grape, and popped it into his mouth.

Kelly reached for the steaming beverage. "What's next? Are you going to the palace today?"

"I do not think so, at least not yet. If I return now, there will be many questions about how I survived the poisoning. But we cannot afford to wait. Rayja might be in grave danger. I must find a way to warn him."

"Can you sneak in undetected?"

"There are secret ways in and out of the palace. Getting inside is not the problem. Trying to reach Rayja is. There are always people near him."

"Can you send him a message?"

"The only one I trust is Narena."

Kelly pursed her lips. "How about me?"

He looked at her like she had three heads.

"Get me into the palace, and I can give the message to Rayja."

"Rayja does not know you. He would never listen."

"Then the message has to be something only the two of you would know."

"And what if you are caught?"

"I can flub my way out of it, I'm sure."

"No. It is too risky."

"We haven't got that many options, Jarek." She thought for a moment, taking a sip of her tea. "How large is the staff in the palace?"

"Very. We have well over a hundred servants."

"There's your answer. You can sneak me in, and I'll pass myself off as one of your staff."

Jarek frowned and gazed into his cup as if searching for another answer. "We will wait until tomorrow morning, just before dawn, when there are few guards out. I will get you into the palace, but I cannot wait on the grounds. If I am caught, it will mean disaster for all. Until then, let us hope Narena regains consciousness and will go instead."

"Do you know what you want to tell Rayja?"

"What I wish to tell him, he may not believe. I do not know how he has taken my absence."

"I still don't think Rayja is in danger," she said.

"I do. I have had many nights to think on how everything started. I have no known enemies."

"Whoever was behind your poisoning almost succeeded. Had you come to me a day later, you would have died."

"Exactly. And the killer would be one step closer to ruling the throne."

"Overthrowing a ruler is usually done by force, through war," Kelly commented.

"But my father is loved by his people. They would stand up and fight for him. Plus, we have huge armies. A smarter plan is to kill members of my family one at a time. With me out of the way, there is only Rayja left. Even though my father is neither old nor feeble, if caught unawares, he would be no match for a lone, trained assassin."

Kelly remained silent. It made sense. Like Jarek had said, whoever was responsible hadn't waged war, which meant it was someone on the inside.

She reached across the table and placed her hand over Jarek's. "Rayja could be behind this."

"No. Absolutely not."

"You have to consider the possibility. If you don't, you leave yourself wide open for another attack. I'm not saying he did it. I'm just saying until we find out for sure, we can't eliminate anyone, not even Rayja."

Jarek shook his head. Kelly thought it best to let the issue drop for now. No matter who the killer was, the betrayal would be difficult to face.

"I have a message for you, from your aunt."

"Vanessa!"

"Yes. She said to tell you she loves you, and if you wish to contact her, you can see her in your dreams."

Unexpected tears filled Kelly's eyes. "I'll have to give it a try. But if I can't reach her that way, I'll be able to see her next month."

Jarek frowned. "What do you mean?"

"Well, the following full moon. Narena can send us back then. Now I know how to help her, and with a hand from Aunt Vanessa, she can send us both back to the twenty-first century. By the time the subsequent month rolls around, you'll know who was trying to kill you. You can come back with me."

Jarek evaded her gaze. Oh God. She assumed he wanted to go back with her once the killer was caught and life in the palace returned to normal. He'd said they would never be apart. Maybe he thought Narena wouldn't send him forward again.

Surely he didn't expect her to stay here? Come on, as nice as Leisos was, it didn't compare to the twenty-first century. There was so much more in her time. Her freedom, her aunt. Not to mention more opportunity to get ahead in life and the convenience of modern living.

"What?"

Jarek rose and walked to the hearth, keeping his back to her. "Do you not like it here?"

"Well, yeah, I guess so. It is very beautiful." She had to be careful. This was his homeland, and she didn't want to insult him. "But I have a job, a life."

"You would not have to work here. I would provide for you."

"Wow, a kept woman," she joked, but the lack of response made her change her tone. "It is very nice of you to want to provide for me, Jarek, but I don't think I could handle that for long. I'd get too bored. I'm used to taking care of myself."

"There are many things you could do to keep busy."

Kelly went to his side. She consoled him with a gentle touch. "Being kept active is only part of the reason. Like I said, Leisos is very nice, but it's not my home."

He lightly touched her hair. "But it could be."

"Are you saying you don't want to come back with me?"

"No. I would go anywhere with you. I will not be apart from you again."

"Which warms my heart, but there is something you're not telling me. I can sense it."

Ominous silence lengthened as he looked down with sadness pooled in his eyes. "You cannot go back, Kelly."

She scoffed. "Of course I can go back. Well, not without help, I know that. And I know I have to wait until the next full moon."

"No, you do not understand. You cannot go back to your time. Ever."

Wariness crept up her spine. "Are you planning on keeping me prisoner?" She took a step away from him.

"Never. You are my *akitra*, my love. You are free to come and go as you please here."

"Well, it would please me to be able to leave when the time comes. Why are you being so stubborn?"

Jarek grasped her shoulders. "David..."

"I can handle David. Once I get back and tell the cops he tried to kill us, he'll be locked up for years. Don't worry."

"Kelly, you cannot go back because David is dead, and the police think you killed him."

Chapter Thirty-nine

So, she was running from the law. Now she knew how the guy in *The Fugitive* felt. Too bad there wasn't a one-armed man to pin David's murder on.

Kelly gazed across Leisos' sloping hills where she had been for the past few hours—the same spot where she met Laisa and Ravell. She'd fled here after Jarek told her she wouldn't be able to go home again. Ever.

He tried to stop her, tried to explain it was for the best, but she wouldn't listen. And he couldn't very well follow her. His face was too familiar. For now he had to remain hidden, which was just as well. It gave her time to think things through.

How had her life become so complicated? It appeared every time she turned around, there was another obstacle thrown in her path to make things more difficult. It didn't seem fair.

But then, life wasn't fair, was it? If it had been, her parents and Stephanie would still be alive. She could've advanced in her career, gotten married, maybe even had kids. And she would never have been brought to this place. Never would have met Jarek. Never would have known his love.

What a trade-off. She gave herself a mental shake. Enough of the pity party. Jarek and Narena depended on her. The only people who relied on her in the future were her boss and co-workers. Not because she was Kelly, but because she filled a position—one which would be occupied by the next morgue intern.

Maybe there was a difference to be made here, in this time, with these people.

She rose and dusted grass off her plain cloth dress. Well, at least she didn't have to worry about keeping up with the latest fashions here.

It was time to head back and check on Narena. Jarek needed to explain the layout of the palace. If she were going to play the part of a servant, she would have to know her way around.

"Move over, Mata Hari. Kelly's going into spy mode."

Narena was awake when Kelly returned. She went to her bedside and checked her pulse.

"As you can see, I am very much alive," the sorceress said.

"With all the tricks up your sleeve, I'm just checking to make sure," she replied with a grin. "Welcome back. How are you feeling?"

"Can you not tell?"

Kelly quirked an eyebrow. "Very funny."

"Although I am weak, I will be fine. Jarek tells me of your plans to get a message to Rayja. Are you sure you can do this?"

She shrugged. "Hey, compared to the last couple of days, it'll be a piece of cake."

Narena grabbed her hand. "You must be very careful, Kelly. Trust no one."

"I do not like it," Jarek said, stopping beside her and sliding a possessive arm around her waist, still playing the role of protector.

"I agree, but we have no other choice. Since it may be difficult to reach Prince Rayja at first, you may need to be there for a few days. Which of the palace staff you will be part of? Possibly a kitchen girl? Or a maid?"

"It would be best if she had nothing to do with the cooking."

Kelly poked him in the ribs.

"Besides, Rayja does not frequent the kitchen as much as I. He enjoys riding and goes out every day. You could work in the stables."

"Me? Around horses? You've got to be kidding."

"You do not like them? You rode one last night."

"I didn't have a choice. Thank God the car was invented. I don't care for horses, and they're not too crazy about me either." Kelly put her hands on her hips.

"The stables are sizable and you could easily hide there." His eyes traveled up and down her body. He tilted his head to one side, touched her blonde hair. "But I think I may have found a solution. How do you feel about impersonating a man?"

"*Excuse me?*"

"There are no women in the stables, therefore you must be in disguise."

"What?"

"It will be much safer than trying to corner Rayja alone in the palace. You could hide in one of the spare stalls. The head foreman of the stables is away most of the time, either in the pastures or across the land to purchase other horses."

"My hair is long."

"Tied up, stuffed under a cap, no one would know."

"And what, pray tell, do you expect me to do with these?" she said, pointing to her breasts.

Narena chuckled. "We can bind them."

He grinned. "That will be my job."

Kelly's gaze flew back to Narena. "You agree with this?"

"As time is of the essence, I do not think we have much choice. I am sorry, Kelly, but for your safety, it sounds like the best option."

"I don't like horses." She enunciated each word.

"Have no fear. You would never be allowed to associate with the stallions in the stables. Only the head trainers and the foreman have contact with them." Jarek's assurance came with a grin.

"Great. Just great. Not only do I have to dress and act like a man, I also get to shovel shit all day," she muttered, shaking her head.

Darkness gave way to pre-dawn light as Jarek and Kelly slinked through shadows of the ten-odd outbuildings of the palace. Jarek stopped along side of one of the stables and whispered in her ear, "You need to be very quiet. We cannot afford to spook the horses or raise an alarm."

He gazed into Kelly's blue eyes, and his heart clenched. They would be apart again. Fear for her almost made him turn around. If she were discovered, she would be at the mercy of her captor.

Kelly brought her hand to the side of his face in a gentle caress. "Don't worry. I'll keep my head down and my eyes and ears open."

He kissed her briefly but with passion. His fingers trailed across her cheek. He never knew he could love someone so much.

Grabbing a handful of dirt, he smeared it over her exposed skin. Her eyes flew open wide. His fingers touched her lips. "People would notice your face is too pale and delicate." Kelly scowled in distaste.

He held her close, wishing there was some other way to get a message to his brother. "You will come back to me." He cringed inwardly at the brusqueness in his voice.

Her eyes fluttered. "I'll be fine," she murmured, stepping out of his embrace.

The loss of contact left him cold. When she made to turn away and walk to the front of the stables, he touched her arm. "I love you."

Her faint intake of breath pulled at his heart. A soft smile lit her face. "I love you, too. Give me three days. If I'm not back, send in the troops."

She walked away, and the darkness swallowed her. Anxiety hammered at him. There was no one she could turn to in the castle. No way to get word to him if something went wrong. Alone and unprotected, anything could happen. Worst of all, the killer was within the palace walls.

Three days. Kelly could be dead in three days.

Chapter Forty

She would never, ever get the stench of horse manure out of her nose. Kelly threw a bale of straw down in one of the stalls. Her whole body ached from the physical exertion of working in the stables all day. And bits of straw had found their way under her clothes, making her itch. Thank goodness she didn't have allergies, or she'd be in big trouble.

A sigh left her lips on completion of the last of her chores. She'd been at it since before six this morning. After arriving at the stables, she'd hidden in one of the empty stalls and watched the men's comings and goings. Once their routines became apparent, she waited, biding her time until she could slip out and work unnoticed.

She overheard talk the foreman was away for a few days. After a while, she left her hiding place and began mucking out some of the dirty hay. Her ploy worked for a bit until someone saw her and questioned who she was. Grasping for a lie that would hold water, she said she was a distant relative of the head foreman, and he'd told her she could have the job.

The man who questioned her just shrugged, probably glad he didn't have to deal with the worst of the grunt work.

Kelly kept her head down, making only short, one-word replies or nods to conversations directed at her. The men left her alone once she proved she knew what she was doing and could work without supervision.

Unfortunately, she hadn't seen anyone remotely fitting the description Jarek gave of Rayja. The prince didn't come into the stables that day, and it was doubtful he would go out at night.

"Kel," the man who had found her that morning bellowed from the doorway. She'd given him the nickname Stephanie had sometimes called her. At least it was something she would automatically reply to.

Kelly stepped out of the stall she was finishing up and turned to the man.

"When you are done there, you may stop for the night."

Wow, how generous. She started to point out she was the last one still working but held her tongue and nodded instead.

"You can sleep in the barracks with the rest of us unless Feldar has given you other quarters."

Kelly guessed Feldar was the absent head foreman. She shook her head. "You are kind, but I prefer to sleep with the horses. Thank you." She lowered her voice to make it sound as manly as possible.

The man waved her off and turned to go. "See the cook for your meal," he said over his shoulder and headed into the night.

Kelly waited a few tense moments until he was gone before sagging with relief. She was so tired, she didn't think she could make it to the kitchen, let alone eat. But she needed to keep her strength up.

She returned the rake used to spread straw and trudged out the stable doors toward the back of the palace. Grand torches lit the outside of the massive structure and illuminated the rooms within. Kelly continued on her path to the servants' entrance, which was near the kitchen. Good thing Jarek explained the layout of the place before she came here. No one else had given her a tour.

"Stop."

Kelly froze. Oh God, she was busted. Someone had figured her out. Crap, now what?

"If you come into this kitchen looking and smelling like that, the cook will not let you live to see another day. Stay right where you are."

Kelly let go of the breath she'd been holding, glanced at the older woman who had shouted at her, and dropped her gaze to the floor. It might have been easy to fool the men in the stables into believing she was male, but much harder to fool another woman. She waited, unsure what to do next.

"Have you come in for your evening meal?"

Keeping her eyes cast downward, she answered with a nod.

"Well, speak up."

"Yes, please," Kelly mumbled, shifting from one foot to the other.

"Fine. I will bring it to you." The woman slopped a heap of potatoes covered with thick stew onto a stoneware plate, added a hunk of bread, and brought the food over.

"You'll have to eat this outside." She thrust the plate at Kelly, retrieved a goblet from the counter, and handed it to her. "There is water in the basin near the door. Bring the cup and plate back when you are finished. Do not expect me to clean up after you." She huffed and strode away.

Kelly nodded and sped out the door, stopping at the designated basin to fill the cup with water. Instead of sitting near the entrance where she might be spotted, she made her way back to the stables. The dishes would be returned before her chores in the morning. Right now, all she wanted was to fill the hole in her stomach and get some sleep.

The illumination from the waning gibbous moon pooled at Kelly's feet as she sat in darkness near the stable door. Gazing up at it while munching on the bread, she wondered if Jarek was doing the same thing. She missed him and the security of his arms. His gentle teasing. The feel of his body as they made love. They had only been apart for the day, yet it felt like an eternity. Maybe it was because he was safe,

259

and she was out of her element. The threat of being caught hid around every corner.

Water washed down the last of her meal. After gathering up her dishes, she quietly crept to the empty stall at the back of the stable so as not to disturb the horses. By now the animals were familiar with her scent, so they didn't seem to mind her presence. She wished she could say the same. Kelly unfolded the horse blanket over the hay and lay down.

If she didn't get out within two more days, Jarek would come to the palace, and who knew what might happen. Maybe luck would be on her side tomorrow, and Rayja would come to the stables so she could give him the message.

But when she did find the prince, would she be alerting an innocent victim, or a cold-blooded assassin?

Chapter Forty-one

Still no sign of Rayja. The mid-morning sun struck arrows of heat through Kelly's drenched shirt. Apprehension mingled with sweat and trickled down her skin. Where could he be? Maybe she was too late, and someone had gotten to him. There was no way to tell. She couldn't very well strike up a conversation with the other men and ask them about the prince's welfare. It would be a sure way of getting into deep trouble. She'd have to be content with keeping a watchful eye and open ears.

And she couldn't shake the feeling something was off. At first she thought some of the men working around her were emitting the usual male emotions, frustration with work and the women in their lives, but the sensation was deeper, darker. It gave her the willies.

With a sigh, Kelly pushed her ancient wheelbarrow toward the heap of dirty, used straw at the back of the stable. The stench rising from the foul-smelling husks almost made her gag.

After dumping the load of stinky hay, she returned to the ancient stone structure, welcoming its shady coolness. A hand clasped her shoulder. She jumped.

"What is the matter with you?" Malik, the second-in-command, towered over her. His face darkened with a glower. "I have been calling your name. Did you not hear me, or is your mind in a far-off place?"

"Sorry," Kelly mumbled, avoiding his gaze. As much as she wanted to blast him with the words on the edge of her tongue, she kept her temper in check. For some reason this oaf got pleasure out of giving her orders and making her do the worst jobs. But kicking him in the shins would defeat her purpose. She shifted from one foot to the other, and Malik grabbed the wheelbarrow handles out of her hands.

"Go to the storage shed and get grain for the horses." He gestured with his head in the direction of the building that housed food for the animals.

She went to take the wheelbarrow back, but he gave her a rough shove.

"Stupid boy," he growled. "This wheelbarrow is for shoveling horse dung and straw. There is another in the grain storage."

Kelly nodded and walked away quickly, not giving him another opportunity to manhandle her. She kept a vigilant eye out for Rayja or anyone who might be curious about a slight, fair-haired lad working the stables.

Thank goodness no one else was at the storage building. Heaving open the heavy doors with a grunt, she let her eyes get accustomed to the dim light filtering in from thin slats near the ceiling, and stepped into the gloomy room. Tall wooden bins lined the walls, each with a sliding door about two or three feet from the base. She scanned the room for the wheelbarrow to transport grain to the stable. Nothing. Maybe someone had left it leaning against the structure outside.

She stepped out, rounded the corner, and made her way to the end where a low murmur of voices rose from behind the building.

Kelly hesitated. The area appeared to be deserted. The grain storage was well away from the main part of the palace, and since nothing else was close, there was no reason for anyone to be there except to get grain.

Or to conduct a private conversation.

She stopped, closed her eyes, found her center, and cleared her mind. Her empathic power reached out to the two male voices.

One of them was nervous, frightened maybe. He was trying to keep hold of his fear. The other projected a foreboding darkness, almost evil. Trepidation wiggled its way up her spine. Something was going on.

She inched forward silently, as far as she dared, to the end of the building and listened.

"Why have I not heard about the demise of Jarek?" Anger whipped through the clipped words.

"Soon, Lord. It will be soon."

Even though the response was obviously meant to placate the other man, the speaker couldn't hide the quiver in his speech. Kelly closed her eyes again and concentrated on the voice. She felt the man's fear escalate to panic. He was deathly afraid. But of what?

"Are you hiding something from me, healer?"

"No. No, my Lord. Jarek is a strong man. The poison is taking longer than expected."

Her eyes snapped open. Lord? A title used for royalty. Was this Jarek's father? Could he be the one behind all this?

"It is time for the next step," the bitter voice continued. "I want you to start giving Rayja this potion. It will addle his brain and make him confused. I will introduce Selaya to him. She will comfort him, care for him, and he will come to care about her. In time, she will become irresistible and he will ask for her hand. After they are united, Rayja will meet with a terrible accident, and I will become ruler of Leisos."

"How am I to give Rayja the potion? He will not take it willingly."

"I do not care how you do it! Just see that you do!"

"But what of Lord Daylen? He is still king."

"When the time comes, it will give me great pleasure to kill my brother with my own hands."

Oh crap. She needed to contact Rayja. Now. He was in real danger.

The men were leaving. If she didn't move, she'd be caught. And it was a sure bet they wouldn't let her live.

Kelly hastened to the front of the building and slipped inside. It would have been better to see what the men looked like, but at least she had an idea who they were. She huddled in the shadows and waited for them to leave. Now that she knew who was behind Jarek's poisoning, the desire to get away from the palace tangled with her promise to deliver the message to Rayja. His life was in danger, but not immediately.

The response the royal healer gave regarding Jarek puzzled her. The healer didn't say Jarek was missing from the palace, which meant he hadn't told Lord whatever-his-name-was that Jarek had escaped. Why?

Kelly waited a few moments longer, hurried outside, found the wheelbarrow, and propelled it into the storage shed, up to one of the bins. She pushed the two-foot square sliding door up. Her thoughts whirled as the grain flowed.

Rayja had to be warned. Today.

Even if it meant mounting one of those awful four-legged beasts in the stable and searching the king's lands for him. Her butt clenched just thinking about it.

Chapter Forty-two

Kelly wasn't sure what was worse, galloping across the countryside on the back of a smelly, four-legged beast, or falling on her ass in a pile of manure in front of the spitting image of Jarek. Once her heart stopped hammering in her chest, she stood up and stepped gingerly through the wet dung on the stable floor. Rayja laughing his head off didn't help her mood.

Arms crossed and lips pursed, she waited for him to regain his composure. Thank goodness no one else was around.

"Ha, thank you." Rayja chuckled, his face still animated. "I have not laughed so much in a long time. I gather you are unhurt."

"I'm so glad I could amuse you," Kelly retorted. He was the reason she'd fallen in the first place. When she had her back turned, he'd walked in and surprised her. She lost her balance and landed in the pile of manure.

Rayja's smile dropped. He narrowed his eyes, placed hands on his hips, and regarded her with an air of disdain. "It would be wise to refrain from speaking one's mind when in the company of royalty, boy, unless you desire a thrashing."

Kelly rolled her eyes. This wasn't a good start, but she didn't have the luxury of playing nice. His life was in danger, and so was hers if she got caught. She dispensed with the pleasantries and got right to the point. "I'm not a boy, and it was your fault. You startled me."

Rayja dropped his arms, and his brows shot skyward. "What

foolishness is this? You are a maiden? Why are you dressed so and working in the stables?"

"Because I didn't have any other choice. Believe me, it wasn't my idea, but it doesn't matter now. I need to give you a message."

"From whom?"

"Jarek."

Rayja's eyes darkened. He snagged her arm, squeezed it almost to the point of pain, and yanked her to him. "What did you say?" He towered over her.

"I have a message from your brother, Jarek."

"That is impossible. Jarek is in the palace. He has no need to send me a messenger, let alone a female."

"If he's in the palace, why haven't you seen him?"

"He is on death's door and not allowed visitors. I do not appreciate this trickery."

"It's not a trick. Jarek's not in the palace, and he's not on death's door."

"You lie. When I have you whipped within an inch of your life, you will tell me who really sent you." Rayja pulled her toward the front of the stable.

Kelly struggled against his iron grip. Although Jarek and Rayja were identical twins, Rayja was slightly shorter and had the body of a runner. But he didn't lack for strength as he dragged her forward.

"Wait. When you were ten years old, you almost drowned at a nearby lake."

He stopped and jerked her body even closer. "That is common knowledge. Anyone who knew us as children was aware of our escapades."

"But they don't know why you almost drowned. There was a fight over a girl named Laleen. You both liked her. Intent on winning her over, Jarek told Laleen you thought she wasn't pretty. You pushed Jarek into the lake, but he dragged you in as well. While under the water, you hit your head on a rock and would have drowned if Jarek hadn't saved you. After that, you both decided Laleen wasn't worth it."

Rayja stilled. Eyes wary, he released his grip on her arm. She took a step back. His hand lifted to the faded white line on his right eyebrow and traced it with his finger.

"That's how you got the scar."

His Adam's apple bobbed twice. "Jarek is not in the palace?"

"No, and he isn't dying either. Rayja, you must trust me."

"I do. Only my twin knew what happened that day. He is the only one who could have told you. Jarek is well?" His eyes glittered with hope.

"Yes, he is fine, but it's you we are worried about. Your life is in danger."

"From whom?"

"Your royal healer and your uncle."

"That cannot be true. You are mistaken."

"No, I'm not. I heard them."

"Why did Jarek not come to me? I must speak with him."

The murmur of approaching voices drifted through the open stable doors. She and Rayja could not be seen together. There would be too many questions.

"There's no time to explain right now, but I'll take you to him tonight."

"Why can we not ride out now?"

"It would look a bit strange, don't you think, a prince and a stable boy on the same horse? It has to be after dark. Do you know the secret entrance near the wall?"

"Yes. I will meet you there when those in the palace retire for the night. Then you can take me to Jarek."

Kelly nodded and walked to the rear of the stable. Rayja casually strode forward, then switched direction to the animals at the other side of the building. As he passed Kelly, he whispered, "It would be preferable if you bathe before we leave." He continued to one of the mounts. He murmured to the beast, caressed its nose, and left with a smirk.

Kelly restrained herself from sticking a foot out when he passed the manure pile.

Kelly's heart rose into her throat. In the shadows, she hunched herself into a ball, covered her face, and prayed she wouldn't be spotted. A guard had stepped outside of the palace to relieve himself. He whistled an off-key tune. Her legs cramped. Geez, hurry up already. Finally, he ventured back inside, and Kelly was underway again. She kept to the darkness and sprinted across the open expanse between the palace and the wall. Once there, she followed the wall to the far end of the grounds and easily located the hidden hole.

She huddled against stone, jumping at every noise. Each minute lasted an eternity.

What time was it?

Fatigue from the day's tasks weighed heavy on her body, but she couldn't afford to fall asleep and miss her opportunity to get away from here. And if she nodded off, guards could catch her. They usually patrolled within the palace walls, but that wasn't to say they didn't check the grounds as well.

She rested her head on folded arms. When she got back home, she would sleep for a week.

Home. She didn't have a home any more. No thick warm comforters or fluffy pillows. No place where she would feel safe.

A shuffle of dirt snapped her head up. It didn't sound like an animal scurrying through the night. The footsteps were light, as if the person was trying to be quiet. But was he or she coming from outside or inside the wall? No hoof beats. A guard? Or Rayja on foot?

She squeezed her knees together. The steps stopped, changed direction and came her way. Her stomach dropped. She clamped her lips together to smother a tiny whimper. Kelly tried to use her empathic power to get a sense of the motive behind who was coming, but she was too afraid to breathe.

Chapter Forty-three

Narena glanced up from her stool near the fire. "If you do not stop your endless pacing, I will turn you into a toad."

Jarek halted in his tracks, giving the sorceress a strained smile. He'd been restless ever since he left Kelly at the stables. He shouldn't have allowed Narena to talk him into the scheme of his *akitra* infiltrating the palace under disguise as a boy. If Kelly got caught, there was no way for her to send word to him. And if she were harmed, there would be no place on earth for the person responsible to run. He would hunt them down and kill them with his bare hands.

The pacing resumed.

Narena rose and stood before him. "Stop, Jarek."

"I cannot abide this waiting." His throat tightened. "What if something happened to her?"

She rested a calming hand on his arm. "I would sense if something was wrong. She is my kin, Jarek. We share the same blood. I would have felt it. Come. Sit with me. There is something we need to discuss."

She poured tea into two cups. He numbly relented and brooded before taking a gulp. He noticed something different in Narena's eyes.

"What is it?" Panic shortened his breath.

She paused. "For some time I have felt a darkness, a great, evil presence growing stronger every day. I had passed it off as man's malevolence, but now I believe it is something more, something spiritual."

Jarek sucked in his breath. Evil in man he could deal with, but he had no clue how to combat it in any other form. "You believe we have evil spirits among us in Leisos?"

"In a sense. I believe there is evil magic here."

"But, how is that possible? You are the only sorceress in all of this land. No one else can conjure magic — good or bad."

"So I had thought, but that may not be the case any longer. I cannot be certain without proof, but what I feel cannot be denied. There is something out there, something that wishes harm to the people of Leisos."

A light tapping at the front door stopped any further discussion. Both heads turned as it opened, and two figures slipped inside.

Kelly. He tamped down the instinct to run to her. Instead closed the distance between them in two strides and pulled her to him. He held on tight until the lump in his throat cleared, and kissed the woman he loved with all his heart.

"Ahem. It is good to see you too, brother."

He broke off the kiss and stepped away. His twin stood before him. Joy, relief, and brotherly love drove him forward to embrace Rayja. When they separated, they clasped wrists and touched foreheads.

"You are safe..."

"You are well..."

He and his brother spoke at the same time, their voices so in sync, it was as if they were one person.

Narena came before them and bowed her head slightly. "It is pleasing to see you are well, Prince Rayja."

"Sorceress. I should have known you would be involved in this," he replied warmly.

"Come. Sit down. We have much to discuss." She led the group to the table. "Would you care for tea?"

Kelly took a seat. "Please tell me you have something with a bit more punch. I haven't spent two days in a stinking stable, working my fingers to the bone, to sit and have tea with friends. No offense Narena."

The sorceress laughed and moved to the far wall. She took down a wine skin and picked up two other cups before returning to the table.

Kelly straightened in her chair. "Hey, I thought that was filled with water."

Narena winked as she gathered up the two cups of tea, tossed the remaining bit of the liquid into the flames of the fire, and then poured wine into all four.

"A toast." Jarek stood. "To a successful mission."

They clinked cups and took a swallow.

"Don't count your chickens yet. There is a lot you don't know. And some of it, you won't like," Kelly said.

"Before we get into the details, Jarek, you must tell me what it has been like putting up with her." Rayja nodded to Kelly. "When I first came upon her hiding by the wall, I thought she was a fiery demon by the way she fought me."

"I keep her in line," Jarek said, in mock seriousness, earning him a jab in the ribs from Kelly seated beside him.

"I thought you were a guard because you came on foot and not on a horse," she said to Rayja, then turned to Jarek. "I haven't told Rayja a whole lot. Just that we met while you were 'away.' I thought it best to leave it for now."

"As much fun as it would be to spend the evening spinning tales, we should hear what Kelly has to say. Rayja must be back in the palace before dawn, or his absence could cause alarm," Narena cautioned.

"You are right, my friend. We will have time to reminisce later." Jarek nodded to Kelly.

She glanced down at the table, and when her eyes connected with his, he saw something he never expected. Regret. "I know who poisoned you, who orchestrated it, and why."

"More than one person is involved?"

"When you came to me, you were quite ill from hemlock poisoning. You said it had gone on for some time. That makes sense. Had it been all at once, the poison would have killed you instantly, not produced a long illness, which is what they wanted it to look like. That being said, it had to be someone on the inside who could slip the poison to you over time."

An insider? Although he had suspicions, it was disheartening to hear them confirmed. "Who was it?"

"The royal healer."

He slammed his fist slammed onto the table.

"He would not act alone," Narena surmised.

"You're right, he didn't. He was under orders from another."

"Who?"

"Our uncle," Rayja spat out with a grimace.

"Tavarian?" Jarek felt like he'd been punched in the stomach. He sat back, mouth open, scanning their faces. This must be a joke. It couldn't be his uncle.

"I'm sorry Jarek, but I overheard them talking. Although his name was not spoken outright, he said it would bring him pleasure to kill his brother, the king. I gather your father has only one brother?"

He nodded silently, still trying to comprehend the news.

"There is something else. Your uncle thinks you're still alive. He questioned the healer as to why he hadn't heard of your death. In fact, when I met Rayja, he didn't know of your disappearing act."

Narena spoke up. "So we know who, but why?"

"To rule Leisos."

"But what of the king?"

"I know it's confusing, so I'll start at the beginning. Your uncle—what's his name? Tavarian got the healer to slip Jarek hemlock. The poison initially manifested as an illness, but with regular intake over time, the accumulation of the drug would have killed him.

"I learned earlier today once Jarek was out of the way, the royal healer was to give Rayja a potion. The potion was meant to confuse and make him impressionable, which would pave the way for Tavarian to introduce Rayja to a woman named Selaya, whom he would eventually marry. Once they were married, Tavarian would kill your father—" she nodded to him and his twin, "—and then Rayja would have an 'accident,' leaving Leisos in your uncle's hands. What I don't get is why all the cloak-and-dagger? If he was after the throne, why not kill your father outright?"

"Although we are a peaceful people, the king still has an army and is well loved. It would be unlikely Tavarian would survive if he claimed the throne in such a brutal way, and the people found out," Narena answered.

"I will kill him with my bare hands." Betrayal sliced Jarek to the core, not to mention what it would do to the King. He felt ashamed he actually considered his father was trying to kill him.

Rayja grabbed his arm. "I will have him first."

Jarek stilled under Kelly's touch. Her brow knitted, and she stared across the table at Narena.

Kelly leaned forward. "What is it? What's wrong?"

"Nothing is wrong," the sorceress whispered.

"Don't lie to me. I can feel it coming off you in waves. I can sense your fear."

Jarek's gut clenched. The sorceress had never shown fear of anything. Not even when she sent him forward in time. But there was no mistaking the alarm in her eyes. He turned to her. "Narena, this is no time for secrets. If you know something, you must share it with us."

The woman reached across the table and squeezed his hand. She took a breath, her beautiful violet eyes, darker, haunted. The emotional pain swimming in them stopped his heart.

"Remember our conversation earlier, when I spoke of sensing something evil?"

He nodded.

"I now understand." She turned to Kelly. "The potion meant for Rayja, did the healer create it, or was it given to him?"

"Jarek's uncle gave it to him."

"And what was its purpose again?"

"It's supposed to confuse and addle him, make him susceptible to suggestion."

"It takes great knowledge and power to create a potion like that. A healer does not have this type of knowledge. It can only come from magic. And since I did not create the concoction, it had to have come from another source."

Kelly gaped. "You're saying Tavarian knows magic?"

"No, he does not. But the woman, Selaya does."

"You are certain? How?" Rayja asked.

"Because Selaya is my daughter," she whispered.

Chapter Forty-four

The silence filling Narena's home was instant and deafening, as if time had stopped when the sorceress broke her news. For a fraction of a second, there was no movement, no breath.

Then all hell broke loose.

Voices clamored around the table, and Kelly literally crumbled under the strain of the emotions pouring off the others. Astonishment, anger, hurt, frustration, angst, and betrayal bombarded her.

She was going to explode.

"Stop!" Her voice rang out, silencing them. "Please. Stop." Curling her arms around her middle, she hunched over, trying to shield her body from the onslaught.

She needed to gain control of her mind, even out her ragged breathing, and slow down the erratic beating of her heart. Jarek opened his mouth to say something, but her hand went up to stop him. She inhaled deeply. Within her mind, the image of a tree became her sole focus. She concentrated on it until calm returned.

"Please keep your emotions under control. They're crippling me. Yes, I know we need to talk about this, but let's try and do it calmly. I'm sure Narena has an explanation. Let her speak."

The sorceress's head hung down, her long ebony hair covering the sides of her face. She sat motionless, and with a sigh, studied each person.

"It is true. Selaya is my daughter. But I have had no contact with her since she was born, and I would never do anything to hurt any of you or the people of Leisos."

With a grim set to his mouth, Rayja sat back in a huff, arms folded.

"It is a long story. One I wish not to delve into too deeply right now."

"When was she born?" Worry lines formed between Jarek's brows. "I do not recall you were ever with child."

"Remember the time when I did not frequent the palace. I had told you it was because I needed to care for my mother who was ill, but the real reason was I could no longer hide my condition beneath my clothing. I had to stay away."

"But you gave no indication, said nothing. I did not notice your belly growing."

"Although we shared many secrets as children, Jarek, some things cannot be spoken of, even between friends. For that I apologize, but you must believe it was not out of deception."

"You gave the baby up, didn't you?" Kelly couldn't imagine the heartache such a decision must have caused.

"Yes. My mother thought it best, for a number of reasons. I named the child Selaya, and the *midwisfel* promised she was placed in a good home."

Rayja leaned forward. "Are we to believe you never once made contact with your own child?"

"I had my reasons, which have nothing to do with the situation at hand. At least I did not believe so at the time. Now I am not so sure. However, Selaya is involved, and since I am her mother, I must fix it."

"What are you going to do?" Kelly sensed hurt and anguish radiating from Narena. She felt sorry for her. Not just because the sorceress was her kin, but also because she was a woman forced to give up her child.

"Find her and reason with her. I must stop her from helping Lord Tavarian."

"I'll come with you," Kelly said.

"No. I need to do this alone. Please understand. It is safer if you stay. You are all very important to me and to the people of Leisos."

"But I'm not from Leisos, and you are very important to me as well." Unease inched up Kelly's spine.

"My kin, you have no idea how much that means to me, but you must stay here and help Jarek."

"Help me how?" he asked.

"You have to convince your father that his brother has set out to murder your entire family to gain the throne."

Rayja stood so quickly, the chair toppled back. "But we have no proof. We only have what Kelly has heard. It would be quite simple for both the healer and my uncle to denounce these accusations."

Questioning glances flashed around the table.

"Kelly will be your proof. I gave this some thought while she was on the palace grounds. As I mentioned earlier to Jarek, I have suspected evil nearby, but I was not certain. I am still not entirely sure it is Selaya who causes my trepidation, but we cannot take the chance. Either way, I must leave tomorrow and find her.

"While I am gone, you, Jarek, must take Kelly to the palace and introduce her to the king. She has the power to convince him of the truth."

Jarek motioned for Rayja to sit. "Vanessa said Kelly has powers. Now you claim them as well. How will she be able to convince my father, Lord Daylen, we speak the truth against his own brother?"

Pride spread across Narena's face. "Kelly is an empath. She senses feelings from others. Her power is even stronger when she touches another. She can sense if someone is lying."

"Neither my uncle nor the healer would ever admit to treason. It would mean certain death."

"I cannot tell you how to go about making them confess. If you do not succeed, Lord Tavarian will be alerted, and he will find another way to gain the throne. If he has Selaya's help and convinces her to aid him, it could mean dark times for the people of Leisos and the end of the royal line. Do not underestimate the lure of power. It can corrupt even the purest of hearts.

"Rayja has to return to the palace before dawn. It is advisable to leave soon," Narena reminded him.

"Since Rayja's life is in danger, we should confront our father as soon as possible," Jarek said. "It would be best if we were all in the palace tonight. Kelly and I will sneak in through the hole in the stone wall. Once inside, we will find a place to hide."

"Keep yourself hidden within the palace until the right time. It is of utmost importance no one knows you are there," Narena warned. "Do not forget, the healer has lied to your uncle. Lord Tavarian still believes Jarek is alive and at the palace. The healer will be cautious. He is probably searching the palace for a place Jarek may be hiding. He has deceived Tavarian for a reason. You must be very careful."

"And what about you?" Kelly asked.

"I have much to do before I leave tomorrow. I need to speak with you. Come, we will leave the men to discuss their strategy."

Kelly followed Narena to the other room and sat next to her on the bed. The sorceress rearranged a stray lock of hair behind Kelly's ear. The gesture filled her with love and twisted her heart at the same time. A wistful smile lifted the corners of Narena's mouth, but her gaze held a touch of sadness. She took Kelly's hand into her own.

"Tell me, what do you sense?"

She focused on Narena. A mixture of emotions emanated from the sorceress's soul.

"I feel your love and encouragement. They override the hurt and fear you are trying to suppress."

"You are correct. I do love you, my dearest kin. And I have great faith in your ability to help others. You have come a long way from the woman who appeared in my home only a short time ago. Your inner strength has grown, and I am very proud of you."

"This sounds like one of those 'I-may-never-see-you-again' speeches."

Narena continued as if she hadn't heard. "The more you use your power, the more it will grow. Do not be afraid of it—it is a wonderful gift that will help you in more ways than you can imagine."

Dread balled in her chest. "But you're coming back, aren't you? You'll be here to teach me and help me."

"I am not sure when I will return. Until I do, use my home as you see fit. If you need help, call upon the Goddess Rehema. She will guide you."

"What if I need a friend to talk to?" she whispered. It could be a long time before she saw the sorceress again.

"Your aunt is only a thought away."

"Yes, I know. The last two nights I've been so exhausted, I haven't had a chance to contact her in my dreams."

Kelly conjured the courage to ask Narena a question plaguing her mind. "When I first got here, you told me we all make decisions that can be difficult, but sometimes they work out for the best. You were talking about giving up your baby, weren't you?"

"Yes."

"Why do you have to be the one to go after Selaya?"

"Because if I had kept her, things would have been different," Narena said.

"True, but not necessarily better than what they are now. Would you be what you are, where you are, if you had kept her?"

"I am not an oracle. I cannot give you the answer."

"What makes you think Selaya is using dark magic?"

"When I was a foolish young girl, a handsome older man named Torrin captured my heart. He had the lure of danger about him. The aura of darkness was compelling to someone raised by a strict mother. As a wizard, he saw my potential as a sorceress. With persuasion from my mother, he became my mentor. Torrin taught me everything I know. Soon his teachings turned into something more, and we became lovers.

"Unfortunately, I did not see what type of wizard Torrin was. When I found out he delved into dark magic, I confronted him. He was ashamed and said he would no longer follow that course. I believed him and persuaded him to use his magic for good. After I got with child, I found out he had lied and continued on his sinister path. I left him shortly after. The lure of dark power was stronger to him than my love."

"Did he know you were pregnant with his child when you left?" Kelly wanted to wrap her arms around her friend.

"I did not tell him myself, but it is possible he found out. I never saw or heard from him again."

"He never came for the child?"

Narena shook her head as tears welled in her eyes. "I do not know. My child was taken soon after she was born. The *midwisfel* worried about the difficult birthing. After the delivery, I became very weak, barely conscious. I remember she placed the baby in my arms and asked if I had chosen a name for her. I kissed my newborn daughter's wrinkled, pink skin and whispered her name, Selaya. I do not recall anything after, as I became delirious and fell unconscious. When I awoke the next day, I asked to see her, but my mother had decided it was best to take the child away before we could bond. She wanted to spare me more pain. The loss of my little girl has haunted me to this very day."

"And now you think Selaya has also followed the path to dark magic?"

"Torrin's blood flows through her veins. It is possible. Now do you understand why I must find her? If she has taken to using her powers for evil, I must convince her to turn back. I failed with Torrin. I cannot fail with her. I will not."

"She'd be just a child, not even a young woman. How could someone so young have turned to evil?"

"My daughter was born twenty seasons ago," Narena said.

Kelly gaped.

"I am a sorceress, Kelly. I may look young, but I am much older than you think. So, yes, it is very possible she was lured by evil."

Kelly gathered Narena close, and they embraced for a long time.

Jarek poked his head into the room. "We need to leave soon before it becomes light."

Narena nodded. "One more moment." Jarek left, and Narena clasped Kelly's hands again.

"The people of Leisos are peaceful and kind. There is need for a good healer in our village. Your medical knowledge from the future can aid you. Plus, you have your powers."

"But how can my empathy help them?"

"You will learn to sense physical pain and identify its source. With patience, concentration, and training, you will also be able to heal them."

"Heal them? How?" Her mind raced. She couldn't heal people with a touch. That was evangelistic, praise-the-Lord, tent-healing. Not medical, scientific disease curing.

"When I said your abilities can grow, I meant you will be able to draw out the disease just as you can draw out the emotions of others. I sense great power in you, great potential. So did Rehema, or she would not have come to you. As a true empath, you will be able to take pain and illness away, absorb it into yourself, and then dispose of it.

"But be warned, Kelly, use this healing gift only when there is no other choice. Your confidence must be absolute. Only then will you have enough inner strength to call upon your magic and dispose of what you absorb. If you cannot, there is no other healer here to aid you. Be very careful."

Kelly nodded. This was way too much to take in. She was just getting used to reading people's emotions. Now Narena suggested she could actually heal people with her powers. She would deal with that ability later.

For now she had to say goodbye to another member of her family—albeit a very distant relative, but one she had grown to care for in a short span of time. Would there ever be a period in her life when family would surround her again? She truly hoped so.

The task ahead for the sorceress was a difficult one, and she prayed Narena would not come to any harm. Kelly rose from the bed and embraced her friend. Her heart ached at the thought of never seeing her again. Narena had taught her so much about magic, forgiveness, and love. She would always be grateful. "Thank you for everything."

"I only brought to the surface what was in you, my kin."

Narena turned away and walked to the other room. Kelly followed a few paces behind.

"We must hurry," Rayja said.

"Prince Rayja." Narena stood gazing up at him. "I am sorry your family was betrayed. I bid you farewell for now. Good luck in your task. Be safe and be well."

Rayja tilted his head in acknowledgment. "I will bring the horses," he said and slipped out into the night.

Narena turned to Jarek, a tender smile on her face. "And you, my friend. I hope it will not be long before we see each other again. I entrust you with the safety of my kin. See that no harm comes to Kelly. She is like a sister to me. Trust in your feelings as well as hers. They will guide you. Be safe and be well."

"I wish you a safe journey, Narena. May you be successful in your quest, my friend." He hugged Narena and stepped away.

The soft clopping of horses' hooves drifted from the other side of the door. He signaled to Kelly once and exited.

The two women embraced again.

"I don't know what you have to do, but if you need my power, you know how to reach me. I truly hope this works out for you, Narena." Tears filled her eyes, and a lump threatened to close her throat. "I owe you so much. How can I ever thank you?"

The sorceress smiled. "You have given me more than you will ever know."

"Will I see you again?"

"What do you think? Be safe and be well, Kelly."

Kelly hugged Narena quickly then walked into the darkness. The tears she had held at bay finally let go.

Chapter Forty-five

By mid morning, the palace was alive with activity. Rayja's bedroom, the only place that wouldn't be frequented by staff, provided a safe haven for Kelly and Jarek. The few hours of sleep Kelly stole weren't enough. Her eyelids drooped, and her brain felt fuzzy. She needed to stay alert.

"I will approach Father today and tell him of this deception," Rayja said.

Jarek nodded. "He will command an audience with Tavarian and the healer, and we will confront them."

"I don't think that's such a good idea," Kelly piped up. "Yes, we need to have your uncle and the healer there, but I don't think we should tell your father about this. At least not yet. What if he lets our knowledge of Tavarian's plan slip out? Or worse, what if he doesn't believe you? We have to keep the element of surprise. If your father demands an audience with Tavarian, it may tip him off, and he'll make a run for it. Then we're no further along than we are now. The threat against taking the throne will still be there."

"I see in modern times things are much different. Women can think as cleverly as men," Rayja commented.

Kelly quirked her eyebrow. She had a big job ahead trying to convince these men—especially Jarek's twin—how capable women really were.

Jarek caressed the small of her back. "How do you suggest we get our uncle to the palace without raising suspicion?" Ever since the three of them had left Narena's place, he couldn't seem to resist having some type of physical contact.

"Don't you have family dinners in this time?"

Both men chuckled.

"They are more like feasts, which require a great deal of preparation. But perhaps there is another way to get our beloved uncle to grace us with his presence." The corner of Rayja's mouth lifted in a grin. "We can always go hunting."

"Agreed," Jarek said.

Rayja continued. "Once I tell Father, he will send a messenger with a hunting invitation for tomorrow morning right after dawn. It should not arouse any suspicion."

"What about the healer? How do you intend to get him in the same room?" Jarek asked.

"Leave it to me. When our uncle and Father are together, I could pretend to be confused. Father will, of course, send for the healer and Tavarian will think my condition is the result of the potion and not suspect subterfuge. Our problem will be how to get you both there."

Kelly sighed. "Great, another night of no sleep."

"Have no fear, my love." Jarek's eyes blazed. "We can retire early here, and I will make sure you have no problems sleeping."

Heat flashed through Kelly, sending delicious waves of anticipation racing through her. When Jarek looked at her like that, she couldn't wait to see his incredible body, feel his hands on her. It had been too long already.

Rayja cleared his throat, breaking the intimate spell. "I plan to retire late in the evening to give you time alone. You should be safe here for now, but take heed. The healer is still looking for you, Jarek, and he may slip into my bedchamber to search. Best the two of you stay hidden until this is over. Unfortunately, since I left notice not to be disturbed, you will have to endure my presence for most of the day."

Jarek's groan echoed the one inside Kelly's head.

Well, she traveled back two thousand years to have this man. She guessed she could wait a few hours more.

"I had better get you to bed. You look as if you could sleep where you are."

"You want me in bed for other reasons." Kelly shot him a playful grin.

"As pleasing as that sounds, you do need your rest. We will rise very early tomorrow, and you must have your strength in case you are called upon to prove Tavarian's deception."

Rayja rose from the settee near the windows where he would be sleeping later. He'd offered Kelly and Jarek the huge bed.

"I will give you some privacy. No one should bother you here." He walked across the expanse of polished wooden floor to the door and slipped into the hallway.

Jarek took Kelly's hand and led her to the large bed. The mattress stuffing was a mixture of hay, wool, and feathers. Adorned with massive feather pillows and silk bedding, it was sinfully comfortable. A girl's dream.

Jarek drew Kelly into his arms and nuzzled the tender spot on her neck below her right ear. Waves of desire pulsed down her spine as she slid her arms around his neck.

"I thought you said I should get some rest," she teased.

"After." The word came out in a sexy rumble. Illicit images sprang to her mind.

He blazed a trail of heat along her neck and lower to her collarbone. Fingers threaded through his silky hair. She drew his head closer to her breast.

With arms supporting her back, Jarek eased Kelly to the bed and slid the shoulder of her dress down lower.

"You have no idea how much I want you. How long I have waited to hold you in my arms and make love to you again and again." His voice was pure male sex. Deep, edgy. It hummed through her blood, shortened her breath.

"I thought your brother would never leave." She gasped as he tweaked her nipple. Her back arched.

"Ah, so you have missed me as well," he murmured, sliding his hand down past her waist until he reached the hem of her dress. He pushed the fabric higher. His hand glided over her thighs, farther and farther up her leg. With each agonizing inch, heat pooled in her belly.

"Maybe a little," she teased breathlessly.

"We shall see how much." His hand reached the apex of her thighs and stroked the tangle of curls there. Her soft folds were already wet with anticipation.

He groaned. "You hunger for me."

"Yes."

Jarek inserted one finger. A moan escaped her lips. He silenced her with a deep, passionate kiss, driving all sense from her mind. Tightness built and madness descended as a second finger joined the first. His thumb found her most sensitive part. Crazy with lust, she lifted her hips off the bed, in a silent plea for more.

"Jarek, please." She gasped against his lips. She pushed his head back to gaze into his eyes.

"What is it you desire, my love?"

"I want you."

"I am right here."

"No, I want all of you, in me. I need to feel your skin touching mine. I need you to fill me."

"I can do no other than comply." He pulled the dress over her head and tossed it to the floor. He eased back, withdrew his hand. She whimpered. He tore off his clothes.

Jarek leaned over and gazed down at her bare form. "You are so beautiful, my akitra. I will always and forever be yours. I said it before, and I swear it to you again, we will never be apart. I will not allow it."

He lowered his head to suckle on one of her nipples.

"Oh God, please. I can't hold on much longer." Her body writhed. She clutched bed sheets. Her hunger for him was all consuming. She needed him. Now.

Jarek sat back, parted her thighs. As he lowered himself to her, his brown eyes blazed with heated desire. The tip of his manhood nudged her threshold. She lifted her hips off the bed to allow him better access. He took the signal, leaned down to kiss her, and thrust deep inside.

He filled her. Totally. Completely. She stretched to encompass all of him, wondering at the incredible feel of him in her. She squeezed her inner muscles. His eyes widened in surprise, then darkened with desire. As he pulled out to the very edge, he locked his gaze on her. He waited for a moment before plunging in deep and hard. He repeated the motion, and with each thrust, his eyes blazed.

Her world was about to explode. Heat rose as he withdrew and pushed back into her. As he quickened his pace, their breathing became more ragged. Beads of sweat glistened along his arms. The tightening in her belly built. Tingling in her arms spread. As she rode to the edge, she wrapped her legs around his waist. Her body burst into a million pieces, and she cried out his name as Jarek found his release.

His body shuddered with the orgasm, and he collapsed on top of her, leaning on his arm so she wouldn't be crushed. They lay trembling together. He snagged her and rolled onto his back so her body draped over him. He trailed fingers down the side of her face, gazed deep into her eyes, and kissed her with sweet tenderness.

"I love you, Kelly," he whispered, tucking a strand of hair behind her ear.

She placed a kiss on the tip of his nose. "I love you too, Jarek."

"Since we are both in agreement, we will become betrothed." He brought her down beside him and nestled her close.

Wait a minute. Betrothed? What the hell was that? Some kind of marriage proposal? It was a statement, not a question. Kelly levered herself up to give him a piece of her mind, but he'd already fallen asleep. She had a good mind to smack him awake and demand an explanation. He could have at least asked her to marry him. She hesitated before lying back down and resting her head on his shoulder.

Wasn't marriage what she wanted? And if so, why wasn't she thrilled?

Chapter Forty-six

Kelly hadn't expected to sleep that night but woke the next day before dawn to gentle shaking. She started. Disorientation clouded her brain until she remembered her location and what she and Jarek needed to do.

Jarek said softly, "We do not have much time, and you need to get dressed."

Thoughts of last night's lovemaking came galloping back. Along with Jarek's betrothal statement. They would have to discuss his announcement later when they were alone. Dealing with the threat against the throne came first.

Kelly glanced around the room. "Where's Rayja?"

"Checking on something and will return shortly."

She nodded and slid from the bed. Jarek held out her dress, and she slipped it over her head. One day she would have her own clothes instead of having to rely on the charity of others.

Rayja knocked once, slipped into the room, and stood near the door.

Kelly ran her hands through her tumbled hair. Without a mirror, she hoped it looked presentable. She was going to meet a king in the next hour, and it would be nice to at least look decent.

Jarek smiled down, kissed the top of her head, took her hand and went out the door.

No one spoke as the trio made their way down the hall, keeping to shadows along the walls. Rayja led them through a maze of hallways and stopped in front of a door that looked like many of the others. He signaled for quiet, eased open the portal, and peeked inside. When he brought his head back, he nodded and opened it wider, allowing Kelly and Jarek to enter first. He followed and closed the door with a soft click.

"Find a safe place to hide," he instructed.

Kelly and Jarek crept around the room to a large, tall cabinet along one wall. They opened it and slid between the heavy robes. Rayja made to seal them in.

"Wait until my signal before you make your presence known," he advised.

Jarek nodded and reached for his twin's arm. The two men clasped wrists before Rayja closed the door. Soft footfalls signaled his departure. Total darkness surrounded them.

Kelly spoke for the first time since awakening. "How long do you think we'll have to wait?"

"Not long. It is just before dawn. Father will come to this room soon after he dines. This is where we keep some of the hunting weapons," Jarek whispered next to her ear.

"If worse comes to worse, you can always skewer your uncle," she commented wryly as she settled against the clothing.

Jarek grunted, leaned back and took her hand. He brought it to his lips, placed a gentle kiss on the back. She appreciated the comforting gesture. He lowered her hand but did not release it.

Time crawled by. Anticipation of what was to come gnawed at Kelly's brain. Before now, she hadn't had time to think of what she would do to prove Tavarian's deception. She wasn't like Narena, a sorceress who could call upon her powers to make a show and prove her point.

292

Her mind stuttered, thinking back to her arrival in Leisos. She'd already called upon her power when she sensed malice from the father of the hurt little girl. And when she got Laisa to admit her fear of getting married. She wouldn't make a big deal of her ability. If she had to prove herself, she could. Just without a lot of fanfare.

Kelly's confidence grew, and she closed her eyes to find her center. Her power built like a bright shining ball of warmth. It flooded her body. She could do this.

After a short while, the door to the room opened, and heavy footsteps sounded. Kelly held her breath. What if the person opened the cabinet door and found them there? It would ruin everything.

Jarek must have heard her intake of breath because leaned over to place a kiss on her temple.

She took a slow, quiet, deep breath and relaxed.

After what seemed like ten minutes, there were more footsteps, and a booming voice rang out.

"Tavarian. You honor us with your presence. We shall be successful on this hunt."

"Brother. I am honored by your request. It looks to be a fine day."

Kelly recognized Tavarian's voice from the palace grounds. What he had in mind for Jarek and his family made her skin crawl. Jarek stiffened at his uncle's words. She squeezed his hand.

"Is it just you and I, then?" Tavarian asked.

"No. We wait upon Rayja. He asked to join us. Surely you do not mind?"

"Of course not. I enjoy the company of my nephew."

"Do you require food or drink before we set out?" Jarek's father offered.

"No, thank you. I have eaten well in preparation for the morning ahead. Tell me, what do we hunt today?"

"Whatever we see," replied the king. "I hear deer are aplenty right now. Maybe we shall be graced with good fortune, and neither of us will come back empty-handed."

"And what about me?" Rayja's voice drifted from across the room. "Am I not to bag one of my own, or will I be forced to share yours, Father?"

The men shared a good-natured laugh.

"I thought you would have been here by now, Rayja, considering how much you were looking forward to this morning," the king commented.

"Really?" Tavarian's voice held a note of surprise.

"I would have, but I am feeling a bit strange lately," replied Rayja.

Kelly smiled even though Jarek couldn't see her. Rayja was setting the trap. Would Tavarian fall into it?

"What ails you, my son?"

"I am a bit disconcerted, confused. I do not understand it."

"Perhaps you should stay behind," Rayja's father suggested.

"And miss a chance to best my father and uncle in sport? Surely not."

"I would feel better if you remain here. Maybe we should call the royal healer?"

"Really, father..." Rayja began in false protest.

"Humor me, my son. If he says it is nothing, then we shall all go."

Heavy footsteps echoed and King Daylen's voice rang out. "Guard!"

"Sire?"

"Send for the healer at once. I do not care if you must rouse him from bed. Prince Rayja is not feeling well."

Now Kelly knew where Jarek got his authoritative streak. A quiet murmur of voices seeped through the cabinet's closed door. She wondered what Jarek was thinking. He was probably anxious to confront his betrayer.

Fast approaching steps shuffled into the room.

"You requested my presence, Lord," a thin, weak voice spoke out. The healer. Kelly recognized the voice from the other day.

"Yes. Rayja wishes to accompany us on our hunt, but he feels ill. What is your opinion, Healer?"

"Oh. What ails you, Prince?"

"I feel a bit odd. Off in a way. Confused and not at all like myself." Rayja laid it on, as if he was concerned but hesitant.

"Really?" Panic and confusion laced the healer's words.

"Yes. Are you surprised?"

"Well, I, er..."

"You shouldn't be," Rayja baited him.

"Rayja, what are you talking about?" King Daylen asked.

"Ask your brother, Lord Tavarian."

"Me?" Tavarian sounded shocked.

"What is the meaning of this, Rayja? Explain yourself," his father demanded.

Rayja's voice rang clear and strong. "Am I not supposed to be befuddled, Healer? Is that not the effect the potion was to bring upon me? Oh, but wait, you have not given it to me yet, have you? You have not had the chance to slip it into my wine. Unlike my brother, I will not fall victim to your treachery."

"What the devil is going on here?" the king bellowed.

"Your brother has conspired with the healer to poison Jarek and now me. He plans to kill you and take the throne of Leisos."

"You lie."

"You are insane."

"It is impossible."

The accusations rang one on top of another in a cacophony.

Jarek shifted from one foot to the other. Kelly let go of his hand and grabbed his arm.

"Silence!" roared the ruler of Leisos. In a more subdued but still harsh tone, he continued. "Son, these are accusations of treason. Jarek has not been poisoned. He is only unwell."

"Is he, Father? Why not see for yourself."

That was their cue. Kelly and Jarek stepped out of the cabinet to the amazed and shocked faces of the men across the room.

"What is the meaning of this?" Tavarian spat, looking from Jarek to Rayja. His eyes darted to the healer and filled with hatred.

"Jarek?" King Daylen gasped, eyes wide with shock.

"Yes, Father, it is I," Jarek said, striding toward the king.

The two men shared a long embrace and broke apart. Essences of confusion and joy warred from his face as the ruler looked to each person in the room. "Explain."

"Rayja speaks the truth. I was poisoned. The healer, who was sent to cure me, is the one who administered the poison all along."

"No, no," the healer stammered.

Tavarian stepped forward. "For what purpose?"

"To remove him from the line," answered Rayja. "Under your orders."

"What?" King Daylen staggered.

Tavarian jutted out his chin. "You have no proof. I would never do anything against my family."

"Ah, but we do have proof." Jarek turned to Kelly, who stood behind him. "This is Kelly. She is related to Narena."

"Narena has no kin," countered the healer.

"Yes she does," Kelly said, tilting her head up. "And I can prove it." She turned around and lifted the hair off the back of her neck.

"She has the birthmark of Narena. Only the sorceress's kin have this mark," Jarek said.

"So, she is from Narena's line. That is of no consequence," Tavarian pointed out.

Jarek smoothed Kelly's hair back into place and turned her around.

She speared Tavarian with an accusatory glare. "I overheard you speaking with the royal healer two days ago on the palace grounds. You asked why there was no news of Jarek's death. You had ordered the healer to poison Jarek with hemlock. Then you gave your cohort a potion to use on Rayja to make him confused and susceptible to suggestion. When the time was right, you planned to have him meet a woman named Selaya, hoping eventually they would marry. After they did, Rayja would have an 'accident' and die, and then you would kill your own brother. All for the throne of Leisos."

Tavarian reared back. "That is pure fabrication. Who is this person you so readily believe? She claims to be kin to the sorceress. So what? You have no proof of her claims."

King Daylen looked at his son. "Jarek. It does my heart good to see you are well, but Tavarian speaks the truth. What proof do you have of these accusations? Do you believe the words she has spoken?"

As she stood next to him, Kelly felt the turmoil within Jarek. She sensed he was torn at the notion of hurting his father with the truth, but there was no choice. He was also disgusted and angry.

"Kelly is an empath," Jarek said. "She can sense the feelings of others and is able to tell when people lie."

The king faced her. "Prove your power. Tell me what I am feeling."

"That is easy. Even I can sense you are shocked and outraged." Tavarian didn't move from the king's side.

The king held up a hand to stop his brother and nodded to Kelly.

She closed her eyes and found her center, forcing all doubt from her mind. She inhaled once and let the breath out. Calm filled her. She opened her eyes, touched the king's sleeve, and concentrated.

"You feel great joy at seeing that Jarek is well, but also sadness because he accuses your brother of betrayal. You are also proud of Rayja for speaking up."

Tavarian pointed to her. "See, she only repeats what I have said, using different words. There is nothing new here."

"What else can you tell me?" he asked softly.

Kelly concentrated harder, focusing all her energies to the hidden depths of the king's soul. He hid an emotion buried very deep. She strained to reach for it, digging farther into him.

"You feel anger and resentment toward your brother," she said.

"Yes, that is true."

"Of course it is true. We are brothers. It is normal."

"Because he tried to take your wife away from you. The woman you loved. You had to fight for her and didn't believe Tavarian could love her as much as you did. You're angry because she felt you didn't trust her." Kelly whispered the last sentence, the words fading away with pity.

"You are correct," he said sadly. "Only someone with a true gift would see something I kept buried for so long. I believe you. And also what you say regarding my brother."

Tavarian shook his head, wide-eyed. "Daylen, I would never, never—"

"Healer." Daylen swung to face the quivering man and pointed a finger at him. "I give you one chance. Is what the empath said true?"

The man's face paled as his gaze leapt from Tavarian to Daylen and back again. His head swiveled between Jarek and Kelly in confusion. He hesitated and nodded, bowing his head.

"Kelly, can you sense if the healer just lied to save himself?" the king asked.

She walked to the man who had poisoned the one she loved. It took all her resolve not to hit him in the face. Her empathic power was her weapon, and she would wield it with pleasure.

She grabbed the man's hand, held it tight, and concentrated. All of it was there — the deception, his desire to please Tavarian, panic at being found out, and confusion at seeing Jarek alive. And something else. Fear. Unrelenting fear. She steeled herself against the strength of the emotion.

Kelly tilted her head. "What scares you so much?"

The healer's face blanched, and he trembled.

"Guards!" King Daylen's voice was furious.

Four men raced into the room, hands on their swords.

"Take the healer away and lock him in a cell to await my sentence." He dismissed the whimpering man with a flick of his hand. "Put Lord Tavarian in chains and lock him in a separate cell." He turned to his brother with a sneer. "Tavarian, I charge you with treason against the people and throne of Leisos. You will be placed into a brazen bull until you are dead. Take him away."

"Wait." Kelly went to the healer, who still would not look at anyone. "Why didn't you tell Tavarian Jarek had escaped?"

The man's eyes twitched from Jarek to Tavarian. "I thought he would have me killed. I did not realize the prince was no longer in the palace. I thought I could locate him."

"If you live in the palace, how could Tavarian kill you?" she questioned.

The healer stammered, "He...he is not..."

"Healer. Best think about what you are about to say," Tavarian warned.

The quivering man went mute. The king nodded to his men.

Tavarian bucked against the guards' hold on him. "Daylen, this is not over."

The struggling men were escorted away amidst pleas and threats of vengeance. Silence filled the room in their absence.

"I am sorry, Father," Rayja said. "I knew you would find it difficult to believe me, and this was the only way we could provide proof."

"I understand, my son. You are not to blame. I am. When the healer claimed Jarek was ill and not allowed visitors, I should have gone to see him with my own eyes. I should have known what Tavarian was doing. He had betrayed me in the past."

Jarek went to his father and held him close. The men's faces were lined with grief. It seemed the king had aged ten years since Kelly met him an hour ago.

She moved to a window and allowed the men time to grieve together. The combination of the healer's words and the emotions she felt from him tumbled around in her brain. The man's fear had been so strong, she couldn't pinpoint what scared him more — Tavarian, or the thought of spending the rest of his days in a cell. And the way Tavarian cut him off suggested there was much more to the story.

She shrugged, found a chair, and sat down. The energy required to read everyone's potent emotions had wiped her out. Maybe with practice, she'd get better and stronger.

Jarek knelt at her side.

"I am sorry I put you in such a position, my love. You did so well, and I am very proud of you."

King Daylen and Rayja joined them. She rose on steady legs. She started to voice her opinion about what she felt from the healer, but thought it best to leave it for later. It wouldn't change the outcome anyway.

"And I thank you for the assistance you gave to both my sons. You seem like a remarkable young woman. I look forward to hearing how you came to be in the company of my supposedly dying son." The king smiled at her.

"It's a very long story, sir, and I am happy to tell you, but I'm starving. Can we eat first?"

The three men roared with laughter and led her out of the room toward the kitchen.

Chapter Forty-seven

A couple of days later, Kelly sat on the stool in front of the fire at Narena's home. It had been an emotional time. Lord Daylen sequestered himself as he dealt with the betrayal of his brother and the threat of treason against the throne.

Tavarian's execution was yesterday. His last words as the guards yanked him from the room still haunted her. "This is not over." Jarek didn't think it meant anything. She wasn't so sure.

The healer was charged with attempted treason, but because he turned against Tavarian, he was spared his life — to spend the remainder of his days in a cell. If it had been her, Kelly would rather have faced death than rotting away alone in a dark, moldy dungeon.

She and Jarek had explained a few things to his father, but they didn't mention his trip forward in time or her trip back. However, Rayja accepted the notion of time travel after a bit of coaxing, but they decided the king didn't need to know. It was best to leave some things alone.

As an explanation for his absences, Jarek told his father Narena had taken him to a far-off place — which technically was true — where Kelly healed him. Since the sorceress was his trusted adviser, there was no reason for him to doubt anything.

Rayja had suggested Selaya might pose a future threat. Was it possible she wanted the throne for herself? No one would know until the mysterious woman was caught.

Kelly's gaze drifted to her hands. No longer implements of investigation, they were now tools for healing. She focused on her ring finger and rubbed absently at the imaginary sensation of a band of metal.

She couldn't go back to the palace just yet. There was still the unanswered question of whether to marry Jarek or not. They hadn't spoken of it. The time hadn't been right, and Jarek had been busy getting back into the swing of living in the palace. Feeling like she was intruding, she left early in the morning and walked to Narena's home to see if there were any clues as to where the only surviving member of her family had gone. Wherever her friend was, Kelly hoped she was okay.

God, she missed having family. It would be nice to have someone to talk to right now. She was so tired. Maybe she could try and communicate with her aunt while she slept. Even seeing her face would be better than nothing.

She walked into the bedroom, lay on the bed, closed her eyes, and concentrated on Vanessa. Power grew, filling her up until her body and soul were nothing but light.

The image of her aunt wavered in her mind, blurred, and then sharpened to crystal clarity.

"Aunt Vanessa? I know you can only hear me, but if you don't mind, I just need to work some things out."

Tears appeared at the corners of Vanessa's eyes.

Kelly sighed. "Jarek sort of asked me to marry him. Or rather, he proclaimed we were betrothed. No romance. No fanfare."

Her aunt quirked an eyebrow, and the corners of her mouth lifted.

"I love him, but I don't want to lose who I am. I assumed we'd live in the palace, but he hasn't said. And it's so big. How am I supposed to help people if I live in the palace? No one can reach me there."

The woman smiled silently and tilted her head as if to say, "What are you going to do about it?"

"I guess if I really wanted to, I could find a place to set up shop."

"We found out who was trying to poison Jarek. It was the royal healer under orders from Jarek's uncle. But as they led Tavarian away, he assured them the situation wasn't over. It worries me."

Aunt Vanessa's eyebrows knitted together.

"Oh, and Jarek told me he had to kill David. I know David threatened us, but I didn't wish him dead. It's sad, really."

Vanessa nodded, her image shimmered and faded. She reached for Kelly.

No, she couldn't leave yet. They'd only just made contact. Mist blurred Vanessa's face, and their hands almost touched. "I love you," Kelly whispered as the spirit-like form of her beloved aunt dissipated.

Kelly awoke to a gentle kiss on her lips. Beside Narena's bed, Jarek greeted her with a loving smile. "I did not realize you spoke in your dreams."

Had it been a dream, or had she really communicated with her aunt? Narena had said Vanessa's gift was to receive messages, but she couldn't reply to them. Maybe the conversation had only been Kelly's subconscious allowing her to find answers to her dilemmas.

"How did you find me?" She rubbed her eyes to shake off vestiges of the dream.

"Since this is the only place you would know to go, I took a chance. Why are you here?" He sat down beside her.

"I needed some time to think."

"About what?"

"Our relationship."

Jarek hesitated and tilted his head. When understanding dawned, he smiled. "I see. You speak of our betrothal."

"No. You're speaking of our betrothal. I haven't been formally asked yet."

"But I did ask you. I said we were betrothed."

"That isn't being asked. That's being told."

"Is it not the same thing? The result is the same."

"The result is only the same if I say yes."

She stood and walked out to the fireplace in the main room. This was getting nowhere. Did he live in the cave man era with the apes? Couldn't he at least ask her if she even wanted to marry him?

Jarek rested his hands on her shoulders and turned her around to face him. "What are you afraid of?"

She hesitated. "I'm afraid of losing myself. I don't want to be known as 'Jarek's betrothed'. I want to be known as Kelly."

"You are that and more. You are an empath with amazing powers. You will become a healer to the people of Leisos. You are my friend, my savior, and most importantly, you are my *akitra*. There is nothing more sacred to me. You will always come first."

Kelly leaned against him. Isn't this what she always wanted? Someone to love her? A soul mate? With him, she could have that and more. But she wasn't going to let him off that easy.

She stepped away with her hands on her hips. "I still want to be asked properly."

A grin tugged at his lips, and he stifled it, as if trying to remain serious. He cleared his throat, took her hand in his, and spoke very solemnly. "Kelly, will you be my first and my only, the healer of our people, and stand beside me when it comes time to lead this land? Will you be my *akitra*, always and forever?"

When he bared his soul like that, how could she stay mad at him? A slow smile spread across her face. She opened her mind and soul to Jarek's emotions. Pure love washed over and through her.

As she leapt into his arms, she grinned. "I thought you'd never ask."

THE END...

Acknowledgments

My incredible editor, Alissa Huelsman-Bell (the grammar queen), your patience was limitless. Thanks for holding my hand, for challenging me and helping mold my story into something I'm proud of. To Dr. J. who made sure I cured Jarek instead of killed him. Cover artist, Taria Reed, who's stupendous talent turned my vision into reality with cover model Alyssa Edelman. And most importantly to my very good friend, author and fellow WOW girl, Dianne - who pushed, prodded, told me I could really do this and taught me more about writing than any course or workshop ever could - thank you.

ABOUT THE AUTHOR

Pat is a playwright and award winning author who has had a love affair with the written word since childhood, many times immersing herself in the stories of Enid Blyton and Carolyn Keene. An active imagination gave inspiration to short stories and her first play as a teen.

Her full-length play The Truth About Lies was staged at a regional theatrical competition in 2006. She was selected in the "One of 50 Authors You Should be Reading" contest in 2012. One of her novels achieved a finalist slot in the 2013 International Book Award Contest - fantasy category. She was also one of the winners of the 15th Annual Writer's Digest Short Story contest for A Holy Night.

Although still in pursuit of a place truly called home, Pat shares her life with her husband and three cats, all of which claim rule over the house at one point or another. Besides dreaming up the next novel, she enjoys traveling, baking, camping, wine and of course reading - not necessarily in that order.

You can find her on Facebook, her website patriciaclee.com or send her an email at authorpatriciaclee@yahoo.com